Tales
of the
Sley Siblings
Volume One

Edited by
K.A. Hough
&
Lillian Ehrhart

Table of Contents

Good Bones

K.A. Hough

K.A. Hough is a Canadian writer and editor who balances her passion for exercise and science with her love of cookies and nonsense. She has a voracious appetite for reading, especially for rediscovering the classics: everything from Austen to du Maurier and Atwood to Wilde, as well as modern humorists like Douglas Adams and David Sedaris. Her guilty pleasures are Mammy Walsh and Inspector Poirot.

In her spare time, she follows her husband around the world, wrangling three energetic kids and a codependent dog, runs, and drinks tea.

∞

She found the first one in the chimney.

The fireplace's rough stone facade caught on her sleeve as she lifted the steel screen out of the way. Heavy iron fire dogs lurked in the shadows of the blackened interior, coated with years of soot. Squat, imperious, ridiculous; more suited to the mausoleum she had grown up in than this little house.

Gen rubbed her wrist across her cheek, a futile attempt at getting her dark curls to stay back behind her ear, since they'd already escaped from her headband. She reached out and ran her yellow rubber-clad thumb over the andiron's rounded top; despite leaving a substantial charcoal smudge on the pad of her thumb, it remained a flat black, no gleam of silver or brass.

She sat back on her heels, and exhaled—not a sigh of despair, exactly, but of fatigue, of feeling foolish and over-whelmed. The old house loomed just as squatly around her, dusty and dirty, so what had drawn her, then, to arguably the dustiest, dirtiest feature? Now she shuddered, remembering the mucky nastiness she'd discovered under the kitchen sink this morning, of mould and mouse droppings. The fireplace, at least, was just soot. Soot and ashes were somewhat clean, for dirt, she supposed.

Her glove left another grimy streak on her jeans, which had been clean—James had pressed them this morning. She reached now for her flashlight, to shine into the yawning, im-penetrable opening above the box of once-grey brick, striped black with ghosts of past fires.

"It's old," Erik had said, even before she pulled him up the front walk. "It's too old." But he had let her drag him by the hand, up the creaky steps onto a decrepit porch, where the real estate agent fidgeted with the lock, peering at it under the lan-tern-style lights that hung on either side of the heavy oak door.

"But this porch—"

"Needs fixing." He was too late. A far cry from the balco-ny of her sleek penthouse, Gen already saw two Adirondack chairs over there, with brightly bohemian pillows squashed against their backs. And a porch swing on the other side; two places to sit together and relax with a cold beer and a cold glass of wine, respectively, on a summer's night, sort of like this one. It would take some time, but didn't they have all the time in the world?

When the door creaked open, and the agent flicked on the lights—not that many were needed, since the house was so small. The windows were curtainless and let a good bit of streetlight in through their dirt, the dust motes streaming through a cramped entryway that opened up to a kitchen to one side and a living room to the other. "The floors! The fireplace!" Erik rolled his eyes. He didn't stand a chance against all this character.

The real estate agent referred to the building inspection: a modern update was going to be in order for the kitchen and bathrooms, but the plumbing was surprisingly sound, the electrical safe… upgrades would be cosmetic only: it had good bones, even if it was dirty and neglected.

"And ours." Gen squeezed his arm, her fingers and thumb almost meeting around his thin bicep, and he grinned down at her, brushed a cobweb out of the air beside her.

"Yours," he corrected.

"*Ours,*" she insisted. It didn't matter that she'd paid for it. What mattered was that RG hadn't, not directly, anyway.

⊂⊃

Erik couldn't get out of his trip, he said. He'd be back on Thursday, and Gen had to pick up the keys alone. She could have waited till he came back, but she didn't want to.

"There's too much to do," she insisted. "I can get to work cleaning and have it halfway presentable by the time you get back."

"And carry myself over the threshold," she muttered now, the porch creaking underfoot. As the door swung open, musty air wafted over her, and her stomach sunk. Gen she had a feeling of oh-dear-what-have-we-done followed by this-is-all-my-fault. An urge to run back home welled, which she quashed, followed by a lesser urge to pick up the phone and ask James to have the place cleaned, top to bottom. With James on it, the house would be sparkling by sundown.

But, no. She wanted—she needed—to do this herself.

She took a step back to breathe; her upbringing may have accustomed her to the strange, had attuned her to accepting the unnatural or even disturbing 'vibes' of a place, but here, away from her family, she didn't want to feel anything… wrong… especially not this early in the morning, not while she was alone.

Shake it off. She did, stepped over the door frame, and… *not bad.* Nothing but a friendly, filthy old house, no secrets, no mysteries. She dropped the keys on the window sill, and walked through the main floor: definitely not huge—the whole thing could easily fit into her apartment—but big enough for the two of them. A living room, one corner of which would function as a small dining room too, and kitchen. A teeny powder room and the door leading to the basement. *No thanks.* That exploration could wait for Erik. Narrow stairs off the living room led up to two bedrooms and another bathroom. She wasn't going to sleep here till he got back, anyway, not least because the house was empty. She'd order beds and furniture tonight. And curtains.

Back to her car, where she unloaded a bucket of cleaning supplies, a broom and dustpan, a mop and bucket, all shiny new. A box of garbage bags, and some new rubber gloves. She paused before entering again, this time tying her hair back, and felt a grin tugging at the corner of her mouth.

It's ours.

She pulled on the gloves. The kitchen, even the swampiness under the sink, had come together fairly quickly: a morning's work. The old counters could be replaced, but the cabinets were sturdy and just needed a lick of paint… she could ask James, but Erik had a guy; he always had a guy. Clean, cold water poured nicely out of the tap, and the linoleum tiles… well, they looked better now that they were swept, and they'd probably look even better once she had mopped. They'd need to be replaced, too, but not right now. Gen added it to her list.

She stopped to consider her next move: the bathroom was the smartest choice, being so small and essential, and mentally braced herself before peeking inside again. *Filthy, yes, but not bad.* Tiles, pedestal sink, toilet… all the important bits in white porcelain, easy enough to clean, she discovered, easy to turn it from a dirty horror to quite a functional space. She even cleaned the little window, and was pleased at the additional change that had on the feel of the room. Quite a feeling, effecting such a transformation from dirty to clean. She stretched her aching hands out as she rolled her shoulders. The soreness felt… good. She almost felt cheated at never having experienced this before; maybe she wouldn't pity James from now on - after all, he got to have the fun of turning dirty to clean on a daily basis. She decided she liked this sort of hard, physical work. Gen wrinkled her nose at the cobwebs in the corners; she would have a vacuum delivered for tomorrow.

She had worked through lunchtime, but she wanted to keep her momentum. So, with the two smallest rooms looking almost livable, she'd wandered into the living room, pulled the flashlight from her backpack, and found the skeleton wedged in the damper.

⌘

She thought it was a mouse at first, but the long, spidery-thin filaments, ending in claws, revealed it to be a bat, a small one at that. Its flesh had all but disintegrated, the impossibly fragile delicacy of its frame feeling weightless in her open hand. The skeleton was intact, perfect, and had come fluttering down in a shower of soot. She cradled it carefully for a moment, then pushed back to her feet and carried it to the kitchen. She placed it gently onto the counter, on a square of paper towel, rinsed her greyed gloves in the sink. She returned to the fireplace.

She hefted the firedogs from the fireplace, grunting a little at their weight, and lowered them with a whimper onto the already-dented/scratched floors. The broom's long handle was awkward and unwieldy, but the cloud of soot it raised from the depths of the firebox was… satisfying. She dumped the dustpan into the garbage bin that sat just outside the back door, coughed into her elbow, and went back in for more.

Three more trips, and the fireplace was swept clean enough. The rest of the living room looked worse in comparison, and Gen realized quickly, when the dark wood gained darker stripes, that she'd done things the wrong way round. Glad that Erik wasn't there to raise his eyebrow, not saying anything but *thinking* it, she kept at it, sweeping back and forth until the smears blended in or spread throughout the rest of the room — she wasn't sure which — as the sun crested and started its descent. Shadows lengthened, and as the windows darkened, the main floor looked cleaner and cleaner. The mop water had to be changed over and over, but eventually, it poured out a light grey instead of a brackish black.

She upended the bucket for the last time just past nine, and left it outside with the mop, leaning against the railing to dry. She peeled off the gloves as she stood on her (*her!*) back step for a moment, thrusting her hands in her back pockets, breathing deeply. The air was better here than in the city, and the overgrown postage stamp of a backyard would be a project, but it was hers to do, and Erik's too, when he was there, the nights that he was home and couldn't sleep. She could picture him out here, digging and planting.

A star peeked out from behind the cedar in the north corner, and she walked towards it. Such a small yard, but as Gen walked slowly around its perimeter, she recognized plants from Daddy's old greenhouse: foxglove, nightshade. She let her fingers trail over the edges of the leaves, almost touching them. This would be her happy place.

She was parched and hungry, hadn't eaten or drank all day, so consumed by her mission. Tomorrow would be just as gruelling, maybe more so, with the windows to do, and the bedrooms. And curtains. She rolled her eyes. Obviously, she'd have the curtains hung.

She rubbed her palms up over her cheeks, then snort-laughed as she pulled them away and saw the state of them. In spite of the rubber gloves, soot and grime had caked under her fingernails and fallen into the whorls and lines of her fingers and palms. She could only imagine what she must look like, or what Erik would say if he saw her. She paused to wash her hands in the freshly clean bathroom before leaving, laughing out loud when she caught her reflection, and, still giggling, splashed water on her face and rinsed out the sink as the drops fell grey. No curtain shopping tonight, then.

She locked the door behind her and drove back to her apartment, still chuckling. Her shower waited, and it was going to feel *amazing*.

⊗⊗

The next day, she arrived just before dawn. A different star twinkled by the cedar as she let herself into the house, trailed by delivery men that carried a stepstool and a vacuum cleaner.

She had woken up sore and a little hungover. James had left a plate for her in the fridge, and she had eaten it cold, ravenously shovelling in the small piece of fish and serving of steamed vegetables, washing it down with first a large glass of water, then opening a bottle of Chablis. Much better. A second glass for a well-deserved celebration, she thought. She regretted it today, but maybe it was the result of yesterday's dehydration and hard work. Every joint hurt, and she winced as she pulled on a clean pair of jeans and a long-sleeved blouse, whose thin material caught on a rough spot on her palm. She frowned at this, and drank her tea quickly — it was too hot, but she forced it down anyway, and ate her slice of dry toast. She grabbed a heavy glass from her cupboard, and headed to the house.

The morning passed much slower than the day before, with trips up and down the new stepladder to saturate each window with a spray that smelled like vinegar, then watching lines form in the dirt, dusty rivulets that she wiped away with paper towel, repeating the exercise until the paper towel stayed clean. The change wasn't as drastic as she'd hoped; anything left would be on the outside. James could do that. Gen's hands felt dry, smelled like vinegar; there was clearly a hole in each of her gloves.

She vacuumed the cobwebs from the door frames by the front door, and found another tiny skeleton tucked at the very back of the front hall closet, immaculate as the one that still reposed on the kitchen counter, but this one was curled up, wrapped in the remains of its wings as if it had lay down for a nap and just faded away.

In its state, the flesh fully gone from the bones, the eye sockets empty and white, it would have had to have died at least a month ago, maybe two.

She picked it up as gently as she could, amazed at its fragility and strength, brushed the dust from its long, slender fingers, the little bleached fangs, and placed it beside its friend in the kitchen. "Do you guys know each other?" She filled her glass and drank thirstily before continuing, ignoring the hunger pangs from her stomach.

She peeked into the bedrooms, noting the nooks and crannies of the high baseboards in rooms whose wallpaper was old and peeling, another project for a quiet week, maybe, once she recovered from this one. Or, better yet, perhaps James would enjoy the challenge.

The bathroom was worse than she had remembered. A formerly-white clawfoot tub graced a dirty black-and-white tiled floor, and the toilet had rust inside the bowl, and a jagged crack bisected the mirror over the vanity. She sprayed at the dingy window, but after three paper towels, there was still not much improvement in the clarity of the glass. Sighing, Gen looked at the tub and toilet, and the grout discoloured underfoot, and turned to toss the crumpled-up paper towel into the garbage bag she'd left in the hallway. The light darkened suddenly, and she looked up as rain spattered against the glass. *Good.* Wiping her hands on her jeans, she turned on her heel and left the room.

Three hours passed, maybe four, before she sat down, crossing her long, stiff limbs and bowing her creaking spine in front of the fireplace. The rain still splatted down outside, but inside was cosy and warm, the bathroom sparkling, the bedrooms and upstairs hallway clean. Even the light fixtures had been emptied of their accumulation of insect victims and wiped out. Her hair was still a little damp from dashing from her car to the drapery store, and back; the thick, light-blocking curtains, a deep purple velvet for downstairs, black velvet upstairs, would be measured tomorrow and installed early next week. Erik would get a kick out of them.

The little fire crackled away, casting shadows on the walls around her. James had set out a little picnic of fruit, cheese, nuts and bread before he'd left. He had even cleaned the mop and bucket.

⚜

"What do you think?"

"You did all this?" Erik's smile was incredulous, his pointed teeth flashing in the firelight, and Gen extended her hand to show him her small beginning of a callus. "It's amazing. You're amazing." He pulled her into a tight hug, and she felt his body against hers, strong and skinny, her hands running over his knobbly spine and the sharp angles of his shoulder blades. He barked out a laugh. "And the curtains! They're perfect!"

The sun had set an hour or so before she picked him and his suitcase up from his basement apartment, sparse and empty. He didn't bring anything else, what little of it there was. The table, the bed, the two chairs… he simply walked away from them. How many nights had she crawled into his bed near dawn after a night out at the clubs? He didn't like her apartment, bright and cold and high, or its large windows… so they stayed at his. In the mornings, she'd leave him sleeping in total darkness as she tiptoed out. Six months of this, arranging her life around his desires, his schedule, and now, they could be together all the time.

She'd made sure that it was perfect: the bats placed in a shoebox on the top shelf of the front-hall closet, the vacuum tucked away beneath, the large, red-patterned rug in the middle of the living room, a couch and chair with throw pillows, all in a casual design that belied their cost. The little wooden table with four chairs in one corner, and another fire, unnecessary in the warm night, but homey. Dinner, staying warm in the oven. Wine on the counter, and two glasses waiting to be filled. Perfect. James had done himself proud.

⁂

The rich smell of earth, blended with the mint of the pennyroyal, surrounded her like a dream. The first star had just begun to emerge from behind the cedar when Gen stood up, dusting her pants of dirt, leaving her trowel and gardening gloves in the space she had cleared around the small, glossy-leaved plant to try to stop its spread.

"Good morning," Erik whispered behind her, and she jumped.

"Good morning, sleepyhead," she said. "That was quite the sleep-in."

Erik smiled, his ghostly skin glowing in the moonlight. "Jet-lag," he said. "Do you want to go out?" he asked. "Or invite some people over?"

Why not? she thought. James had stocked their fridge while she browsed the botanical grimoire he'd brought over—clearly stolen from her oldest brother's library—and a platter like the one James had made for her a few nights before was well within her capabilities.

⁂

They gathered in front of the fire, the woman's flame-red hair flickering as if its mirror, the shadows that fluttered across her fair-haired boyfriend not quite hiding his unease as they sat together on the sofa. Gen had already forgotten their names. She sat on the rug by the chair, her thin legs tucked beneath her, her back resting against Erik's shins, his bony hand conferring not unpleasant chills as he stroked the back of her neck.

The woman's laugh was too loud, a little shrill, and Gen tried to keep her face composed. *Where did he meet them,* she wondered, *and how long did she need to entertain them before she could have her house and her boyfriend all to herself again?*

"A little music?" From this angle, looking up, Erik's face was angular, almost skeletal, His skin seemed to be the only surface in the room unwarmed by the fire, stubbornly maintaining its cool pallor. His canine teeth, always pointy, looked longer than they had even five minutes ago.

Gen knew—of course she had known, had felt it the first time she met him, understood that they could only ever meet after dark, that his tastes ran to what RG called "interesting," but she had never seen him like… this. Charming, easy. Dangerous. His eyes glimmered at her, and she swallowed, nodded, then rose to her feet. Erik's tongue flicked out for an instant, wetting the centre of his upper lip, and her breath grew shallow.

The man could feel it too, she realized, his glance darting back and forth from her to Erik, his hands clenching his knees. Gen turned away and crossed to the Victrola, not an old-fashioned one with a horn, like the one in RG's library, but a cabinet style, still anachronistic, but not nearly as expensive. She kept her back to the room, letting her fingers glide over the album covers on the bookshelf, pausing first on a modern record—the Seekers—then skipping back a few to pull out her Bartok. *Perfect.*

She took her time, sliding it out of its sleeve, holding the black disc by the edges and tilting it back and forth to catch the orange glow from the fireplace, the black shadow crossing in front of it. The woman giggled. Gen placed the record gently, precisely, onto the spindle, clicked the switch, and lowered the needle arm to the revolving narrow black band at the edge;

a shout of static exploded from the speaker, then the first quiet piano notes sounded. She rested her hands on the sides of the cabinet, seeing that they were trembling, wondering how it was that they hadn't been a moment before when she put on the record. Or maybe it was just the flickering light that made them seem—

A scream cut the air, but she didn't turn. Instead, with shaking fingers, she turned the volume knob. Loud. Louder. She could still hear the crackling of the fire, the couch scraping back, the screaming, the gurgling… the pleading and shouting. Shadows leapt across the corner in front of her. A glass broke—*My rug,* she thought, picturing the wine seeping into it, nevermind what other liquids were probably already staining her couch and pillows.

"Please," a voice said, hoarsely. "Please." Those snapping, crunching sounds would drive her insane, she thought. Her knuckles were white on the edge of the cabinet, and when Erik spoke—"Gen"—she imagined that she were a statue, that if she stood still just a little bit longer, that none of this would have happened.

"Gen." She released her fingers, one by one, and turned, stiff as a marionette, rotating on the spot. She found Erik's eyes and held them, refusing to see what was around him, what was on his face and splattered on his shirt. He extended his arm to her. "Join me."

No. But she went, pulled to him. His hand was a foot away from hers, then an inch, then—

The man, bloody and torn, lunged between them, throwing his body at Erik's. Wounded as he was, he was larger, and his mass fell heavy against Erik's lean frame. They crashed against the fireplace, a sickening sizzling preceding the burning log they knocked from the grate, and it rolled out, stopped by the leg of the couch. Gen stood, her eyes wide, tracking the struggle, the remaining log that burned brightly, a sharp branch that jutted out towards the room like an accusation, the couch… and what lay on the couch, motionless and mangled, the red hair no longer shining in the firelight, become a darker, dull, sticky mop.

She took a step back, then another, as the rug began to smoke and more black fumes emanated from the couch, trying not to look at the horror in the fireplace, the man's body collapsed on Erik's, holding him down among the logs and embers, all burning hair and bubbling flesh and screams.

☙❧

The police were kind, the firefighters kinder, checking her over, treating her burns, wrapping her in a scratchy grey blanket. "Poor thing," she heard one murmur to the officer with the notepad, their faces streaked with black grease. "Home invasion, by the looks of it. A fight, her boyfriend impaled. She's lucky she got out alive."

"Is there anyone we can call for you?" Gen thought about RG, about the look he'd give her when he showed up, if he showed up at all, then even more fleetingly about Charles. She shook her head.

"No, no-one."

The house had burned quickly; by dawn, shivering and now alone, Gen gazed upon its smoking skeleton, the blackened chimney rising out of the wreckage like a crooked spine, the morning star winking out as the sky brightened. Three new sets of bones lay where they fell, cleansed black by fire.

☙❧

Gen let herself back into her apartment, stumbling into the hall bathroom where she avoided her soot-grey reflection, her blouse stained with ashes and blood. She stripped it off, her eyes downcast, her mind filling in the details of the bandages that covered the forming scars. Her breath started to come in shaky sobs and she crumpled her shirt up in the sink, scrubbing and scrubbing as the warm water burned hot on her ruined skin. She dropped her head and shoulders, then threw the sodden wad at the trashcan, leaving a trail of dirty water in its wake. Suddenly starving, she walked towards the kitchen, where she found a covered plate, the steak and baked potato on it still warm. *Could have used this earlier,* she thought, a ghostly smile on her lips. Standing at the counter in her bra and jeans, she sliced into it, watching as dark red blood oozed out. *Perfect.* She ate quickly, and headed for the shower, leaving a trail of dirty footprints and smudges of ash on the counter around her bloodstained plate. James would clean everything up later.

Hell House Call

William Sterling

William Sterling is an independent author, screenwriter, and the host of the Killer Mediums podcast. His stories tend to play in the realms of "popcorn flick horror" with high body counts, absurd set pieces, and soft spots for unexpected endings. His latest novels include STRING THEM UP, which is a small town murder puppets novel, and DEAD MEN'S CHESTS, a pirate horror novel which will be published by Dark Lit Press in 2024.

❧

Kevin stood at the end of the long gravel drive, rubbing his temples and trying to come to terms with his situation.

Before him stood Sley House: tall, dark, and seeming to lean slightly to the left, though no ruler or protractor would ever agree with that observation. The house liked to play tricks on people like that. It would lean this direction or that direction, until some naive fool tried to prove the lean, when it would straighten back up. It would get cooler, or hotter, until you busted out the thermometer. It would get darker and spookier until you questioned the hairs on the back of your neck.

Kevin *hated* it here.

So why, oh why, was he back again?

Each year as he left, he swore that he would never return. But then each April he made this same trek up the gravel drive, and each year he hated his lack of self-control just a little bit more.

Kevin shuffled his feet. Shifted the bags in his hands. The bag in his right hand—the heavier one—was full of receipts and banknotes and To-Do items which the firm needed the Sley siblings to address with Kevin, the poor bastard, who was selected as the firm's representative. Nobody at the firm wanted to take on the Sley account, Kevin included. And yet for some reason, it always fell to him. Maybe his bosses hated him. Maybe there was something about his demeanor that the firm thought made him uniquely suitable for dealing with the Sleys. Maybe, at this point, it was just a tradition thing.

God only knew.

With a groan and a sigh, Kevin trudged forward and climbed the steps to the door. He rapped on the entrance using the cast-iron door knockers that looked, disturbingly, like a pair of goats' heads.

From inside the house, his knock was answered by the sound of shattering glass and an unholy scream.

A beat, as Kevin set his suitcase down by his feet and adjusted a second bag in his hands. The one with his clothes and toiletries.

"Genevieve! The lawyer is here."

"Ah! I'll get the door."

"No. Genevieve. The *lawyer* is here."

"Oooh!"

"RG, put some clothes on."

"CLOTHES ARE A SYMBOL OF THE OPPRESSOR."

There was another sound, like more glass shattering, followed by a long pause before finally the door opened to reveal Charles Sley, standing alone, in the foyer. Charles wore a broad, disarming smile and a glorious, full-bodied mustache on his face. Across his shoulders, a fine tweed jacket and the unmistakable air of a pompous academic wafted about him.

Kevin smiled, politely, but fully aware that his smile hadn't reached his eyes. Oh, what Kevin wouldn't have given in that moment to be back home in St. Louis. Away from the Sley siblings and their monstrous house.

"Kevin! How very good to see you. Is it April already?"

"That's what the calendar tells me."

"Well, come in, come in! Unfortunately, I cannot say that the house has been expecting you, but you are welcome, all the same. You know how things get around here. Busy, busy, busy. Time just seems to slip away of its own volition sometimes."

Kevin nodded and glumly crossed the threshold, as he had been instructed.

The foyer looked the same as Kevin remembered from previous years. A wide staircase rose before him, curving up to the second floor, playing with some of the same illusions that the house's exterior enjoyed. The staircase's steps were all uneven, each step a little bigger, or a little smaller, than the one before it. That was, until you went to climb the staircase, of course. Then it was all perfectly uniform. Overhead an oversized chandelier hung, suspended from the three-foot-high ceiling with its hundred bulbs casting faint glimmers of light across the space. Enough for one to see by, but somehow, despite the number of bulbs, never enough to truly brighten the room. Shadows lurked in every nook and cranny, holding their ground against the chandelier's affronts.

"This way, my old friend," Charles instructed, as he gently guided Kevin to a door to his left.

"I see your bag is fit to bursting this year. Many notes from the outside world?"

"Yes. Lots of…um…items that need attending to. Where are your brother and sister?"

"Making themselves presentable. As I said, the time got away from us today. Genevieve is in the process of seizing it back."

Kevin raised an eyebrow but asked no questions.

Charles was, and always had been, an odd duck, wielding questionable turns of phrases from books he'd read, but never worked into a conversation himself before, barren of their intended meanings. Bastardized by social blindness.

Kevin followed the strange man into the East Wing of the manor, slipping through room after room as Charles led him through the labyrinthine Sley House. A dining room made way to an annex for the kitchen, made way through a smoking room until, finally, the pair landed in the library.

Like they had the previous year, and the year before that, and the year before that, and the year before that, Kevin and Charles planted themselves in two high-backed lounge chairs, facing each other. Charles' usual chair was worn to the point of destruction. The leather was cracked and faded from where his back and ass had rubbed against the seat year after year. Stacks of books were piled on either side, each as high as a man standing, the individual books all dog-eared and bookmarked to hell. It had likely once been the mirror image of Kevin's chair, which still stood tall and regal. The leather shone with polish. There wasn't a single crack or blemish to suggest it had been sat in before.

Kevin sat down in it, fully certain that nobody had touched the seat since it had borne his own weight twelve months prior.

Kevin set his bag on the table between the two chairs and settled in, the chair accepting him awkwardly, uncomfortably, the piece of furniture so used to being left alone that it struggled to remember its purpose when required to host an occupant.

"So, what do you have for us this year? Good tidings, I'm sure?" Charles began, hands folded in a steeple on his lap.

"A mixed bag, I'm afraid. As usual, you and your siblings' affairs are…" Kevin paused, unzipping his bag, and removing a folder, using the action to buy himself enough time to find the appropriate word, "…complicated."

"That we are, my old friend. That we are."

"So, let's dive straight in, hmm? Are Genevieve or RG going to be joining us? Or will it just be the two of us again?"

A howl echoed from somewhere deep within the house, the shrill cry reverberating through the air vents to reach Kevin and Charles where they sat.

The hairs on the back of Kevin's neck leapt to attention, but Charles looked around calmly, as if the nerve-shattering sound was perfectly natural. Like somebody opening the fridge in the next room over.

"I believe that sound is RG being predisposed. And Genevieve shan't be joining us. As you're aware, it isn't her place to worry about the finances of our household. She has her mind preoccupied with other affairs."

"How very old fashioned of you." The words slipped from Kevin's mouth before he realized he was uttering them, and the horror he felt at making such a direct snipe at his client ripped through his gut.

But Charles simply smirked at the comment. Did not challenge it.

"So first on the docket," Kevin dove in, hoping to redirect the conversation back to business. "The money that usually arrives, to fill your account each year. It doesn't seem to be available."

"The funds will come. Don't worry about that."

"Yes. Well. I appreciate your confidence, but my understanding is that the money comes from your…um…deceased parents. Maybe like an endowment or something? I asked around the office and nobody has been able to explain it to me. But anyhow, if it's an endowment, then the payments should be consistently regulated. And they're not. Last year the money appeared in late March. The year before that, early March. The year before that, late March again. And now it's April. And your accounts are running nearly bare. So I just wanted to make sure that–"

"As I said, the funds will come," Charles interrupted with a bored huff. He looked like he'd barely paid half a mind to what Kevin was saying about him going broke. Like somebody was discussing the weather.

"Well. If you're sure?"

"I'm sure."

"But I don't see–"

"What's next on your list?"

Kevin cleared his throat, watched Charles curiously for a moment, then shuffled the papers in front of him.

"Very well. Next up, I suppose this could help with our previous topic. The Miskatonic University still has the Iron Maiden that you sent them on loan. They have a pair of requests for you concerning the item. First, they would like to inquire, again, about how to open the device. They have brought in several experts on medieval mechanisms, and everybody ensures the University that the device has not rusted shut, or been sealed in any identifiable way, and yet the accursed thing just will not cooperate. And your brother, RG, was able to swing the device open with ease when it was first delivered. If you could, kindly, advise them, they would like to, secondly, extend their loan of the Iron Maiden another year so that it may be properly displayed for their students."

"Did they ask it to open nicely?"

"I beg your pardon?"

"The Maiden. Did they ask it to open nicely? Or did they just paw at her with their grubby mitts, expecting her to spread apart with nary a moment for foreplay?"

"I don't understand."

"Tell them to woo the Maiden, my dear Kevin. But for their second question, of course we can extend the loan."

"Very well. I'll tell them to…as you put it… 'woo' the Iron Maiden, and I'll let them know that you're amenable to extending the loan. That will get us another month's worth of cushion in case your endowment stalls further."

"It's not an endowment, but the funds will come. Stop fretting about that, Kevin."

"Sir, it's literally my job to fret about that."

Charles groaned, bored, and waved at Kevin to continue.

"Okay. So. Next, the air drop of 37 cattle into the center of the Namibian Desert has been completed. The pilots wanted to note that they placed the cattle at the exact coordinates you specified, but that there was nothing there. No huts. No watering hole. Just sand and confused livestock."

"Correct."

"Umm…okay?"

"And there were exactly 37?"

"Yes."

"None pregnant? Not 37 and a half cattle?"

"Not as far as I'm aware."

Charles shot Kevin a look.

"No, sir. Probably no pregnant cattle. Good grief. Next time I can get a vet to confirm before we send them across, though."

From deeper in the house, the howl came again.

"Should you go check on that? It sounds like RG might be, I don't know, hurt?"

"Hmm? That? Oh, no. That's fine. *Probably* no pregnant cattle." Charles rolled the word "probably" around on his tongue like it was spoiled food. "Well, I guess we'll see about that sooner or later."

"What? How, sir? The cattle are in the desert. And in all likelihood, dead by now."

⊱❈⊰

"Oh, they are most certainly dead."

"Then what did their numbers matter? If we just sent them to die? We had assumed a band of nomads were scheduled to pick them up or something."

Charles smiled at Kevin. A sad smile that suggested Kevin would never, could never, hope to grasp the depths of the question they had asked. A child inquiring about String Theory.

"Let's move along, shall we?"

The two of them kept at it like that for hours, until the sun through the big bay window turned a soft shade of pink and the shadows from the trees outside stretched their wavering patterns across the Sley Library's luxurious hardwood floors.

Noting the hour, and the pit in his stomach, Kevin assessed and checked his bag one more time. Found it empty. All the stacks of papers had been signed, stamped, and organized on the little table beside him.

All except one.

He turned the notice around in his hands and frowned at the words. He knew what they said already but made a show of reading through the page again. Let Charles watch him frown at the page, hoping the importance of this last item might be imparted through the show of attention he was giving to it.

"So. Lastly. The firm has requested… No. I'll go ahead and put it plainly. The firm has more or less demanded that I recover the Chest of Gadon from you while I am here. There have been multiple inquiries about the chest from the federal government, and just a month ago, our offices were the un-amused hosts of an FBI raid. The warrant presented listed nary but one item: The Chest."

Kevin could already see Charles frowning.

"Now, we hold our clients' privacy and information sacred above all else. And we were able to push back against their search and seizure attempt this time. However, we all agreed when you were grandfathered in as our clients, with the pass-ing of your parents, that we would coordinate and facilitate all *legally permissible* activities that you, your brother, and your sister chose to engage in. But that legal permissibility is a hard line that our firm is not willing to cross. As we discussed last year, if the Chest needs to be turned over to the authorities, then we strongly, strongly advise that you relinquish it to my care and allow me to coordinate the transfer of custody for you. If you can hand it to me before I leave, then it can be out of sight, out of mind, for you and your family, and I'll promise to get a just and fair monetary compensation for the piece when it is forfeited. That will help resolve your financial woes as well as getting the law off our backs. Win, win, win all around. What say you?"

Charles didn't answer. Not at first. Instead, he made another little tent with his fingers and turned his face towards the window with its setting sun. The shadows from the branches outside made little zigzagging patterns across his flesh, causing his face to appear fractured and segmented. The lines wobbled and contorted like a bed of snakes when he finally did talk.

"I'll tell you the same thing I told you last year, my dear Kevin. The Chest of Gadon is not an item that can fall into mortal possession. Though it lies in the belly of this house, to imply that me, or my siblings, HAVE the thing is like suggesting that a man HAS a breath of air. If these federal agents that you speak of are so desperate to obtain it for themselves, I would like for them to first define what it is. Tell me what the Chest consists of, and why it is, as they say, illegal, for me to possess it, and I will consider their demands with an iota of seriousness. Until then, they can kindly fuck away."

The curse hung in the air, changing the temperature of the room with its bite and the poison that Charles' tongue had imparted on it. Usually so even keel and even tempered, to hear Charles speak in such a way underscored his deathly frustration with the affair. It made Kevin completely overlook the "last year" part of Charles' comment.

His words carried the same message of serious importance that the paper in Kevin's hands carried.

"Do NOT return without the Chest. Not again."

Kevin's boss had written the message by hand, in red ink, at the bottom of the acquisitions form. Kevin's boss never hand-wrote messages. Never used red ink.

So here sat Kevin: Between the unstoppable demands of his corporate overlord and the immovable object which was Charles Sley's "fuck away".

He gulped. Shifted uncomfortably in his seat.

"But sir, I–"

"No."

"Well maybe if you–"

"I said no. Again."

"There are ways to–"

"My dear Kevin, you either aren't listening to me, or you're willfully ignoring my words. I have said no, and the matter is settled in my mind. I believe supper should be prepared by now. If you will drop this nuisance of a matter, we can go to the Dining Room and have a pleasant meal together. If you insist on bringing the Chest up, even one singular time more, I shall have to ask you to leave. But I do not want to ask you to leave, my dear old friend Kevin."

Kevin frowned. Tapped the top of his stack of receipts and forms, now all accounted for save one. He looked again at his boss's red handwriting.

"Yep. Okay. I'll leave it alone," he lied. "Let's eat.

☙❧

Dinner was, as it always was in the Sley House, exquisite and strange. It was a vegetarian platter, of that much Kevin was certain, but otherwise, he had no success in identifying the things being placed before him.

Something that might have been an oddly shaped mush-room, wrapped in a deep purple pepper.

Citrus fruits with bright orange, ridged peels.

Potatoes that were dark brown, inside and out, which were

soft and steamed and which folded apart as he applied the slightest pressure with the side of his fork.

And the wine. Napa Valley eat your heart out, the wine was to die for.

Kevin tried to mind his manners, eating slowly, savoring the flavors, but it took all of his self-restraint not to tear through the delicacies like a fox in a chicken coop.

On the far side of the table, Charles regaled the barely listening Charles with stories about his most recent excursion to Budapest, in pursuit of rare new books for his collection. He spoke of musty, half-forgotten halls in ancient libraries. Scouring the black markets and local bookshops for some tome or another, a deep cut from a philosopher whom Kevin had never heard of.

Kevin had just cleaned his plate and was reaching for seconds when RG came wheeling into the room, showing himself for the first time all day. He barely cast an eye at Kevin as he entered. The man was shirtless, covered in splashes of blood and dashes of, based on the smell, fecal matter. There was hardly a square inch of clean skin visible anywhere beyond his hands, which he used to quickly scoop some of the mushroom-like dish onto his own plate.

"RG, I am certain that I requested that you put a shirt on earlier! And what are you covered in? Do you have the jar?"

RG scoffed at his younger brother and reached for the fruits.

"No time for shirts. Have to keep moving. Only came upstairs because I was getting dizzy. Couldn't keep my hands steady any longer. Have to eat something to…"

⚬

RG paused for a moment, cocking an eye at Kevin, who waved like a shy child and tried not to breathe through his nose. God, the stench was unbearable.

"Hello, Master Sley. We met last year, but twelve months is quite a long time to remember a face, I'm sure. My name is Kevin. I come from the–"

"Shit. You're the lawyer, aren't you?"

"I am."

"Whelp. I'll be seeing you again soon, I suppose. *Adios* to you both. Charles, enjoy playing with your friend. Some of us have work to do."

"RG! Wait! Do you have the jar?" Charles asked as RG lowered his hands to his wheels.

"'Course I have the jar. What do you think I am, daft?"

RG spun his wheelchair around with a frightening speed and slipped from the room soundlessly.

"Yes. Well. Good to see you, Mr. Sley," Kevin called to the man's back, but there was absolutely no telling if he was heard. RG wasn't going to slow down to reciprocate pleasantries. But his stench lingered still, and Kevin suddenly found himself without any sort of appetite. His desire for second helpings died a cruel death.

"Well. Ah. I hate to eat and run, but it was a long drive this morning and I'm quite tired. If you wouldn't mind, I think I'll retire to my quarters."

"Yes, yes of course. You must be quite at the end of your rope by now. Driving all this way, then spending hour upon hour talking through our finances. It's understandable. The same room as last year has been arranged for you again. You'll find fresh linens on all the sheets. Do you remember the way?"

"Yes, down the East Wing. Second floor. Third door on the left."

A curious look entered Charles' eye and his smile appeared sad.

"Quite the memory you have, my dear Kevin," Charles complimented.

"I thank you for your hospitality."

"I thank you back for your tireless dedication to my family and our affairs."

"I suppose I'll see Genevieve in the morning?"

"Perhaps. If history holds true, though, I suspect Genevieve will be at large long before breakfast."

Kevin, in the process of rising from his seat, paused, considered Charles' strange words, then shook the comment off.

Kevin had had enough of the Sleys' riddles and oddities for one evening. He wasn't going to get sucked down some new rabbit hole of "what did you just say?"s. He had work to do.

"Your suitcase has been brought to your room already, and you know that if you need anything, anything at all, you just need to ring the bell, correct?"

"Correct. I remember. Pleasant dreams, Charles. I'll see you in the morning."

Charles chuckled at that. Probably at the *pleasant dreams* comment. Probably.

Kevin exited the room through the large double doors that led back to the Sley House's foyer. The staircase with its uneven steps greeted him, seeming slightly shorter, slightly less steep, than it had previously, as though it was a gentle giant, bowing down to allow him to ascend.

"Come on up to bed now, Kevin," the staircase beckoned.

But Kevin could not.

Instead, Kevin crossed along the foyer and, after scanning each surrounding shadow to make sure nobody was lurking about, spying on him, he slipped into the opposite hall.

The West Wing.

He guessed that the house would be laid out the same on

this side of the manor as it had been laid out on the east end. He was wrong. A wholly new pattern of doors, halls, and paintings spread before him—narrower than the East Wing had been. Shorter. It felt cramped in this hallway, like he had passed through the mouth of a snake and was now making his way down a long, slender belly towards its narrow tail.

Kevin retrieved the final note from his employer from his pocket. Looked at the red writing for strength. "Do NOT return without the chest. Not again."

Kevin crept forward on his tiptoes, trying to be as quiet as a mouse so as not to alert the Sley Siblings to his scheming. He would spend the whole night if he had to, working his way through room after room of this wretched house, until he found the Chest of Gadon. He had been shown a picture of the piece back at the office. A dark, mysterious object, roughly the size and shape of a jewelry box. It had a cast iron lock affixed to the front and ornate carvings decorating the top. Images of a large, tentacled creature being worshipped by early humans wrapped around the front and sides of the chest. At least, that's the way it looked in the picture. But the picture was roughly thirty years old. Nobody had seen the chest since Charles' father "borrowed" it from the Miskatonic. There was no telling what state the chest would be in now.

Kevin wandered the West Wing of Sley house with aimless purpose, opening this door, then that door, poking his head inside and assessing his environment with quick, sweeping glances. Here was a bathroom. Surely no valuable chest would have been stored in the loo. There was the music room, with a grand piano that looked barely touched and a large family portrait hanging overhead. But alas, no chest. Kevin opened then closed each door gently, praying with each reveal that he would not accidentally stumble across RG hard at work. Or Genevieve doing…whatever it was that Geneveive did.

Door after door was opened, then closed, until Kevin stumbled across the Greenhouse.

He did not have to open the door here to know what he had found. Floor-to-ceiling windows replaced the walls beside the greenhouse, and looking past the vegetation, Kevin could see the night sky glistening, dark, through multiple panes of glass. Inside, flora and fauna of all conceivable shapes and colors sprouted. Reds, yellows, blues, and some colors that Kevin struggled to define blossomed as roses, lilies, tulips. Kevin froze in his pursuit of the chest, distracted by the beauty of the greenhouse.

The sound of trickling water greeted his ears. Small waterfalls had been constructed around the greenhouse, lending a white noise ambiance of tranquility to the environment, and Kevin, completely entranced by the vibes, strongly considered abandoning his job altogether to bask in the oasis. The door handle was right there. The flowers were calling to him. Enticing him.

Genevieve passed by the window, walking right past the space where Kevin had pressed his nose to the glass. Her back was to him, and that was the only thing that saved Kevin's cover from being blown as he threw himself down, to the ground, snapping out of his trance.

What had just happened to him? He had never been enthralled by plants before. Had he? Why had Genevieve's garden been so alluring? So attractive? So familiar?

Through the glass, Genevieve's humming could be heard, lilting and serene through the hazy gurgling of the waterfalls.

Kevin took a deep breath and, staying low so that the greenery from the room could help shield him, scuttled forward to the closest door available. He flicked the handle around and slipped inside without bothering to check which room he was entering, nearly falling down the stairs on the other side due to his haste. His grip on the door handle was the only thing that kept Kevin from caterwauling down into the darkness, and he pulled the door shut, much harder than he intended, in his panicky flailing.

Ka-chunk.

Surely Genevieve had heard that.

Kevin stood, hand still gripping the doorknob for dear life, balance hanging over the dark stairwell behind him, listening for sounds that his cover had been blown.

⁂

But there was nothing. He thought, maybe, that he could still hear Genevieve humming along, tending to her garden.

He let out a hiss of air, pulled himself forward, and found his footing again.

A staircase, hmm?

Leading down to a basement?

This seemed promising, Kevin decided. The Chest of Gadon could be stored in a basement. Sure.

He felt the walls to his left and his right, fingers poking and prodding through the perfect darkness in search of a lightswitch that wasn't there.

Blast it. Phone flashlight it was.

But as Kevin reached down towards his pocket, he turned away from the door, facing the darkness that he was about to descend into.

He slapped at his pocket spastically, pulling his phone out too fast, failing to get a decent grip on it before the phone went flying out of his hands, into the darkness. He heard it bounce once, twice, three times as it tumbled down the steps.

Kevin should have run. He should have thrown the door

back open and rushed to Genevieve's Garden, claiming he had gotten turned around when looking for his room. It would have been an easy sell. The Sley House did not like making navigation easy.

He should have done anything, gone anywhere, besides down those stairs.

And yet, Kevin followed his phone down, down, into the unknown space below. He tested each step carefully before stepping down, his right hand pressed firmly against the stairwell's walls to orient himself, his left hand clutching his bag like a weapon. Above him, he sensed something else in the darkness. Hovering just above him.

The ceiling for the staircase, perhaps? Pressing in on him like the walls pressed in on the hallways elsewhere in Sley House?

Possibly. But Kevin didn't think it was the ceiling that he was sensing.

No.

Whatever he sensed above him in the darkness seemed to be breathing. Heavily. Perfectly in time with Kevin's breaths so as not to be obvious, but still there. Still watching. Still stalking him down step after step after step.

"What am I doing?" he whispered, clutching his bag against his chest and hoping that he didn't really feel the tickle of air, of breath, pass over his balding scalp.

He reached the bottom step and felt around with his shoe for signs of his phone. Bumped it with his toe and reached down to retrieve it.

Overhead, Kevin felt the air shift as the thing from the darkness lowered itself in unison with him, bending at the waist, reaching towards his device. Maybe the thing was a foot overhead. Maybe six inches. Maybe it was right on top of him, tasting the hairs that stood up on the back of his neck.

Kevin couldn't tell.

He could just feel it there.

Right there.

With trembling fingers, he picked up his phone, flicked the light on, and spun around.

But there was nothing. Not beast nor creature. No eyes, glowing in the dark.

Kevin's rational mind went to work. He had imagined the eyes, for sure. Imagined the feeling of being stalked as he made his way down the stairs. What a silly thing to believe.

He forced himself to chuckle. Tried to convince himself he wasn't truly petrified with fear as he slowly swung his light around the room.

The space below the house looked like a workspace. Half-finished projects of wood, steel, and wires were strewn about, surrounded by all conceivable manner of tools and utensils- some recognizable, like the table saw and a jackhammer. Some mysterious; rods full of lava-like fluid that bubbled and rolled back and forth as Kevin watched, maybe reacting to the light from his phone?

Kevin sighed. A workspace, like a bathroom, was no place to house the Chest of Gadon.

Or so he thought, until his phone glinted off something in the back of the room. A padlock, old in design, yet polished and maintained enough that it glistened and shone in response to Kevin's phone.

Was that the same padlock from the picture? The one that was supposed to seal the Chest of Gadon, but now lay, un-clasped, on this nondescript workbench?

Of course, there could have been thousands of such locks in the world. Millions. But Kevin knew, deep in his gut, that this was the lock from the picture. In a rush, Kevin crossed the room and grabbed the discarded clasp.

He pocketed it without thinking and looked around for evidence of his real quarry. Where was the chest, then?

If the lock was any indication, then the chest had been opened. He racked his brain, trying to remember if he'd read anything about the chest being opened before. What was inside. In the flurry of tasks he was meant to pursue with the Sleys, he had neglected to fully do his research on the chest, and could only recall the haziest of details. He knew what it looked like. He had believed that would be all he needed to know. *Do NOT return without the chest.*

From this angle, Kevin could see more of the workroom. The space opened up to his left and to his right in a great, gaping expanse that Kevin's light could not reach the backs of. Thick concrete pillars held the manor up, overhead, but otherwise Kevin was struck by the impression that the entirety of the Manor's square footage might be accounted for here, sans the walls, the doors, and the hallways that squeezed in on a person on the main floor. Down here there was just openness, like a warehouse where oversized cargo was expected to travel back and forth. Here and there, more machines were scattered about. Kevin recognized a wood planer, large enough to fit an entire tree through, to cut boards for construction. He took a few steps into the dark expanse. Now there was something that looked like a turbine coming into view in the darkness, clicking softly, but not visibly moving.

Kevin gave the turbine a wide berth, pressing his back against one of the concrete columns and rotating around it, trying to keep himself oriented to where the stairs were. It would be so easy to get lost down here…

His flashlight found the chest. Sitting in the middle of the floor, completely isolated, abandoned, the thing was just sitting there.

It looked so out of place that, at first, Kevin second guessed his eyes.

Shouldn't a chest like this have been sitting… he didn't know… on a desk or something? Displayed prominently in a location that could reflect its value? Not plunked down on the cold, concrete ground unceremoniously.

The lid was slightly askew, as if the hinges had grown loose or someone hadn't dropped the top back into place quite correctly. The faintest suggestion of a light glowed on the other side of the crack that was created.

Kevin bent over to look at the piece, his back arching, spine pressing against the back of his shirt. Exposed.

The chest was bigger than Kevin had expected. Slightly larger than a jewelry box. More akin to a shoebox. It would be difficult to fit the chest among his bag when he stole it away from Sley House. Perhaps he should leave some of his clothes behind to make room. Empty out a portion of his bag and wedge the Chest of Dagon into the bottom.

He considered his options as his hand reached out, fingers aimed for the lip of the lid.

A crowbar sliced through the darkness, connecting with Kevin's spine right at the base of his neck. The blow was swift. Heavy. Devastating. Kevin's world went black in an instant, before he ever knew what happened.

❧❦❧

RG stared down at the dead lawyer, crowbar in his hands, a scowl on his face. He was glad he'd fixed his squeaky wheel earlier that week. He'd almost forgotten that the lawyer was scheduled to come, and this whole thing didn't work unless RG could glide soundlessly through the darkness of the Sley basement.

"It's done now!" RG shouted, his voice reverberating through the darkened expanse around him.

A click.

The lights in the ceiling popped and hummed to life as, deeper in the basement, Charles entered the basement. Late, as always.

"He's getting more desperate. Came straight down here this time instead of heading to his room first," RG called to his approaching brother. "We need to just put a stop to this."

"No, no. He's a good lawyer. And he doesn't ask questions. Well. Not too many questions at least." Charles stepped up beside his brother and looked down at Kevin's corpse.

"Did you take the lock off the Chest?"

"Nope."

"Bollocks. Must have been Genevieve again."

"Idle-brained girl."

"Quite."

Charles reached down and rolled Kevin onto his back. There was a heavy kerchunk as the lock in his pocket rolled across his body and crashed down to the concrete floor.

Charles and RG exchanged a confused look and Charles fished around, producing the lock from Kevin's pocket.

"Did *he* open it?" RG questioned.

"Surely not. Right? Otherwise none of us would be standing here."

RG glared at his brother.

"Oh, shut up. It's a figure of speech."

Charles used the lock to refasten the Chest of Gadon, but he was very careful not to move the box. Didn't look inside.

"We'll deal with that tomorrow. For now though, pass me that crowbar?"

RG passed the crowbar along to Charles, who pointed the crooked end at Kevin's forehead, adjusted his angle, then sent the device cracking down through the man's skull. The tip of the crowbar punched through Kevin's skull easily. Like a knife through an egg shell.

"Go ahead and get the jar out," Charles requested, and RG turned in his chair, fumbling with a bag on the back until he pulled out an oversized mason jar filled with a strange green liquid.

"Genevieve should be ready in the garden by now, right?"

"We'd better hope so. But based on the look on her face this morning, I think she had completely forgotten he was coming."

RG stayed silent and didn't admit that he'd forgotten about the lawyer as well.

Charles threw his weight into the side of the crowbar and Kevin's head tilted up, his chin straining to rise as high as it would go until his skull finally split the rest of the way open with a pop, his warm, dying brain exposed to the dust motes and damp air of the basement.

Charles withdrew the crowbar and examined the torn skin around Kevin's head. He used the tip of the crowbar to punch at a few places where the skin still tried to hold Kevin's head together. Working carefully, but quickly.

"Looks like you tore part of it up with your crowbar there." RG called, pointing at a spot where his brother's brutish work had ripped part of Kevin's brain away.

"Frontal lobe. Not important. Here, help me…"

Charles shoved his fingers down, around the grey, wrinkly mass, worming his digits into Kevin's skull until his hands were wrapped all the way around his brain. RG wheeled over and grabbed Kevin's feet, popping the locks on his tires and heaving backwards as his brother hoed forwards.

With two grown men pulling in opposite directions, Kevin's brain tore free from its brainstem. It plopped down into Charles' lap as he fell backwards.

"You're getting faster at that," RG commented as he unscrewed the lid of the jar and extended it towards his brother. Charles slipped the brain into the jar and its strange liquid. There was a hissing sound, and bubbles from the liquid began congregating around the brain, like fish investigating a new toy in their tank.

"Many thanks, brother. It's not a talent that I would prefer to practice, but still. Things being the way they are…" Charles shrugged. "I guess it's a good skill to have. Think I should put 'brain surgeon' on my resume?"

RG rolled his eyes and recapped the jar.

"The devil do you need a resume for?"

RG turned his chair around and wheeled back towards the ramp that led upstairs.

"You never know!" Charles called back. "The way Kevin has been going on about our finances, you'd believe we're almost out of money. That we'd need to consider getting real jobs sometime in the near future."

RG scoffed at that. Didn't dignify the idea with an answer as he rolled up to the garden, leaving Charles to mop up the mess they'd made.

The Chest of Gadon sat where it always sat, at the point where Charles' star charts insisted it was safest. In the center of all of RG's runes, painted on the walls and the ceilings of the basement in invisible ink. There to protect. Not to be seen. Not to be questioned or understood. To remove the box from that spot? To allow what was inside to venture outside the realm of the defenses they had constructed? To go back to

Miskatonic University? RG shuddered to think of the devastation that would result.

But who had opened it?

Bigger problems for different days, RG supposed.

⚮

RG rode straight to Genevieve's garden, knocking the door open and startling his sister with his abrupt entrance.

"It happened again?"

"It happens every time. Kevin is dedicated to his job. It makes him a good lawyer, but a boring quarry."

"I like him."

"Of course you like him. You made him."

"Speaking of which."

Genevieve pushed a few ferns out of the way and peered into the center of her garden where a massively overgrown cabbage-like figure waited. Four feet high, four feet wide, a disturbing dark green color that was turning brown around the edges of the leaves, the vegetable-like growth stood in stark contrast to the flowers and vibrant colors of the plants surrounding it.

Genevieve pulled a small mallet from her tool belt and, after poking around at the cabbage for a moment, selected the perfect spot and gave her creation a thwack.

The plant groaned and shivered. Its leaves parted slowly, folding open to reveal the pink, meaty interior that the wilting leaves had been covering. And seated in the center of those folds: Kevin.

Or, an approximation of Kevin.

His skin was sickly green. His limbs wound around each other like noodles, the bones not quite hardened yet. But in his face, and in his overall build, the thing was recognizable enough as Kevin.

"Not your best work," RG commented as he passed the jar with Kevin's brain across to his sister.

"No. No it's not. But it'll do. Nobody outside this house will know the difference."

Genevieve reached forward and pulled "Kevin's" hair apart, revealing an opening just large enough to slide a brain into. She pulled Kevin's grey matter from RG's jar, and RG was secretly delighted to see that his bubbles had repaired all the damage done by Charles' careless butchery. Kevin's brain looked healthy and whole and fully restored as RG's sister slipped it down, into the gash in her creation's head. To RG, it looked like she was pushing spoiled Jell-O into a soggy, hairy cantaloupe. The squelching sounds didn't help. It took Genevieve a moment, but she eventually pulled her hands free, the brain in place, among the husk she had created.

"You know it would be easiest if we just locked the basement, right?"

"Since when does our family care about easy?"

Genevieve groaned.

"And besides. We tried that in 2008, remember? We turned Kevin away and then we had the authorities breathing down our necks for the next three years."

"Strange how killing a man is somehow easier than playing by the world's rules."

"The world's rules are stupid and make no sense."

"Preaching to the choir, brother."

With Kevin's brain seemingly seated in its new body, Genevieve folded Kevin's hair back into place and gave him a loving tap between the eyes.

Kevin awoke, groggily, and looked around, taking stock of Genevieve's Garden and the odd plant that he was laying in.

"Off to bed with you, sleepy-head. You've had a devil of a

night."

Kevin blinked. Looked at RG. Looked at Genevieve. Then did as he was told, slipping his legs free from the unfolded cabbage and trudging out the garden doors, hand fumbling at his side, looking for the bag of paperwork that wasn't there.

"Remember, down the East Wing. Second floor. Third door on the left!" Genevieve called after her creation, and Kevin waved a hand in acknowledgement just as the doors closed behind him.

CRESO

The next morning, Kevin woke up with a disorienting, piercing hangover. Though he didn't remember drinking anything with dinner the night before, this always happened to him when he stayed at Sley House. Something about the atypical cuisine, perhaps. Some spice that the Sleys had procured from South America, or a seasoning from Indo-China, must set off his allergies.

Sure. That was probably it.

Kevin rose from bed and found his suitcase neatly placed in front of the room's heavy oak dresser. He pulled his clothes on, checked his reflection in the mirror. Found himself looking a bit green around the gills, but otherwise presentable, and checked his bag to make sure all of his paperwork was still in order from the previous day's wheelings and dealings. The papers were, as far as Kevin was aware, all present and accounted for. Signed and dated and ready to be presented back to his boss at the firm.

Well done, Kevin. Another successful run through the old Sley House. Now to just excuse himself before Charles invited him to a breakfast filled with whatever foreign toxin was causing his headache. He would bow out gracefully, his work complete, and then slip away into the morning sun to take a taxi back to the city.

But glancing out his window, he found the Sleys were a step ahead of him already.

A yellow taxi waited at the end of the Sleys' front drive. Parked and idling just at the end of their gravel road, as if anticipating Kevin's swift retreat. As if he woke up at precisely this time and made precisely this exit he visited the manor. Did he? For the life of him, Kevin couldn't remember.

He made his way downstairs and politely thanked Charles Sley for his help with the paperwork the previous day.

"Not at all, my lad. Happy to have everything in order once again!"

"And I'll phone you the moment your account receives its money, gets settled again."

"Don't bother, my boy. The money will come. It will be fine." Charles said with a dismissive wave of his hand.

"Well I must be off and running. You know how it is."

"Same as it always is, I'm assuming."

"Give my best to RG and Genevieve. I'm sorry I did not have the pleasure of more of their company this time around. Perhaps next year, if I'm sent back out."

"Oh yes, next year most certainly. We'll be counting on it."

"Farewell, Charles."

"Farewell, Kevin. Safe travels."

Kevin slipped out the front door, past the goats-head knockers and walked away from Sley House feeling the same way that he always did when he walked back down that gravel drive.

Sley House was odd. Confusing. Scary. And yet, in some ways, for reasons Kevin could never pin down, it always felt a bit…homely? Comfortable?

The clientele was frustrating. The house itself, creepy beyond words. Kevin hated it here. And yet for some reason that he couldn't explain, he knew that he would always come back.

Always.

The Unwelcome

Kay Hanifen

Kay Hanifen was born on a Friday the 13th and once lived for three months in a haunted castle. So, obviously, she had to become a horror writer. Her work has appeared in over forty anthologies and magazines. When she's not consuming pop culture with the voraciousness of a vampire at a 24-hour blood bank, you can usually find her with her two black cats or at kayhanifenauthor.wordpress.com.
Twitter: https://twitter.com/TheUnicornComi1
Instagram: https://www.instagram.com/katharinehanifen/

CREO

R G inspected the summoning circle he'd painted onto his lab floor a few months ago. He knew he really should have a permanent one put in, but the metal ones were elevated just enough to be a pain for him to wheel over when it was not in use, and his parents would have killed him if he'd etched it into the ancient wood flooring.

"RG," he could almost hear his mother say, "That wood comes from a now-extinct species of oak. If you so much as scuff it, I will haunt you for all eternity."

In his mind, the paint was a compromise. Genevieve had told him that this particular brand wouldn't damage the wood, and his little sister was the expert on this sort of thing. The one drawback of a paint circle was that they periodically had to be repainted. Between his wheelchair and the maids and visitors to his lab scuffing it with their shoes, it would start to wear away. He would be fine as long as it was unbroken, but he made sure to repair it every time it looked shabby. What kind of occultist would he be if he let a demon run wild because of an improperly maintained summoning circle?

If that ever happened, he knew that Archibald Horne, the head of his local occultist society, would never let him hear the end of it. The Sley family had made many enemies over the centuries and had suffered through many attempts on their lives, from demons to rival businessmen to fellow occultists to—on one memorable occasion—their family dentist. Ever since the founding of the occult society, there had been a rivalry between the Hornes and the Sleys. They were too similar to get along: old money, ties to the supernatural, and a desire to stay in power. Over the centuries, the cold war between them would occasionally heat up—one would sabotage the other's experiments, one would blackmail the other, and there was even the occasional murder attempt on each other—but RG had made an effort to keep things civil, a favor that Archibald refused to return.

Such is life.

Eager to run his experiment—so that he could prove a point about the mutability of arcane forms—he missed seeing that a sliver of paint between two floorboards had been scraped away.

Two days before, their maid, Eleanor, had gone into his lab to dust his beakers and clean up any forgotten dishes from the meals RG had taken up there, so that his studies would not be interrupted. After working there for the better part of forty years, Eleanor was used to the strangeness of her employers, so when she stepped inside, blinked, and found herself outside with her arms full of RG's discarded dishes, she simply shrugged and went about her business. She'd been subject to the residual magic of one of his experiments and the strange results of entering his lab many times. Once, she'd entered a brunette and left a blonde. RG was fascinated by that, of course, and peppered her with questions. A week later, it returned to the same shade of brown, much to her disappointment. Blondes really do have all the fun.

She'd assumed that a memory spell cast over the room caused the brief blackout, but that was not what happened. When she stepped into that room, something had overtaken her. Though she fought against it, her body moved of its own accord, grabbing RG's scalpel, and using it to slice a thin line along the slats in the wood. Then, she continued, business as usual with dusting and picking up the dishes.

Though RG was usually abundantly cautious when conducting his experiments, he had not noticed the hairline fracture in the circle and continued with the ritual. Genevieve was a consummate bleeding heart, so the sacrifices for such things could not be living, like he had wished. Instead, he settled for thawed frozen mice from a pet store. They still had enough blood for him to conduct his rituals.

The syllables of the chant rolled off his tongue as he sliced open the mouse's belly, letting the blood and intestines tumble into the circle. "Y'iah Y'iah Rgak Thulum Tok!"

The air dropped in temperature as a sudden breeze blew through the room, rustling papers and sending loose items flying. His chant rose to a crescendo as a red, glowing mass pulsed and twitched. "Y'iah Y'iah Rgak Thulum Tok!"

Abruptly, the impossible breeze stopped, and in the center lay a squalling creature. It wasn't the demon he'd intended to summon, but it would do nicely for his purposes. In a way, it almost reminded him of a giant, hairless cat; its skin wrinkled and folded in impossible shapes, and its midnight eyes held galaxies of knowledge.

"I bind you to me, demon," he said, picking up a silver collar to clasp around the creature's neck. But it vanished in a puff of acrid smoke. "What on earth—?"

He wasn't able to get much farther than that before the demon reappeared with a yowl, its raptor-like claws tearing into the flesh of his arms. The force of it knocked him from his chair, and he landed with a cry, curling as best as he could without the use of his legs to protect his vital organs as it raked at his skin.

"RG, is everything—" his brother, Charles began, opening the door. He stopped short, surveying the strange scene in front of him with a look of abject bafflement. "—okay?"

"No, no, close the—" he tried to say, but the demon was too quick. It darted between his brother's legs and out the door, sending Charles tumbling to the ground, and letting a demon loose in this labyrinth of a house. "I had it all under control."

Charles pushed himself to his feet. He'd be feeling that ache for a while. "Clearly," he retorted, setting RG's chair upright.

"Just shut up and help me back into the seat," RG grumbled. "We have to catch it before it kills someone."

"Should we let Gen know?" he asked.

RG rolled his eyes. "She'll never let me live this down. Let's see if we can catch it ourselves first."

Charles raised his eyebrows. "*Our*selves? Why should I help you clean up your mess?"

"Because you're the one who let it out of my room to wreak havoc on our ancestral home," RG snapped.

Charles sighed and patted the top of RG's head. "You can turn lead into gold, but you cannot seem to grow a sense of humor."

He flinched away from the touch. "Start being funny and perhaps I'll grow one." Rolling to the door, he turned to look over his shoulder at Charles. "Enough fooling around. We need to find that thing before someone gets killed."

❧

Sarah was hopelessly lost. It was her fourth day on the job, and this stupid place was a labyrinth. She needed a map just to find the toilet, but instead had been left on her own to navigate this stupid, creepy mansion. The ancestral portraits glared down on her from every wall, making her feel as though she was intruding on a private family meeting.

Something rustled behind her. She froze, listening, but heard nothing. It was just her imagination kicking into overdrive because she was ostensibly alone in a mansion so gothic looking that even Tim Burton would call it excessive.

She reached the end of a hall and had to choose left or right. Closing her eyes, she tried to mentally retrace her steps, then glanced down each one for something familiar. Nothing on the right side. Nothing on the left. She wanted to cry. She wanted to scream. She wanted to break a window and escape, never to return. Thirty dollars an hour plus health insurance was not nearly enough for this nonsense.

Maybe if she found a window, she could open it and just walk around the exterior of the building until she found the servants' entrance. It wasn't much of a plan, but it was better than spending an eternity in this maze, feeling like Theseus hunted by the minotaur, and—

There it was again, the rustling. It seemed closer this time. What was it that Eleanor had said when she was first hired? "If you feel like you're being watched, look over your left shoulder. You're more likely to see that which cannot be seen and be better equipped to deal with the threat." She hadn't signed up for unseen threats. She'd signed up for doing dishes, laundry, and enough dusting to make her empathize with Sisyphus.

Fear sucked all the moisture from her mouth as she slowly looked over her left shoulder and saw what had been following her: a pink, wrinkly thing, with floppy, batlike ears, and gleaming talons. She screamed and ran, not caring which corridor she was headed down or if she could find her way back. She just needed to put as much distance between herself and that… thing as possible.

The smell hit her as it grew closer—sulphur and sweat and the sickly-sweet odor of rot. She could feel its unnaturally hot breath on her neck like the exhaust from a car, and she wanted to throw up. Instead, she pushed her legs to go even faster, grateful for the first time that her mom had forced her to sign up for track team in high school, because its hot breath now wasn't as close as it once was.

But then something leapt onto her back, talons digging in as she rammed into walls in a vain attempt to knock it off. She shrieked again, the panic and pain blinding her to the jaws at her throat until it was too late. They closed around her neck, snapping it. She vaguely registered her legs giving out underneath her and landing on her face with such momentum that her spine seemed to bend in half. She was numb from the neck down, wanting to breathe but unable to will the muscles to do so.

Her dying thought was that at least the paralysis had left her numb to the monster sinking its teeth into her flesh.

CRUED

Charles and RG both heard the scream as it echoed through the halls. RG glanced up at him. "That came from the east wing."

"I'm on it," Charles said, running in the direction and only feeling a little bad about leaving RG in the dust. Someone was in danger, and if he didn't act, they'd be dead. Hoping he wasn't too late, he turned the corner, only to stumble upon a grisly sight. One of the new maids—Sarah, he thought—lay face down on the ground, her neck bent at an unnatural angle. The flesh had been stripped from her back, and meat had been ripped away from her in large chunks. In his younger days, he might have thrown up at the sight, but he'd seen worse since then. Still, it had never happened in his own home.

"My word," RG breathed as he rolled up next to Charles.

"We need to tell Gen and alert the staff of the danger." He pulled out his phone and opened the home security app Gen had insisted they install.

"My wards will protect us from any outside threat," RG had said, his pride wounded by her suggestion.

"Yes, but what will protect them from us?" she'd retorted. Neither of her brothers had a good answer for her, so they installed the emergency alarm system.

The app functioned a bit like an Amber Alert, sending out a mass notification to all phones that they needed to evacuate as soon as possible. Despite their… unusual interests, Charles never really believed that he would have to use it, but Gen had been right. It was handy in an emergency.

She would have received the notice by now, and he was sure that she'd be waiting on the front lawn with her arms crossed in the way that their mother used to do when they were kids.

"I'll be right back," he said, and stepped into the closest guest room. This one hadn't been used in years, so he supposed that it would be alright to strip the bed and use the sheet to cover the body. Poor girl.

When he returned, RG was glaring down at her corpse as though it had personally offended him. Charles spread the sheet over her, the white immediately staining red from all the blood.

"It's my fault," RG said softly. "I didn't check the circle well enough before summoning the demon. I should have been more careful."

He was right, so Charles didn't insult his intelligence with empty words of comfort. He simply just gave his older brother's shoulder a squeeze. "Come on. We need to catch this thing and bind it before it hurts anyone else."

☙❧

Gen never brought her phone to the greenhouse, so she didn't hear the emergency alarm go off. Though she made more of an effort to be modern than her brothers, there were places that were far too sacred for intrusions from the digital sphere. The violins of Paganini and Vivaldi warbled from her old CD player, soothing her while helping to stimulate plant growth. Her wolfsbane seemed to be coming in nicely, as was the wormwood. The ingredient that the Bard referred to as Adder's Fork, but botanists knew as Violet Dogtooth, seemed to be struggling a bit. Perhaps it needed some more sun.

As she donned her gloves to transfer her Chamomile flowers into a larger plot, something entered her greenhouse. Nothing ever crossed the threshold without her knowing about it, and as her special strain of Bluebells tinkled their alarm, she sighed and grabbed her cold iron gardening shears. The Bluebells only went off when there was something unwelcome and preternatural in the greenhouse.

The plants rustled with the entity's approach, and she faked ignorance of its presence right up until it pounced. Whipping around with the garden shears, she drove the blade right into its chest. The entity, a mass of jaws, claws, and wrinkly skin, snapped at her, knocking her backwards. The cold iron did little, so obviously, it wasn't one of the fair folk. But she didn't have enough time to ponder much more than that, as the snapping jaws threatened to rip her throat out.

Grateful for her thick, leather gloves, she held the creature's mouth open and away from her face. Its breath stank of fresh blood, meaning that she likely was not the first one to be attacked.

Closing her eyes, she tried to summon her Boa Vines, but she could not concentrate while also holding the creature's mouth at bay with her rapidly fatiguing arms. There was only one thing she could do: yell for her older brothers.

"Charles! RG!"

It couldn't have been more than a few seconds, but when trying to keep a beast from devouring you, it might as well have been a century before the door swung open and she heard Charles cry, "Genny!"

"Over here," she gritted out. Her fingers were slipping from its slobbering maw, and if he didn't help soon, she'd be its next meal. "Hurry!"

"Beast, I bind you to my will," Charles said and then repeated once, twice, three times. The entity let out a surprised yelp as Charles clipped a collar around its neck and yanked it off her. "Sit," he ordered. The demon sat, much to his delight. "Stay." Turning to her, he grinned. "Just like a naughty dog."

Gen groaned and let herself roll back and lie on the ground. "Was it you or RG?" she asked.

"I don't know what you mean."

She raised her head to shoot him a glare. "Which one of you summoned the demon?"

"You remind me so much of our mother when you glare at me like that," he replied.

She rolled her eyes and sat up slowly, wiggling her fingers and toes to make sure that everything still worked. "This seems more like RG's doing than you. What happened?"

"I'm afraid I'm not sure of the full story myself. It all happened so fast." He helped her to her feet and then to limp out of the greenhouse. Everything ached, and she was almost certain that she'd be feeling all of it in the morning.

RG was waiting outside the door. They were a deeply repressed family, the kind that only said "I love you" on birthdays and Christmases, but she could see the way his eyes appraised her, scanning for injuries. She peeled off her gloves, wincing as the leather disturbed the scabs that were trying to form where the teeth had broken through, and tossed the gloves in the trash. They couldn't be repaired anyway, and she had plenty more.

"RG, please explain what on earth just happened," Gen said wearily. So, he did, telling them about the demon's supposedly impossible escape from the summoning circle and the death of their newest maid. Her heart twisted at the news. Judging by its breath, she had known that the demon had probably killed someone, but that poor girl. No one deserved to die so young and so horribly.

"We'll be paying the cost of the funeral, of course," RG said, as though reading her thoughts, "as well as the expenses of anyone else who she was responsible for taking care of. It's the right thing to do."

"It's the only thing to do," Gen retorted.

"But first, we'll take care of this." Charles jerked the demon's chain, making it mewl miserably.

The poor thing likely had no idea what was going on. One moment, it was in its own dimension, and the next, it was in a strange mansion with strange creatures that seemed to want to bind or hurt it. She wasn't exactly going to lobby for letting it go, but they all could at least treat it with compassion. "Don't do that," she snapped.

Charles gave her a quizzical look. "This thing just tried to kill you."

"Still, it's terribly rude to torture it, don't you think? It's just as scared and confused as we are."

Her brothers both gave her that look. The one that said, *there goes Genevieve being a bleeding heart again.* But all living things must be treated with respect, even the dangerous ones.

Especially the dangerous ones.

RG sighed. "She has a point. Best not to make that thing any angrier than it already is." He wheeled back towards his lab. "Come along. The sigils and supplies required to banish it are up in my lab. We don't have much time to lose."

⚜

It was a pity that they had to send the creature back to where it came from so soon. The prideful corner of RG's mind whispered that he should keep it around at least until the occult society's meeting to show up his rivals, but once an entity has tasted human blood, it's only a matter of time before it thirsts for it again. Banishing it back to its home dimension was the humane alternative to putting it down, which was saved only for those demons whose bloodthirst drove them to claw their way back into this dimension.

He and his siblings took the elevator to his lab, with the creature yowling like a cat in its carrier. Genevieve patted its head, giving it a scritch behind the ears, and, astonishingly, the creature leaned a little into the touch.

"How did you do that?" Charles asked.

She shrugged. "It looks like a cat, so I pet it like one."

RG suppressed a sigh. "Can you please refrain from petting

the demon?"

"Why? Are you afraid it won't seem as fearsome after getting chin scritches?" she asked playfully.

Charles copied her, scratching it under its chin. "Its skin is surprisingly soft. Like peach fuzz." He tilted his head. "From a certain angle, it's almost cute. Like one of those pugs without fur. But you're a little troublemaker, aren't you?" He said it to the creature as though he was baby talking a pet.

"Don't babytalk demons," RG snapped. Mercifully, the elevator stopped, and the doors opened. Preparing the ritual was a simple matter. He ordered Genevieve to form a salt circle around the creature and Charles. He would have used his old circle, but that was apparently compromised, so salt was their safest option. Once the circle closed, he said, "Charles, when I count to three, I need you to remove the collar and jump free of the circle. Then, I will banish it. Make sure to bring the binding collar with you. High quality ones are rather expensive and difficult to find."

"I love you, Charles. Be safe, Charles," Charles muttered, his fingers already undoing the clasp but still holding the collar together.

"One… two… three… Jump!"

Charles leapt out of the circle with the collar in his hand, crossing the threshold of it without displacing a single grain of salt. The demon yowled and ran into the magic circle's invisible barrier. Closing his eyes, RG drew from his power and began to chant, the unnatural sounding words of an undead language rolling off his tongue like marbles down a hill.

His siblings each took one of his hands in their own, forming a secondary circle as they chanted the same words: "Yiak

Nyen Blagath Naok Trov!"

The demon howled and banged against the confines of the circles, but it was no match for the power of the Sley siblings. It vanished into a puff of smoke, and a wave of exhaustion overcame RG, one that he suspected was also being ridden by his siblings.

But they weren't done yet. In addition to taking care of their maid's body, they still needed to figure out who just tried to kill them and why. It certainly wasn't RG, so that only left their most senior maid, Eleanor. They had practically grown up with her, and all three saw her as a mother figure; she was the only one RG trusted to clean his workspace without judgement.

But Eleanor had been working with them for more than forty years. If she wanted to kill them, she didn't have to go to all this trouble when a bit of poison in the afternoon tea would have more than enough. Whoever was truly behind it wanted to make RG look like a fool, but he was no fool. He knew what they were doing. By sabotaging the circle, it would make him look like a failure as an occultist, and he'd be laughed out of the society. They *wanted* him to be humiliated—so he had a pretty good idea as to who was behind this. All he needed was confirmation.

◯

Eleanor paced the front lawn of the manor house, waiting with the rest of the staff for the siblings to allow them back inside. She felt a bit like a schoolgirl practicing a fire drill, something she hadn't done in decades. Maybe this was just a test for the emergency protocol, and everything was fine. But knowing the trouble that her employers regularly got into, she doubted it.

She had been in one of the bedrooms dusting when the alarm went off on her phone, instructing her to leave the building and wait until the Sleys gave them the 'all clear.' As they congregated outside, she paced, worry growing for the siblings. They were all adults now, but she had known them when they were children. They used to roast marshmallows and watch superhero cartoons while she was on break from work. God, she was getting old. Between their magic and their understanding of the occult, they were a formidable group. But still, she had every right to worry.

Finally, Charles and Genevieve appeared in the doorway. "You all have the rest of the day off," Genevieve announced. "But Eleanor, before we let you go, can we have a word?"

Feeling as though she'd just been called to the principal's office, she followed the brother and sister back inside. They led her to the drawing room, where RG waited and fidgeted with his signet ring. "Eleanor," he said.

She swallowed. While Genevieve was kind and Charles was magnanimous, RG had always been the most intimidating of her employers. Deep down, he was just as decent as his siblings, but it didn't stop her from shivering under his cold, appraising gaze. "Yes, sir?"

"Today, a demon I had summoned managed to escape my circle because someone had sabotaged it. It killed the newest maid, Sarah, before we could bind and banish it."

Her body went cold and clammy. Someone had sabotaged his lab and now Sarah was dead? How could this have happened?

And worse, she knew that she was the only person aside from the Sleys with access to the lab, which meant that she was the most likely suspect.

"Have a seat, dear," Charles said, offering her a chair. Her knees gave out from underneath her, and she sat down with a heavy thump.

"Sir, I-I would never—"

"We know," Genevieve said, cutting her off.

"I mean…" Charles began, but RG hushed him.

Genevieve gave Eleanor a reassuring squeeze of her shoulder, revealing the holes in her hands, like stigmata. Without thinking, Eleanor grabbed one of her hands for a closer look. "What happened?"

"Sarah wasn't the only one to run afoul of the beast," she said. "But don't you worry about me. I'm fine."

"I've worked for you for decades," she said. "I-I'd never betray you."

"Not on purpose," RG replied, "but I need you to think back to the past couple of days. Did you notice anything unusual?"

At first, she came up blank. Working for the Sleys meant that just about everything was a little bit unusual, so she had learned to put it out of her mind. But then she thought about her activities around the lab, and the strange incident she'd had recently. "There is… something. I had a blackout while cleaning up your lap the other day. One moment, I'm opening the door. The next, I'm carrying your dirty dishes outside. I didn't think much of it at the time because I've experienced magical aftereffects and the occasional memory charm you've cast to protect your work before. But it was rather strange."

RG hummed thoughtfully while the younger Sleys exchanged worried glances. Eleanor fidgeted with her hands, her nerves keeping them from going still. Finally, RG asked, "Did someone bump into you at any point in the past week?"

Eleanor blinked. This was not the question she expected to be asked. "P-probably? It happens often enough that I don't really remember."

"This one would have been accompanied by a pinching sensation, almost like you were stung by a bee."

Now that she thought about it, there was a moment in the grocery store a week ago. She had been in the baked goods section picking up more pancake mix in anticipation of her grandchildren visiting when a man rather rudely bumped into her, almost knocking her to the ground. Her arm stung as though he'd pinched her along the way or stuck her with a safety pin.

"Hey!" she'd called after him, but he ignored her. His head was low and covered by a baseball cap, but she could tell that though he was not elderly, he was certainly no longer a spring chicken. The skin of his hands was wrinkled, and what little hair she could make out appeared to be salt and pepper.

It was rude, but whatever. People were rude sometimes. RG listened intently, the gears of his mind turning.

"Do you remember any other distinguishing features?" Genevieve asked. "Maybe a tattoo or jewelry like a wedding ring?"

Now that she thought of it, there was something else she'd noticed. He had worn the very same signet ring that RG was currently fidgeting with on his finger. "He had a ring like yours," she replied, gesturing to it.

RG blinked. "An occult society signet ring?"

She nodded. "I'm pretty sure. It stuck out to me because the symbol looked familiar, but I couldn't quite place it until just now."

"Aren't the Hornes also a part of the society?" Genevieve asked.

RG's jaw tightened, his gaze full of barely restrained fury. "Yes, which means that it was most likely Archibald who is responsible for this. He probably wanted to humiliate me in front of them all. The tincture he'd injected you with is something I call the Sleeper Agent. It's similar to mind control, but it's only triggered for one specific action that the caster wants you to do." He placed a hand on her knee. "I'm sorry you were caught in the crossfire of our families."

"Ridiculous old rivalries," Genevieve muttered. "Why on earth are we still fighting with them when all the original offenders are long dead and buried?"

Charles threw an arm around Genevieve. "Because from ancient blood breaks to new mutiny, where civil blood leaves civil hands unclean. I seem to recall that you found the idea of your own Romeo and Juliet story rather attractive in your youth. What was the name of that Horne girl again? Ursula?"

Genevieve ducked under his arm and out of reach with a glare. "Oh, and what about you and that man, Mark Horne? You and your wife both seemed to enjoy fooling around with him."

"He was only distantly related to them, and—"

"Children!" RG snapped, getting their attention. "We have more important matters to deal with than your ridiculous dating history."

While the siblings bickered, a horrible feeling seeped into

Eleanor. If she had been the one to sabotage the circle, then she was responsible for Sarah's death. She had helped the demon free itself. It had killed Sarah, and nearly killed RG and Genevieve. "If you want to fire me, I understand," she blurted out, earning surprised looks from the siblings. Perhaps they forgot she was even there.

"Of course we're not firing you," RG said, his hand still on her knee.

"Assuming that you still want to work here after everything that happened," Genevieve added. "We would understand if you wanted to quit."

Eleanor shook her head. "Never. Even after I die, you'll have to call an exorcist to fire me." That earned a laugh from all three, which was nice, but now there was something else on her mind. She didn't want to seem rude, but she needed to ask, "So, am I free to go?"

"Enjoy the rest of the day," Charles said. "Hell, after all you've been through, take tomorrow off too."

Eleanor smiled, relieved to still have her job. There wasn't much of a market for seventy-year-old maids, and though she knew the siblings would take care of her, she still enjoyed the work.

◌◈◌

All three waited until Eleanor was gone before getting down to business. Charles knew that the feud between the Sleys and the Hornes was fierce, but he never expected for it to turn into an attempted murder *and* an actual murder. He wasn't sure what the rules were for RG's club or if they had enough proof to punish Horne, so it was difficult to come up with a strategy moving forward. He wished his wife was there; she'd always been great with planning.

"We cannot let this go unchallenged," RG said.

"Agreed," Genevieve replied, earning surprised looks from her brothers. "It would be one thing if no one was seriously hurt, but Horne got another woman killed. Sarah deserves to have justice done. Is there a way to trace the magic used on Eleanor back to him?"

RG shook his head. "It would have dispersed after the task was completed." He gnawed his lip. "Perhaps we could simply kill him."

"No," Charles and Genevieve said in unison. She gave a quick jerk of her head, an indication that Charles should speak. He said, "You and I both know that killing him will create an all-out war between our families. It's better for him to stay alive. Is there a way for him to be kicked out of the society?"

"You would have to be able to prove that he attempted to kill a fellow member of the society."

"What if we got him to confess?" Genevieve suggested.

"He'd never do that of his own accord, and he's too savvy for most truth spells," RG replied.

"Well, is he familiar with Wiccan magic? Our areas of study are incredibly different from one another. You know a lot about it through me, but what are the odds that he'd study two disciplines that seem diametrically opposed?"

"Perhaps, but I'm sure he'd still notice if I tried to slip him something in his brandy at the next meeting."

Charles grinned. Perhaps Sarah could receive a little bit of direct justice. "I may have a way to make him less likely to notice it."

☙❧

One week later, RG wheeled his way into the occult society's meeting. Horne was already slumped at a table with a drink in hand, looking as though he hadn't slept in a week, which, considering Charles's efforts in summoning Sarah to haunt him, he very well might have been struck by some spirit-induced insomnia.

"Archibald," he greeted cheerfully as he fidgeted with the special ring he wore for this occasion.

Horne picked up his head and stared balefully at him. The circles under his eyes were so dark that they looked bruised. "What do you want, Sley?"

"You don't look so well," he said, brows knitting in false concern. "Have you been sleeping lately?" And now for the tricky part. He wheeled forward, running over Archibald's toes. The man yelped and tried to pull his foot out from underneath. While he was distracted, RG opened the secret panel in his ring and used sleight of hand to pour the white powder into the glass while also making gestures of apology.

"I am so sorry," he said, wheeling back. "I suppose that I also have not had enough sleep. Did I break anything?"

"No," Archibald gritted out. "Just leave."

"Of course. Forgive me." He wheeled off. One of the secret pleasures he indulged in from time to time was 'accidentally' running over the feet of the people who annoyed him. Sometimes, he just needed a bit of petty revenge.

He watched Archibald finish off the drink. Genevieve said it would be about ten minutes before it took effect, so in that time, RG sipped at wine and nibbled on hors-d'oeuvres while mingling with the other members of the society.

After the ten minutes were up, he wheeled to the podium and grabbed a handheld microphone. Turning it on, he cleared his throat. "Excuse me, excuse me. I'll let you return to mingling in a moment, but I must make a serious accusation about one of our own. Last week, Archibald Horne mind-controlled my maid to sabotage my summoning circle in an attempt to take my life. Horne, how do you respond?"

"I…" he began, but then stopped and tried again. "I…"

"I do suggest that you be honest. I've dosed you with a bit of powdered truth that my sister cooked up for me."

Horne's gaze was absolutely murderous. "Go to hell, Sley." The crowd erupted into shocked murmurs.

"The girl who you got killed has been haunting you, hasn't she? She'll likely stop once you own up to your deed and face the consequences of your actions. Wouldn't you like to get a good night's sleep again?"

"Are you really going to believe Sley over me?" Horne yelled at the murmuring crowd.

RG grinned. He had him. "Then answer the question, Archie. Did you try to kill me by having my summoning circle sabotaged? Yes or no."

"Why should I dignify that with a response?"

"It's a simple question. Answer it and put all this to rest." He cocked his head to one side. "Unless you can't lie about your answer and decided that the best way to get out of this was to act like a bloviating buffoon."

"Fine," he growled. "Fine, I tried to kill you. Are you happy?"

"Well, I will be once you're stripped of your membership

here," RG replied, turning off the microphone and rolling offstage. The elders of the society were already speaking with Archibald, so he hung around to give his full side of the story before heading home. Genevieve's wounds would heal, she and Charles would be happy to hear that the person most responsible for Sarah's death faced the consequences of their actions, and a new maid would be hired tomorrow. Even better, he would never have to suffer through another society meeting with Archibald Horne ever again.

Spinoza's Signet

Jackson Willis

Jackson Willis is a Maryland-based writer fascinated with the bounds of conscious experience and the end of history. In his free time he enjoys reading, playing narrative-driven games, and hanging out with his pet snakes. His work has appeared in outlets such as Neologism Poetry and Fifth Wheel Press.

❧

The hideous barreled beast smells of rotten eggs soaked in vinegar, and Gen wonders how anyone could bear its proximity for long. No matter. After today, she thinks, it won't matter. The silty soil shifts beneath her feet. Gray-green shrubbery and faces steeled with determination dot an arid landscape. Poster-board slogans cut the stifling air. Gen tells herself to take note of these things. To remember where she is. Focusing is difficult with the beast looming at her back. She can feel its tar contents gurgling on the other side of inch-thick stainless steel, like darting shadows beneath a frozen lake.

In their cars, trucks, and SUVs, the cops sit maybe two hundred feet back, leaving a thin slice of no man's land between themselves and the protesters. Exhaustion hangs over the whole affair. Four days in, and nothing accomplished. The adrenaline inertia of the start has faded. Another day will have the cops twitchy, dangerous. Now is the time, Gen thinks, then acts. She doesn't have much on her—scraps for a few makeshift hexes—but it will have to be enough.

The beast moans and gurgles. Gen can't believe no one else seems to hear it. Slipping through the gathered crowd, she nears its round exterior. No one pays her any mind, for she suspects they see only a frail senior citizen. Their disregard suits her just fine. She pinpoints a specific section of the beast and produces a garish yellow thermos from the folds of her olive robe. A few dabs of her gravy-thick corrosive brew should do the trick. The stuff trickles down into each nut and bolt in turn. She could swear it sizzles on impact. Maybe three minutes, she figures, until hell breaks loose.

Wasting no time, Gen turns her attention back to the cops. They'll be an inconvenience. Kneeling, she lets the soil below filter through her fingers. She hones in on each grain. She concentrates on following their ancient imprints. The dark and the dry of it parches her, but she must press deeper. Get down to the wet where it began. Beneath layer on layer of *pillage* and *famine*. Gen finds her answer where the dark concentrates and burns with fevered loss. The unspent rage of souls bound to unmarked graves. With a flick of her wrist, Gen performs a ritual ingrained in her muscle memory, and the dead's chambered energy is unleashed like an iron slug ascending.

From stillness, the landscape explodes. The beast unhinges its jaw and its guts spill out. Dark oil spatters the dirt. Nearby protesters notice first, then shock and panic spread like a wave. Some sprint from the scene quickly as their legs can carry them, likely fearing indiscriminate retaliation. The first cop sees the pipeline's cadaver exactly two seconds later. He takes a step into the strip of no man's land too fast, too hard, and his leg sinks down to the knee. The desert floor, dry clay moments earlier, has gone to sludge all the way down. Two comrades at the fallen man's shoulders yank him from his predicament. Blood drenches his khaki trousers, staining thick and heavy enough to never wash out. Not the man's own blood, though his agitation tells Gen he doesn't know that yet. Countless others in vests and visored helmets swarm for the beast Gen has felled. The strongest and lightest make it a few steps before the mud claims their legs. A truck sputters, its hind wheels spinning in the mire and blinding anyone caught in the path of their arcing slush.

Gen goes about her work on firm footing, faintly aware of the chaos on all sides. Her fingers are drenched in oil now. Allowing the stuff to flush into the soil would be a disaster. The frost hex is doing its work already. Oil slicked on the dirt congeals, then solidifies. As the frosting effect spreads, it seals the wounds of the no-longer-gushing beast. It's a rush job, of course, but it will suffice. Gen breaks off a bit to keep. The crystallized oil has a nice sheen to it, a bit like onyx (this is not why Gen slips a second chunk into a leather pouch). Spirits below having exhausted much of their energy, cops begin to struggle out of the bloody muck. A satisfied Gen takes her cue.

Sweating, nose curled at the pungency of iron, an aching man breaches to the hard surface of Gen's shoreline. The only traces of her presence are fragments of shattered pipe gleaming with caustic brew. When the stuff is later examined in an agency laboratory, puzzled technicians will find traces of unnaturally potent citrus, red ant pheromones, and a vulture's stomach acid.

⚜

"Room Seven's right around the back, second floor," grunts the motel manager. Gen nods and takes the key. A motel was not her first choice. Yet these rural backwaters didn't have many options in the way of lodging, so here she is. Her room is where the man said. Its walls are drab and sickly yellow, the bedsheets bear a tapestry of stains, and the air is hung with the lemony scent of cheap cleaner. At least it's clean. For Gen, a not-entirely-disgusting place to rest her head is good enough for now.

The knock comes at her door around two in the morning. Gen expects the red-blue lights of the law to paint her curtains. On the contrary, the knock has punctuated an otherwise entirely silent blackness. She nevertheless proceeds with caution.

Another knock. Gen moves for the door with a half-full thermos in hand. No traditional weapons, unfortunately. She'd packed light. A look through the peephole tells her it's the manager. She opens the door a slit, leaving the door's chain lock in place.

"Sorry to bother you, miss," says the manager, unable to comprehend how sorry he will be if there isn't an excellent reason for this disturbance. "Got a message for you."

"What do you mean, a message?" The message couldn't be for her. Gen paid in cash and gave no name. It was a force of habit.

"Came in the mail earlier today. Didn't notice until I was going through the papers just now."

"And what makes you think this message is mine?" Gen's curt tone softens as the manager looks genuinely confused. Something is at work here beyond knowledge. She decides to give the manager another five seconds to explain himself.

"Take a look." He slips a sealed manila envelope through the crack. On the front, in pristine cursive: *Dear Sister.* Gen cracks the envelope to reveal a note. The handwriting is Charles', no doubt about it. They hadn't spoken in months. Years? Whatever he wanted now, she was sure it wouldn't be good.

"That will be all, thank you," Gen says and shuts the door.

◌

The place hasn't changed a lick. Crumbling arches and the overgrown vines latticing its walls do not take away from the grandeur of the Sley manor. The house is located in Colorado's mountains today. Jagged rocky precipices form a suitable backdrop for the manor's imposing stature, and mountain birds soar about the spires in futile search for a comfortable nesting place. To pin a particular architectural style on the house would be a fool's task, but the Victorian and Gothic influences are evident. Gen looks up to a barred window and recalls her earliest years spent looking out at the green, yearning. She feels at home, and it is not an entirely pleasant feeling.

"Genevieve." The voice comes from a figure at the manor's entrance, which is at present a pair of large red sequoia barn doors. "You got my message, then?"

"I am here," Gen answers. She refuses to give Charles the satisfaction of explaining his newest arcane methods for letter delivery. He has her email address.

"Yes, well, you'd better come in," Charles says through a bushy white mustache. Between that and his slicked-back silver hair, he affects an echo of Jung or Freud. Gen remembers his interest in psychology, before he'd declared his aims beyond that limited and incoherent field of study.

"Doing well?" Gen tries for small talk, a skill she hasn't quite honed.

"Fairly. You?" Charles walks Gen down a corridor she doesn't remember, which makes her feel more at home than before.

"Fine. You know, seeing the world. Helping out where I can."

"And have your travels been informative?"

"I suppose. There is knowledge out there that cannot be trapped in your library."

"I fear you underestimate my library." Charles leads her into an atrium with a ceiling of rosy glass. Shelves cluttered with nameless relics fill the space. Gen has no recollection of this room either.

"RG has been busy, I see." This was the stuff that occupied their older brother's every waking hour. This was the stuff that pushed Gen away in the first place. What could these artifacts do in service of the world, rather than collecting dust under RG's watchful eye?

"Yes, he's had his hands full lately. In fact—"

"How is your wife?" Gen asks, overcome with the urge to change subjects. RG can wait. She has not come all this way for him.

"She is well. Visiting the grandkids this week. You know how it is."

"Not really," Gen muses, examining the small figure of a gargoyle. The marbled figure was hot to the touch and sent prickles up her arm. Where did RG find these things?

"My reasons for reaching out were not purely social, Genevieve."

"Of course not," she scoffs. The Sleys were not that kind of family. "And what happened to Gen? You called me Gen when we were young."

"We have not been young in a long time," Charles says plainly, resting his hand on a carved doorknob.

"True," Gen admits, though she is the youngest of the three.

"Before we go in, I should warn you," says Charles. His hand has not moved from the knob. "RG is not happy. In fact, his mood is positively foul. He's discovered something. I don't know the details, but I know you should be here for whatever this is. Ready?"

"I suppose." Truth be told, Gen doesn't remember RG having any good moods. Her first memories of the man bear the permanent sneer of his face that had already weathered untold years before her birth. The door creaks open to reveal a laboratory. It is how Gen remembers it, and more. Gloom seeps from every corner. Forgoing lamps and windows, the room is lit by the odd glowing beaker or eerie purple smoldering without a discernible source.

"You're late," RG snaps, lurching from a shadowed corner in his wheelchair. A scowl claims every wrinkle and liver spot on his face, the baldness of his head punctuated by a pair of sharp snowy eyebrows. Seeing RG, Gen thinks maybe Charles and herself aren't all that old.

"There were complications," Charles begins, "and—"

"We're here now," Gen cuts in. "You need our help?"

"Something troubles me." That much is obvious, Gen thinks. The eldest continues, "Over these past months, I have been in pursuit of an item with untold power. You both know of Baruch Spinoza?"

"The prince of philosophers? Key figure of the Radical Enlightenment?" Charles asks the rhetorical questions like a puppy begging for treats.

"He famously wore a signet ring," RG goes on. If he can hear anything outside his own voice, he doesn't show it. "A familial symbol, we are told. The signet bears his initials and a single word: 'caute,' or caution."

"An ironic motto, considering his radical views," Charles remarks as an aside to Gen, but loud enough for RG to hear.

"The ring disappeared soon after Spinoza's death. No one could find any trace of the thing until it resurfaced without explanation five months ago. Rumors of Spinoza's signet surviving have since triggered a mad race among occultists around the world."

"That hardly seems sensible," says Charles, "What value does this ring hold for the mystic? Spinoza was the least mystical philosopher out there. The man railed against superstition and miracles. He had no respect for the occult—and certainly no affiliation."

"The forces at work beyond our cosmic veil exist independently of our notions. It does not matter whether Spinoza believed in them. He nevertheless served their purposes as much as any loyal acolyte."

"Because he embodied the perennial philosophy of unity," Gen pipes in. She doesn't want the others getting the idea she's clueless.

"Spinoza introduced a geometric formulation of the One," says RG, "His 'God' is nature, an absolute being containing all the universe's attributes. He penned in Latin what others had put down in Sanskrit and Pali. Everything is connected, every supposed individual is an expression of one and the same essence."

"And this view is what gives his signet ring power?" Charles asks, skeptical.

"Our world is a paradox," RG answers. "Unity versus difference, monism versus dualism, the one versus the many, the trunk versus the branches. Both elements are necessary. When one side of the spectrum gains enough power, it threatens to throw everything out of balance."

"Of course," Gen says with not a little sarcasm. She knows RG well enough to detect when he's holding back. She knows what kind of person her brother is. A keeper of the balance he is not.

"Spinoza's a prophet of the trunk, and yet he never properly channeled his power," RG blunders on. He speaks with an intense sense of purpose, as if each word is the most important any human being has uttered. "He lived a meager life, refused to publish his masterpiece, and died young with little to his name. His considerable accumulated energy needed somewhere to go. A receptacle. Why not the ring that stamped each of his letters?"

"Makes sense," Gen says, "Now where's the catch?" This is not the first time RG has obsessed over some arcane relic. Gen expects it will not be the last. This is his world, not so much hers or even Charles'.

"The signet's power is clearly lost on you." RG sounds agitated. Charles was right, their brother's mood *is* particularly dour. No, there is more to it than that. Something more disturbing.

"I understand the power just fine," Gen retorts. She raises an eyebrow at Charles and his head retreats into his shoulders. Fine. If Charles doesn't have the guts to ask, Gen will voice the question she knows they're both thinking: "Why do you need our help?" RG's face contorts further. Gen's sure he doesn't care for her phrasing. After all, RG never *needs* anyone. Except today.

"War is brewing. Last week, three of my contacts in Amsterdam were eliminated while following a lead on the signet." There it is. Gen can hear it in the way his tongue jitters on "eliminated." For the first time in her life, Gen can swear RG feels fear. It's written on his face and confirmed in his words. The revelation rattles her. What being or primordial force can scare her brother? It cannot simply be a great unfathomable force of evil. RG is no stranger to those; little bottled cosmic horrors probably fill this very laboratory. No, this must be something more.

"You want us to investigate," Gen says, feeling her indifference falter. Whatever has RG rattled cannot be ignored.

"Precisely." RG gives her a toothy, humorless smile. "I must have the signet before some half-competent sorcerer reaches it first. Someone who knows how to draw out the latent magicks stored in the artifact without the prudence necessary to wield it could melt down reality's structure."

"*We* must have the signet," Gen corrects him. RG ignores the comment.

"You both have plane tickets," he says. "There's a house on the lower side of the city—I'll provide the address. Start there."

"Of course," Charles says, given the opportunity to ingratiate himself. "Is there anything else we should know?"

"That's all for now," grumbles RG, which to Gen translates as *of course there is more but I don't have to tell you.* She doesn't press the issue. RG busies himself with metal tools and a squirming specimen on his table. Hoping the thing isn't too alive, Gen backs out of the room and Charles follows.

"What was that?" Charles asks the instant the door closes.

"We don't owe him anything."

"Don't you remember what he did after mother—"

"I'm going, aren't I?" Gen grits her teeth. She doesn't need a lecture from Charles, not now.

"Yes," he relents, "you are."

"Is my garden where it used to be? And the greenhouse?"

"Essentially."

"Wonderful," Gen says with mock cheer, "I need to pack."

◌

As it turns out, there are no reliable spells for jet lag. Gen is dragged along from the Amsterdam airport by Charles. It's not until she's lying in a hotel bed that Gen realizes she's not tired at all. Thoughts run through her head like a choppy river. She thinks of everything but the mission at hand. She remembers the noble truth-seeking ambitions of a young Charles, the illness of their mother, the inherited propensity for madness that touches each Sley family member—some more than others. She thinks of the family wealth; plenty of old money and no discernible use for it. Gen would donate lump sums when it felt appropriate and Charles was a persistent patron of the arts, yet it didn't feel like enough. Their money, their knowledge, their power, it all has to count for something.

After her period of self-imposed exile, doing good where she could, Gen feels no closer to satisfaction. The wonderful and horrifying oddities of the universe no longer hold any secrets from her. Gen's bounty of esoteric knowledge supplies answers for everything save purpose. Exhausted, Gen waits for the aimless thoughts floating about her head to tire themselves out.

At some point the thoughts must grow weary, because the sun is up now. Gen lets out a sigh and stalks to the restroom. Charles still slumbers in the twin bed beside her own. She decides to let him sleep. One of them should be rested at least.

The restroom mirror reflects a face barely Gen's own. When did her eyes bag, her forehead crease for good? She has aged slower than any human has any right to. That doesn't halt the existential pangs.

"Getting ready?" Charles asks from the other side of the door. His voice is annoyingly chipper. Another splash of cold water shakes the morning numbness from Gen's cheeks. They may as well get started.

The streets of Amsterdam are nothing special. Concentric rings of city and bridge littered with tourists hover over labyrinthine canal networks where the real interesting life resides. Gen hears the gurgling dialects of a dozen forms of life, aquatic and amphibian, screaming to be heard over each other. Eels flit through crevices between pike and carp. In the liminal space between canal and pavement, obese rodents war with pigeons for plastic-wrapped crumbs. A lethargic mouse sprawls under wooden bridge slats beside a still-burning cannabis joint.

"You alright?" Charles breaks her reverie. His eyes search her face for an answer.

"Good. Yes. I am alright." Gen manages in stilted syllables.

"I wanted you to see the synagogue." Charles points to a large cubic building across the street. "That's where our man Spinoza was excommunicated just about 400 years ago."

"Wonderful."

"He was only twenty-three at the time." Charles comments, "Mother took ill when he was young and his father passed two years before the *cherem*, the excommunication judgment. He had a brother, too. Ran a business together. After the *cherem*, they couldn't speak again. Otherwise his brother could be expelled from the community along with him. Can you imagine?"

"Sounds dysfunctional." It's not hard for Gen to see what Charles is getting at.

"Quite," says Charles, "though I suppose it worked out in the end."

"The man died young and poor."

"The human mind cannot be absolutely destroyed with the body, but something of it remains which is eternal." Charles quotes with the cadence of rote memorization.

"You've done your research." Gen had busied herself in the garden during their preparations instead. "Hey, where is this place anyway?"

"Almost there." Charles glances at an address scribbled on the back of a tourist pamphlet. Below the address, Gen can see he's heavily annotated a simplistic map of the city. "That's the building." Gen follows her brother's pointed finger diagonally across the street. A brick apartment building with nothing particularly notable about it. Exactly the sort of building favored by residents of the mystical otherworld. "Follow my lead," Charles says before moving to climb the fire escape. Gen takes the rungs one by one until they've reached the top floor. A floor that is apparently windowless.

"Tell me you've got the key," she mutters.

"I've got the key." Charles produces a rusted pocket-watch and thumbs it open. Another flick of his finger, and Gen's staring through an open window. "Localized temporal fracture," Charles explains, "They shored up the top floor in the 90s. After you." Gen hops through the opening. Charles follows, and the window is once again a plain brick wall. The only thing interesting about the room is a short man leveling a revolver at Gen's skull.

"RG sent us." Gen keeps her voice placid. "You'd better have some serious enchantments on those rounds. One shot is all you'll get." The short man lowers his firearm.

"Got plenty of enchantments, but it looks like I won't need 'em. Name's Harmen." The man jerks his head. "This way. RG didn't say there'd be two of you." Gen shares a glance with Charles and rolls her eyes. Dangerous communication gaps were precisely their brother's MO. Reluctantly, Gen follows the man into a second bare room where three limp bodies are arranged side by side on the shag carpet. "Done what I can to keep 'em fresh," says Harmen, "Figured you'd work better that way."

"We appreciate it," Charles says with utmost diplomacy. He crouches to examine the bodies without hesitation. Gen sees the gears turning behind his eyes. "Thoughts, Gen?"

"The left man's bloated, for starters." She leans in to get a closer look. Two men and a woman, all in their thirties or perhaps forties. The markings they bore on their clothing and skin revealed their membership in a local occult order. All novices, by the look of it.

"The right one's bludgeoned," Charles remarks. Bludgeoned is perhaps an understatement. Half his head is mush the consistency of overcooked oatmeal. Bruising swells and purples his limbs. The woman is where it gets interesting. Besides a handful of surface-level scrapes, she appears unscathed. Charles turns to question Harmen. "The three of them were together when it happened?"

"I found 'em all together. Sprawled on a bridge not too far from here."

"Him too?" Gen points to the bloated man. "He drowned." The bacteria in his lungs resonate exactly with those in the canals. She can smell it all over him.

"All of them," insists Harmen, "I can show you if you'd like."

"That may not be necessary." Charles raises a finger. "The woman is still here."

"She's dead. I made sure to check the—"

"What remains is undetectable by scientific means," Charles interrupts, "less than a faint pulse now. Still, there's something locked in the chambers of her mind. Perhaps no one is home, but if I can rattle the door. . ." Gen always told Charles he was better in the field than in the library. She allows a grin as he proves her right. "Gen, you'll need to be ready for this."

"What do you mean?"

"Someone needs to go in," Charles says like it's obvious.

"You're the parapsychology expert."

"I've got to stay and hold the pathways together," he says, "wouldn't want to trap myself in a dead body." Gen hesitates. She would argue if Charles weren't most probably correct. "For this to work, time is of the essence."

"Fine." Gen doesn't need the reminder. "Put me under."

"Gather what information you can," Charles says, bringing one palm to the dead/dying woman's head and the other to Gen's. "And remember, whatever you feel or—"

Chill. A bitter night wind bites at her earlobes through wool. Her heart thrums in staccato. One. More. Step. One. More. Step. Her body judders forth to the mantra. Outside the ringing in her ears, the world is deathly silent. Nightlife has left this bridge barren, as if recoiling from something rustling in the murk. One. More. Step. Not much further, then safety and warmth and reward. No looking back. The cold of the ring makes itself constantly known, burrowing further into the flesh of her palm as she squeezes the blood out of circulation. One. More. Step.

A light tap at her shoulder signals they've been made. The hand taps again, then grips and pulls with riptide force. She stumbles and onemore-steponemoresteponemorestep *she turns to see a friend stumble head-first into the depths beneath the bridge without a splash. A figure all bones and sinew crouches there uttering a whisper that carries. Her other friend— she can't look. Her head is locked in place by salt-dry talons. The figure breathes mist into the small pocket of air between them. Its face is sunken, a human skull vacuum-wrapped in meaty dust. Eyes too large for the other features stare with purpose. She starts the briefest prayer she knows and the figure jerks to one side. A whisper falls from its inverted lips. Not words. A sound. The sound the universe made when it came into being and crawled into the march of time.*

She returns to a womb beyond the womb. There is no attack. There is no threat. The figure, her friends, her own body are simple vibrations in a divine orchestra. Life is play. No need to keep up the ruse. She feels each organ shut down of its own volition, eager to disassemble and fold into a more interesting structure. The united self once laying claim to this body fragments and fades as if its contents are being poured through a strainer. All that remains is the light. The light where all is actual. The light where pain and death are shadows of delusion.

⟳⟲

A body hums the tunes of awakening. Eyes flutter, muscles engage, neurons switch gears. Another hovers over this body and moves in jagged slices. A shell of being fits itself into place, blocking out the pure light. Where the light fades, pain crops up like a weed in the cracks.

"Gen? Listen to me. Follow my voice, Gen."

The body is Gen. Gen is the I. I am Gen. My body aches like hell. One by one, I feel my organs get back to work.

"Tell me what that was," I manage. Charles kneels beside me in the blank room. Harmen sits in a corner. I'm sprawled on the floor. With no small effort, I push myself into a sitting position against the wall.

"You tell me," Charles stammers. "I've never seen anything like it. You had an incredible connection—perfectly synced, just before your body replicated her physical state. All in 20 seconds, give or take."

"I saw what happened on the bridge." Gen tries to remember. The experience feels like a dream. "It's like I was her, and then I wasn't." Charles nods.

"When you returned."

"No. Before that. I wasn't her, I wasn't me, I was something else."

"Amazing." Charles jots something on an inner fold of his brochure. "Transindividuation within transindividuation? This opens so many possibilities. If replication were possible—ah, but the last of her mind has faded. Perhaps you took it with you on the journey back? In any case, it's something worth pursuing at a later juncture."

"Let's not forget I almost died," Gen prods. Her brother can be a relentless academic.

"Of course," Charles blurts, "Did you learn anything to justify the danger? Aside from what we've already covered, obviously." Gen wants to say no, but that isn't true. She has the skeletal figure's scent. If it's still nearby. . .

"I've got a trace of our killer," she says, "It's a humanoid creature. Practically mummified. Lightning fast, though."

"Still in Amsterdam?" Charles sounds hopeful. Gen lets her consciousness expand and bleed into a million feelers. Flora and fauna throw a tight security blanket over the whole city. Gen follows dead end after dead end in a fraction of an instant. Charles watches with bated breath.

"Sorry." Gen shakes her head. "Not here." Then it hits with the screaming rage of a white-hot firebomb. Gen feels its impact ripple through the city like the aftershocks of an earthquake.

"What's wrong?" Charles asks, and Gen realizes her body language must indicate that something is wrong in the way a broken bone bending at impossible angles is wrong.

"Southwest." Gen grips the short man Harmen by the collar of his shirt. "Do you know a village about 50 kilometers southwest of here?"

"You're sure it's a village? Leiden's about that far. Leiden's a real city though."

"No," Gen says, "village." If it were a city, even those less attuned would have felt the impact.

"Let's see," Harmen starts, "There's a few villages just outside Leiden. Warmond, Voorhout, Rijnsburg—"

"It's Rijnsburg then," Charles interrupts. "Spinoza lived there for a time."

"We need to go now," says Gen.

"You can take a train to Leiden, then a bus from there to Rijnsburg," Harmen suggests.

"No time." Gen cannot voice the full urgency without wasting another crucial minute they don't have. "Car?"

"I can get one." Harmen jogs obediently out of the room. Charles gives Gen an intensely curious look. He says nothing. Gen latches onto the trust of silence until Harmen returns with keys and several additional guns.

"We won't need those," Gen says.

"Not for you," Harmen grunts, "Emptied the trunk in case you don't come back."

"We'll return before you know it," Charles replies. Quiet, Gen takes point down the stairs to Harmen's car.

⊂⊰⊱⊃

The skeletal figure is the village. Gen doesn't know how to square it, but this is the only fact she knows with certainty. She tries explaining it to Charles on the drive. It was only the figure once, then it expanded and became Rijnsburg. A whole community compressed in a monolithic black hole of shared purpose. Gen does not comprehend how the entity can be defeated, only that it has to be defeated or Leiden will be next, then the Netherlands, Europe, the planet, and it will not stop there.

"Do you think this could really be the end?" Charles asks, as always more curious than afraid.

"Would that be so bad?" Gen imagines going out in a last fiery clash with elemental forces threatening humanity's existence. No, she doesn't deserve something so heroic. The Sleys are not a valiant breed. The speed of it does tempt her tired spirit. How many joyless years will she endure in the alternative tedium? If the years shape her into anything like RG, she will regret escaping an earlier demise.

Rijnsburg approaches faster than expected, as if it clambered to meet them halfway. Gen can sense the moment their car enters the field. The air changes, feels occupied.

"I can feel it too," Charles says, "like the barriers between individuals have all given in." He's right. Outside, trees swirl into air, one no longer dancing to the other's tempo. A voice drenches the atmosphere. Not words. A sound. Gen's body effortlessly joins the Rijnsburg choir. A fall from herself into something greater. She hovers on the ledge from whence eternity views its domain. The gusting thought of ego, of Gen, drags her back to herself. She relishes the pain that says she is imperfect, an individual. Centered in her body, Gen steps out of the car now rendered useless as its steel frame mingles with asphalt. And Charles—where is Charles? The car is empty as her surroundings. Beneath a violet sky and above a melting substrate, Gen trudges towards the storm's eye.

The barriers begin with titan trees crumbling to form walls in her path. Gen evades these, keenly aware of the moments lost by doing so. Soon the old *Spinozahuis* is in sight. That's when the first human Rijnsburg resident tackles her with limbs splayed and clawing. Gen feels the wind forced out of her gut. She tries to cough but another hand clasps her face. Searching fingers jab around her eye sockets. A tangle devoid of mind piles in. Two more bodies restrain her legs. Each twitching motion meets resistance. Can't reach any pouches. Can't move. Can't breathe.

"Back away." Gen hears the dull thrum of a distant voice. "Last warning." The lack of oxygen has blurred her vision when it becomes clear of shadowy fingers again. Gen sits up and notices blood pouring from her ears. She can almost forget the ache and the ringing when she locks eyes on her savior. Charles approaches at a sprint, a shotgun bouncing in his two-arm cradle. He says something she can't quite make out.

"Thanks," Gen tries. Her gratitude is directed at Charles as much as Harmen for leaving something behind.

"Can you hear me now?" Charles asks. Gen nods. "Good.

We're mentally tethered. It's not total telepathy—we don't have the time or concentration for that—it's more like assisted lip reading." Gen nods again.

"The house?" She asks.

"The house." Charles responds.

◌

The *Spinozahuis* is untouched by reality's boiling collapse on every side. Relief seeps into Gen as she steps through the threshold. The space resembles something normal. Sturdy wood framing keeps the house supported. In each room, transparent museum cases line the walls with various letters and early published editions of Spinoza's work. Except for the skeletal figure lounging in the study, the scene is relatively sane.

"You're both Sleys," the figure speaks in plain words, "We gleaned that from you at first contact."

"We are," says Gen. Charles stands at her shoulder. "Who are you?"

"No longer a meaningful question." The figure waves a hand. The signet ring slides loose on a bony finger. "We are all and nothing. If we may, you probably wish to know the identity of our progenitor. The being who took the form you see here. A sorceress."

"It's a start," Charles says.

"We're not surprised RG did not mention her. There is much history. The years have not been so kind to the woman who abandoned immortality. Did you know RG loved once? He loved her until she threatened his power. Not as a rival. No, as an alternative to his conquest. Live in harmony with the universe or break it until it suits your will—this was RG's choice. It is the choice of each being."

"I'm not going to apologize for RG." Gen takes a step forward to gauge the figure's reaction. She has no illusions about

her odds in direct combat, but if she could just remove the ring.
. .

"You have a choice. Unity's bliss or egoism's pain." The sorceress-figure sits perfectly still while the world folds into itself outside their room. "Take your time."

"Look, Gen." Charles stares with a limp jaw through the room's sole window.

"We bring you home," the figure declares. Through the window, beyond countless soupy gurgling tendrils united under the figure's awareness, Gen saw the place where her greenhouse conjoined with the central Sley family manor. "Our progenitor long wished to bypass this manor's arcane defenses. Now we move without effort. Space within us unwinds its linear mask. Remember your choice" The figure vanishes. Its tendrilled abominations have vanished too, beaching the stranded *Spinozahuis* on the Sleys' front lawn.

An explosion rocks the Sley manor's thickest spire. RG's laboratory. Gen has no energy to ponder morality. She only floats on the inertia carrying her back into Sley manor. Up a flight of stairs, through a twisting hallway, and between the two highest bookshelves in Charles' library. Gen and Charles breach the laboratory where their brother stares down God.

He puts up a good fight. Every glowing rune, accursed instrument, captive hell beast, and sentient grimoire tears chunks from the field of pure being surrounding the nameless skeletal figure. Gen can see it will not be enough.

"Do you dare consider this your doing?" RG roars at the figure. Neither take notice of Gen and Charles. "You believe you can enter this place without my permission?"

"We have done so." The figure envelops an imp under RG's thrall and melts it down to stardust.

"You have done exactly as I wished." RG's teeth flash, frothing with spittle. "The others were a misdirection. Bait to pull you to my domain."

"The perfect whole cannot be resisted." The figure almost sounds saddened. "Divine perfection awaits."

"In these walls," thunders RG, "there is no God before me." With a deft twirl of his fingers, he completes the final touches of an immensely complex spell. Something beams from RG and erases every bit of Rijnsburg the figure has brought along with it.

"You were so close," says the figure, and in a blurred fit of motion flings RG from his seat and across the room. The figure staggers toward RG. Already Gen can feel its power returning. The room begins to blur into itself.

"Give me that," she says, and Charles offers up the shotgun. Gen lines it up with the figure and marvels at her own willingness to kill perfection. Can she live with herself after wiping out an enlightened creature to save a rotted pit of a man? Gen decides to find out after she pulls the trigger. The figure twitches and lets out a final gasp. Not words. A sound.

In the wreckage of RG's laboratory, the signet of Spinoza is the only artifact remaining. Gen watches it dance in the light. Under her guidance, unity could be achieved the right way. The sorceress was a vengeful spirit leading its accumulated godhead astray. With the right center, it could be more. RG stirs across the room and makes Gen's decision easy. She would never become like him. The signet ring makes a *plop* falling into Gen's half-full yellow thermos. She hears a stifled shriek like the cry of a kettle, then nothing.

☙❧

RG doesn't regain full consciousness for nearly a week. When he does, his questions revolve solely around the ring. Charles reluctantly informs him it was destroyed in the battle. RG's face sours before quickly stiffening.

"Probably for the best," he says with a somber brow. Gen wonders if he means it. His next set of questions revolve around the sorceress. Despite honest reports from Gen and Charles, RG remains skeptical about her death. Let him worry, Gen thinks. Let the sorceress-figure keep him up each night for the rest of his unending miserable life. When RG returns to sleep, Gen slips into the hall outside his room with Charles.

"I suppose this is it?" He asks like he's expected this conversation from the moment they defeated the sorceress.

"For now," Gen admits. She's not ready to tend her plants full-time just yet. The world needs more good in it. "Unless you want to come along?"

"I must pass for the time being," Charles says, "I'm sure I don't need to tell you the manor's doors are always open, Gen." Gen nods.

"Tell RG I'm not doing any more of his dirty work."

"I'll include myself as a signatory on that one." Charles smiles. Gen walks out through the oversized barn doors.

"One more thing, Charles. A saying I remembered." In truth she'd spent the last week studying the works of Spinoza. She didn't grasp large chunks of it, but one parting line stuck out: "All things excellent are as difficult as they are rare." Charles lights up at the quote. Without spoiling his fun, Gen amends the phrase in her own head. Perhaps there is excellence in ease as well. Perhaps there is excellence readily accessible to all. Perhaps the woman who shot perfection in the back is no fair arbiter of moral lessons. Gen has no answers. For now, that is enough.

A Very Good Dog

Trevor Williamson

Trevor Williamson holds a B.A. in Modern Languages and an M.A. in Spanish Literature. Trevor is the co-host of the Sley House Presents podcast, which features book reviews, audio fiction, and author interviews from across genre publishing. He co-edited two previous anthologies with Sley House Publishing, and this is his first fiction publication. Along with his brother, Collin, Trevor co-hosts the Books & Badgers podcast distributed by Sley House's network of podcasts. Every weekend, you can find him curled up with a good book in his home in Northwest Arkansas. You can follow his adventures online on most major social media platforms as Sley House Presents.

CB&O

The day I turned twelve, a dog stumbled out of the woods beside our manse, and I made my first friend. I know it seems strange to make friends so late in life, but you must understand how terrible and miserly my father was. And besides, I had siblings, not that they were any good.

The dog had patchy fur, one drooping eyelid and a dry tongue that never quite fit in its gummy mouth. She—at least, I think it must have been a she, for it had no general genitalia that I could inspect—had a habit of limping around with one leg, though the leg with a limp was seldom the same one as the day before. I took to her almost immediately, the dog's strangeness a reflection of my own family's bizarre tastes and inclinations.

My sister hated the thing, although I have never known Genevieve to actually like anything other than those dreadful plants she cultivates in our greenhouse. I suppose she must have liked something about her various husbands, but their serious and deadly allergies have given me cause to believe it was their money that spoke to her most. RG, cruel and intellectual, never gave much thought to the dog except for what he might do to experiment on it. I learned quickly never to leave her alone and unsupervised with my brother for any amount of time—though perhaps more for his safety than hers.

When I took her to my father, his face contorted into a scowl. He inspected her with the same expression one might study rotting garbage or spoiled milk. His frown deepened as the dog locked eyes with him, and his voice croaked out to me alongside the smoke from his pipe. "Son, this dog is not all right."

"Of course she isn't all right, she's half starved and in need of a home. I am certain that with some victuals and affection, she might well recover." I don't know what compelled me to defend the dog so much, except that I had already grown quite fond of it in the slim hours we had spent together.

My father shook his head and grimaced at me. "I won't

allow it in the house."

"Then I shall prepare a house for it all its own. If Gene-vieve is allowed a greenhouse and RG a laboratory in the cellar, then I should be allowed at the very least a small house for the dog outside."

Father pressed his lips together and grunted at me indif-ferently, leaning back from me and the panting dog. "So be it. But it is now your responsibility. You will provide its meals and clean up after it. Take it for daily exercise, give it… affection." He seemed to struggle with the word, as if nobody could love so repulsive an animal as this dog. I never knew my father to have affection for anything or anyone, except perhaps his to-bacco and the lung cancer it gave him.

I took the dog with me outside and set to finding the space where she should live. It took us both the better part of the afternoon, though it was mostly because I couldn't help myself from running through the grounds with the dog, her barking a strangely hoarse and low growl while playfully nipping at my heels. It was a strange and wonderful feeling knowing that we had a bond, only her drooping eyelid hiding her immediate love for me.

We eventually settled on a spot just next to the gate that separated the manse from the woods beside it. With the dog-house so close to the woods, she would be able to come and go as she pleased and still have access to the whole yard beside the greenhouse, where we seemed to play the most. As evening grew closer, I dragged blankets out from the house and set up a fort of old tapestries and tented sticks where the doghouse would later be constructed. We supped outside that night, I with a three-course feast from the house chef, her on the scraps of fat and gristle unfit for the rest of us.

She did not so much as eat as inhale the food I provided to

her, and I giggled all the while she slurped at the grease between my fingers after handing her the food. The gums where
she had lost teeth were slimy and hot, providing no end to my
childish laughter. When we had finished our meal together, I
wrapped my arms around her and inhaled the stale dirt smell
of her patchy coat.

With a sigh, I let her go and she sat beside me in the tent,
her dumb eyes roaming over my features. "I suppose all that is
left to us is finding your name. It's a serious business, naming a
dog. I should think long and hard about what to call you."

She seemed to understand the gravity of this moment,
stilling her panting as if it might distract me from uncovering
the appropriate name for her. I studied her features closely, as
if it might give me some clue. Though her coat was patchy and
her breed completely unknowable, she had one leg covered in
bronze hues. Her name suddenly came to me as if by a strike
of lightning.

"I know exactly what to call you! Henceforth, you shall be
known as 'Empusa,' a dog no longer."

Empusa nodded to me with those drooping eyes and accepted my gift with a regal seriousness. A cackle escaped my
throat and I leaned into her for another hug, which she recip-
rocated by spreading her paws wide across my shoulders. With
her cheek pressed to my ear, I emptied out all the boyish love I
had to give.

That night, wrapped around one another under the cover
of the blankets I stole from the house, we deepened our bond
through a few hours of sleep. As the house clock chimed the
witching hour, Empusa stirred, rousing me from my slumber.
My back felt stiff from the lumpy ground beneath us, and I
propped myself up as the dog scurried beneath the blanket
and bolted for the gate leading into the woods. There, her

hackles rose, and her growls reverberated through her chest into the air like the rumbling of approaching thunder.

I crawled from my makeshift tent and peered through mist that poured out of the woods in long fingers, shimmering in the moonlight. I had long suspected something lived in those woods, but one gets used to blood-freezing howls after so long. We had all been told stories of how horses would wander from the manse stables into the woods only for their meat-stripped corpses to be found a few days later. But hearing tales and seeing monsters with your eyes are two very different things, and for the first time I saw what actually lived in those woods.

Empusa stood in front of me like a guardian statue, illuminated by the light of the full moon overhead. Beyond her, a figure draped in shadows loomed over the open gate between the rock walls that divided Sley House from the woods. I could not make out the form of the thing in its shroud of mist and moonlight, except that it appeared like a great writhing black mass, conjuring up great evils in my mind's eye. Its amorphousness only served to accentuate the waves of malice that rolled from it, though I could not tell toward what or whom that malice was directed. Was it me, for my relative innocence? My family for their acknowledged wickedness? To Empusa, for daring to trespass across the threshold between woods and our estate? Or toward Sley House itself, conjured of brick and wood fired and chopped from the woods beyond?

Whatever its intent, the thing roiled and belched its displeasure as it encroached upon the open gate. Empusa stood firm, barking with increasingly feral snarls. At last, the mist receded, and the thing coalesced into a writhing mass of bladed fingers stretching out toward me.

It was then that a similar transformation undertook my dog.

Empusa reared up on her back legs, her joints popping as her legs suddenly lengthened. Her claws took on the appearance of hooves deformed by great talons, her hair bristling into a coat of fine feathers and sickly pale scales. I scrabbled backward on my bottom as her torso stretched like a serpent's, elongating so high she might have stretched even taller than the home that towered behind me. Across her back, great leathery wings unfurled and blotted out the moon so that I could not make out the transfiguration of her canine head into whatever monstrous countenance it surely underwent.

From Empusa came a terrible, human-like cry, the challenge of a powerful woman as through the throat of a crow. Great and powerful arms reached for the writhing black mass on the other side of the gate, and Empusa and the terror grappled in a bloody fight that raised the fine hairs on my arms like static electricity. They exchanged miserable blows, each gouging the other with talons like sickles and teeth like daggers. The terror began to weaken, to cower beneath the ferocious attack of Empusa, until finally its black lengths fell limp and Empusa began to thrash its corpse around as a retriever would a duck.

It was then that I saw Empusa's glowing eyes, her distended jaw widening into a serpent's mouth. She bore down on the terror of the woods and jammed its body into her widening maw. Within seconds, it had slithered down her gullet, engorging her body, until her mouth had closed around it entirely and she had swallowed the whole of the monster, nary a trace of it or its mist to be found.

Empusa turned back to me and wriggled her massive frame across the gated threshold and back onto our property, wherein she began to undergo a second transformation back into the dog I had met earlier—albeit, with a rather distended belly. I could not comprehend what had just transpired except to think she had saved my life.

Extending my hand to her, I felt her sniff me, then give me a dry lick with her flaccid tongue. I crouched to her and smiled into her dumb eyes.

"Goodness," I said to her. "You *are* a very good dog."

What's In A Name

J.M. Haugen

J.M. Haugen is an aspiring writer in the genres of horror, fantasy, and comedy. A native of the greater American Midwest, he's looking to bring a few thrills, and a few smiles to his readers.

C☙

Charles Sley was no amateur scholar of mythology. Not by any stretch of any fool's imagination. He'd mastered Greek and Latin before his teen years and read the epics of the Hellenistic world, in the *original* dialects. His adolescence had been spent deciphering the tales of ancient Mesopotamia, and he still could recite them line by line. Translations of the life of the Buddha lined his shelves, next to several summations of Hindu canon. Charles knew the names of every god, goddess, demigod, demiurge, and spirit between the coasts of the Iberian peninsula and the easternmost island of the Pacific, and he was nearly as encyclopedic in regards to the Americas. Few were the legends he was unfamiliar with, and rarer still was the mythical figure he'd hadn't heard of at least twice.

"Where *is* that damn name?! Of all the blasted gods in all the world, how is it I can't find *that* one?!" He thumbed once again through the tomes scattered across the table, leafing through pages at breakneck speed. He cross-referenced this or that name, for the tenth time that morning, attempting to blend and twist and warp phrases and terms in languages that bore almost no linguistic familiarity to each other. He re-checked his self-authored charts and diagrams, chasing words through the timeline of civilization's development, attempting to link specters of mythology across eons and cultures. Hours had flown by as he pulled down book after book, drew up new line charts and discarded them alongside the old, and repeated the pattern over and over, till Charles found himself surround-ed once more by towers of literature.

In all his years of reading and research, of thumbing through religious texts and scrolling through scrolls, he'd never encountered a truth he couldn't unearth. No mystery had ever bested him before. The several dozen publications he'd penned, each unveiling forgotten lore and hidden dots of nar-rative parentage others had long failed to connect, were testa-ment enough to his academic prowess. And here Charles Sley stood, nearly pulling his alabaster hair out strand for strand as the *one* truth, the singular theory he'd long held but had never confirmed, once more eluded him.

"BAH!" He swatted a pencil to the far wall and retreated from the family library, availing himself of the early afternoon sunlight pouring into a nearby window. Charles let the warmth course over his face, feeling the wrinkled skin around his eyes and the muscles beneath relax. His wife had said for years he'd go blind, not from the constant reading, but from the constant squinting in effort. *I should probably call her. Letting another month go by* ... He shooed away the thought like he had the pencil. He was close. He knew. He couldn't be distracted, not now.

But where to go next? What tome could he consult that would fill in the missing piece? He suspected that it must have come from the deepest part of Africa, as had humanity itself. Somewhere in the midst of that storied continent was the one name he only knew of by rumor and hint. The name of the one divine figure in all of mythology that seemed utterly past all recollection, despite its prominence.

The First God. The progenitor of all gods in human myth, its aspect handed down in a million different forms and iterations throughout time. Somehow, this single figure had lapsed into oblivion, completely buried in the sands of history, Charles *knew* it had to exist. Every piece of lore and legend he'd read harkened to an earlier story, and *that* to an even earlier tale, and so on. And at the end, or beginning as it were, of all myths there must have stood one character, one name to spawn them all. The "Big Bang" of divinity, handed down from the earliest culture humans had ever developed. If Charles could find it, could prove it existed, not only would he be remembered for all time in academia, but every further anthropological discovery made upon the back of his triumph would be attributable to *him*, and him alone.

He snorted. "Maybe I should go have RG conjure me up the damn name. Would save me at least *one* headache."

The thought of his brother - his disagreeable, cantankerous, occult-schooled, well-traveled, knows-more-than-is-healthy-for-*any*-person, brother - sparked an old memory from when Charles was four or five, and his brother well into adulthood.

He'd always been an adult in Charles's eyes. Back then, he'd been a far younger, still disagreeable but more dashing than dangerous RG, raging over a letter from a "colleague" in Europe. Something to do with a trip he'd taken on a river years before, somewhere in...

"Africa," Charles grinned. It was a long shot, to be fair. A nigh impossible shot, were he being honest. But if *anyone* might have found the name of the most primordial deity in human history, etched into some lost ruin in the jungles of Africa, it would have been RG.

Charles adjusted his tie and suit coat, and turned in the direction of RG's lab. He couldn't remember the last time they'd spoken in more than formal terms. Perhaps this once, he could convince the old sorcerer to talk with him in something approaching a congenial fashion.

❧

"No. Leave." The elder man remained hunched over his desk, never once looking up from the manuscript beneath his hawk's gaze.

Charles did his best to suppress a sigh. "Come now, RG, it shouldn't take more than an hour or so of your precious time. Just one little rendition of your trips through Africa, and I'll leave you be. Scout's honor."

"You were never a Scout, and NO. For the final time. Now get out of my laboratory. I'm in the middle–"

"Yes yes, you're invoking some great rite or working or whatever. Can't it wait a tad to indulge a sibling?"

"It cannot! Thanatos does not wait upon the indulgence of man, but upon the clipping of the thread. And my thread has grown strained these past years, so I must finish all that I've set out to do."

"Oh? Are you about to die, old man?" Charles teased playfully. "You've been saying that since I was grown enough to look you in the eye, and you've yet to keel over. Quite frankly, I don't see the Reaper bothering with your musty spirit any time soon."

"*WHY*, oh impertinent fledgling, do you *always* insist on vexing me whilst I'm engaged in something?"

"I can't help it. You are *always* engaged in something. You're a verified workaholic. I don't recall a time you weren't doing this or that, to the point you couldn't spare two words for friend or family. Not that you had many - or any - of the former. The first words you ever spoke to me were 'not now, my greatest leap is nigh', or some such."

RG lowered the magnifying glass, distant strands of memory coalescing into a coherent picture. "Ah, yes. I'd just deciphered the *true* Simon translation and was examining the invocation for Marduk. You barged in asking for," he said, side-eying his brother, "a story."

Charles laughed, twirling one end of his ivory mustache. "Yes, yes I did! You practically threw me out of the room by the seat of my trousers! I was outraged, so I recall! I even asked the nanny to scold you," he chuckled, adding "Did she ever say anything to you about it?"

The vitriolic elder had gone back to his glass and manuscript. "No servant of ours has ever had the poor sense to interrupt me. Unlike *some*."

"I'm family. Different rules apply." Charles sashayed closer to the wheelchair, not quite placing his rump upon the desk (a capital offense) but leaning just so to cast a slight shadow over the tabletop. "Now then, about that tale"

RG slammed his fists to either side of the open book, rattling everything nearby in a surprising show of strength. "For the FINAL time, Charles! NO!" he roared. "Now take your insolent hide out of this laboratory before I forget our mutual origin!"

Charles did not immediately back away, but close enough. He didn't think RG would go so far as to do something meta-physically drastic, unlike their sister that once, but if the older man did, it would be far more horrifying than anything Gen-evieve could conjure up. He held his hands up in surrender, backing out of the room till he crossed the threshold. He's barely stepped both feet to the other side when an unheard wind slammed the door in his face.

"Damned old magician," he uttered, softly. RG had par-ticularly strong opinions on certain labels, and Charles wasn't about to aggravate the man further. For now, at least. In the meantime, there were other sources he might still check. The Sley family library was, if anything, expansive, and it more than certainly held at least a few more tomes that could be of yes. Granted, none were as old, or as exotic, as any of the sources his elder sibling had access to, but there might yet be hope.

He would have that name, come hell or high water, and he began the trek back to the library through the mid-afternoon shadows, as determined as ever.

∾

"I'm sorry, but what did you just say?" Charles stammered, blinking to accelerate the transition from lamplight to late afternoon sunshine. The sound of his brother's voice had spun him about to confront a blur of radiance shining down upon a patch of darkness. Eventually, his vision adjusted, revealing a halo of light surrounding the older Sley sibling, who sat en-sconced in the library doorway.

"I *said* that I've reconsidered, and will acquiesce to your re-quest," RG repeated. "Assuming you're still interested."

Charles hadn't heard the squeak of the wheels, nor felt the

drop in the room's ambient temperature which always seemed to herald RG's arrival. *How the devil did he sneak up on me again?!* Yet as vexing as the man's sudden appearance was, Charles's annoyance was quickly buried by comprehension. "You'll tell me? Really?!"

The elder scholar sighed as he rolled closer to the table. "Ordinarily, my answer would have been final. However, after a few hours of contemplation, I've decided that it does little harm to recount my old adventuring days."

"And what, pray tell, was the instigating factor in this about-face of yours?" Charles asked skeptically.

RG leaned back, his fingers forming a steeple. "There were several, the most prominent of which is that I finished my work early. Beyond that, the not insignificant breadth of your research assures me that you, more so than most, would appreciate the story I have to tell. Your knowledge of legends and myths is...well, I'd not say 'staggering', but it does have the patina of the impressive. If anyone could make use of my tale, I suspect you'd make a suitable candidate."

Charles twisted a mustache end. "Rare praise, coming from you. Anything else?"

"The inevitability of you pestering me *again*," RG snapped, "was too oppressive a thought to ignore."

Charles snorted. "And there it is. Glad to see I've made an impression, brother. Well," he trailed off, maneuvering a nearby chair to face his visitor. He retrieved a notepad and pencil, seated himself, and settled his eyes onto his sibling. "Let's not waste the rest of the day, shall we?"

"Now," RG spoke cautiously. "You are *sure* you want to hear this? You've no reservations whatsoever?"

A derisive chuckle was the immediate answer. "You needn't concern yourself with my mental well-being. I'm more than capable of handling your tale of terror, if it makes the final connection I've been searching for. I *need* that name, RG." Charles's gaze grew in intensity. "I'm too close to uncovering a primal secret–"

"Oh yes," RG smiled, a sardonic twist to one corner of his mouth. "Your little pet theory. The foundational myth of all myths. A grandiose bit of hogwash."

"And yet, it was none other than you yourself who told me, *when I was three*, of the supposed 'final truth' at the heart of existence. Did you have a revelation at some point that dispelled the illusion?" Charles did his best to keep his eyes locked on the man, and not on the transportation aide the man had been forced into all those years ago.

The older man didn't flinch, or show any expression beyond his usual scowl. "Do you want to hear this or not? That I finished my previous project does not preclude the numerous *other* activities that need my attention."

Charles bit his lip, ambition and eagerness overriding his natural flippancy. He merely nodded, and held the pencil at the ready. RG took a breath, collected his thoughts, and began.

"It was some years ago that I found it, buried in a forlorn site that had not known the presence of humanity in eons..." RG's voice trailed off a moment, memories parading before him. "The First God–such a fascinating trip."

CR§O

I forget the date. It was, I think, perhaps a year or two after our parents had brought you into the world. Genevieve was not even a thought yet, and I was not yet confined as I am now. I had taken to traveling early in my youth, seeking the higher mysteries. My will and efforts were already bent to the purpose I continue to pursue, and as I did not always see eye to eye with our father, our mother suggested my time was better spent away than here on the family estate, exchanging verbal barbs with 'the cowardly fop' as I'd come to call our patriarch.

That year was a particularly momentous one for me, though I was unaware of that as I paraded off a boat and into the wilds of the inner Congo. I had just finished a summer in the sands of Egypt, and as luck would have it I had run across mention of an ancient, long-buried temple, or the very least some forgotten place of worship lost to the jungle. The reference was cloaked in myth and metaphor, but given the range of my studies, and a quick but thorough divination, I was convinced that the place was in fact a convergence.

You know of such places, of course. Stonehenge, the Oracle of Delphi, the peak of Huangshan and the Devil's Tower — all points where the flow and ebb of the world's power converge in a whirlpool of possibility. I'd been to a few by then, had worked wonders within the maelstrom of Nature's beating pulse. But all my research confirmed that this was something special. A convergence like no other, perhaps the actual heart of the world's life force. I'd seen a few such places mentioned in other works, but they were never quite the spectacle promised.

This one, though. I had reasons to believe this was the genuine article. A colleague of sorts assured me that she'd seen a similar tale elsewhere, in a scroll taken from a monk's retreat deep in the Tibet ranges. In our correspondence, we became convinced of what we'd found, and as she was tied up, I volunteered to make the initial discovery. Perhaps, had I waited — but then, given all that transpired later, it may have been a blessing that I went alone.

Ahem. Never mind. Old sentiments, best forgotten. Anyway, the temple. Yes.

My party and I trudged through the forests just southeast of the river's northern bend. I remember being somewhat astonished at how quickly we made the destination. Surely a point as important, as powerful as this couldn't have been forgotten so easily, given its proximity to the waterway. I asked my guide, a local man quite knowledgeable of the area, multiple roundabout questions, but it became quickly apparent that neither he nor anyone in the region knew anything about such a site. As far as he or the two porters were concerned, there was nothing in that stretch of forest other than insects, snakes, and disease. No prohibitions, no ancient warnings coddled in stories...it might as well not have existed, for all anyone knew. I began to doubt, yet I pressed on regardless.

Three days we trekked through those woods. Three days of cutting vines and swatting vermin. One of the porters took a nasty bite from some reptile or other. The others were quick to pronounce him a dead man walking. A quick poultice and an incantation later, the man was right as rain, though it took the promise of more American currency to get the other two to not flee at the sight of me. Damnable peasants. Should have left the fool to his fate and cowed the others into continuing, but I wasn't about to carry the man's load alongside my own.

Finally, we made it. Even all these years later, I'm not entirely certain what I expected to find. A grand edifice, perhaps. A wondrous construction in the style of the pre-Old Kingdom pharaohs. A circle of carved monoliths, not unlike the Salisbury monument. At the very least a sacrificial platform of some kind. What I did not expect was the confounded absence of anything even remotely of interest. There wasn't even a clearing! Just a small hill, covered in foliage no different than the rest of the blasted jungle.

Needless to say, I was...unimpressed, at first. However, what I was not was deterred. I'd scoured more than a few sights that were equally as barren at first glance, and always found something to pique my curiosity, or at the very least justify the expense of the trip. And my conviction as to the site's authenticity was absolute. I knew there was something there to be found. Something tremendous. She...my colleague, that is, had been as equally satisfied as I that there was profit to be had there, if only it could be hoisted up from the grave of antiquity.

We got to work, my party and I; they with hatchets and muscle, I with intellect and esoteric craft. They gave my pavilion a wide berth, no doubt from the smells and sounds issuing forth, and that was perfectly acceptable *to me. I had no need of their companionship, only their effort. With more exact information I'd gleaned from the area, I directed their efforts accordingly, clearing away the flora from the hillside and its surrounding area. After yet another incident with the local fauna, I took it upon myself to clear out the animal life as well. The men were decidedly more skittish in my presence after that, but my methods produced an abundance of viable meat, so they ate well and did not complain.*

It took three days more, but finally the hill sat alone in a small clearing, unobtrusive and demure save for its spot of prominence. As luck would have it, we'd finished on the day before a full moon. I took it as an auspicious sign, a clue from the firmament that I was right, and the hand of destiny hovered close. I prepared all that day, enacting every ward and safeguard I knew. I had no idea what to expect, or what might approach from within that mound. Given past experience, I half-expected a struggle of some kind, and prepared for such. I wasn't at all repulsed by the idea; far from it in fact. The fires of youth burned hot in my veins. I yearned for a contest of wills with some long-dead god, or an attack by some guardian monstrosity. The hubris of a young man, fueled by an abundance of wealth and skill, knows few bounds.

Suffice to say, I was ready, and foolishly eager as the sun fled and the moon ascended. I tried every incantation I knew that was designed to open. Open doors, open mouths, open souls...anything to compel the hill to reveal its secrets. None worked. Hours slipped by. The sweat rolled down my torso, naked and covered in ash and runes. I chanted, I sang, I danced, I commanded, I implored, and by the end I raged. Not once did that little hill acquiesce to my demands. I was, to put it mildly, frustrated.

ⓒ₰

RG paused in his telling to rub the bridge of his nose. Charles took the lull in the narrative to quip "Well, you've always had something of a short fuse, dear brother. I rather suspect you did everything short of attacking that poor little hillock."

"Oh, I did that too. The men had to pull me off the hill before I beat my hands to a bloody pulp."

Charles blinked. "That...seems...a bit far. You've always been temperamental, but I couldn't imagine you going berserk."

A short cackle issued from the older man. "Yes, well, I was a great deal more passionate in those days. Far less controlled, and occasionally prone to such outbursts. It was a failing I'd borne since birth, much to our parents' lament."

"And what changed you, out of curiosity?" Charles knew better than to inquire too closely into RG's past, but he was also not one to ignore a good mystery.

But the old occultist leveled his sibling with look, a glance that spoke of experiences the man would not willingly divulge. "Many...things. None of which are the subject of this tale. Shall I continue, or would you prefer to dig your ink-stained fingers into old wounds?"

The implicit threat was not lost on Charles. "Oh, by all means, proceed."

৪৪৪

Well, by the time dawn was breaking, I had run through as many workings as I knew, or had the resources to invoke. There were grander rituals I could have used, but my materials were limited to what the porters could carry or the jungle provide. Needless to say, I was out of options. Or out of good ones, at least.

I was laying against the hill when the sunrise came. I was unclothed, save for a galabeya I'd picked up in Egypt, and which I had pulled up only as far as my waist. I was dirty, tired, exasperated and humiliated. And I was deeply, deeply vexed. Insulted, might be a better term. That some old mound of soil and moss would defy me...ME. I would have gladly blown the whole damnable thing to rubble at that point, had I the explosives.

But then came the hour where the sun was just tipping over the horizon and a golden radiance began to stretch across the earth. As it began, for just a moment, all became still. I watched the shadows on either side of me elongate. I heard the whispers and cries of the forest around me trail off, as if a congregation drew their heads down in reverence for the morning prayer. For the briefest of points in time, the world was perfectly silent.

Almost.

I heard it behind me. A sort of gurgle, the unmistakable sound of running water beneath me. Or more precisely, beneath the hill I rest on.

The porters of course claimed it was just the river to the north echoing through the trees. But I knew better. I knew what I heard, where I'd heard it. I ordered them to start digging, to uproot that shameless hill. There was some reluctance, at first. However, I was not in the mood to tolerate insolence. My ego was easily pummeled in those days, and it had been bruised by my failure in the night. Those poor souls...ah well. Oh, don't look at me like that, Charles. I didn't inflict any permanent injuries upon them. Physically, at least. After all; I needed them to work. And work they did.

It took a few hours, and three pairs of bloodied hands, but ultimately they tore down the hill, and lo and behold, there in the crust of the earth lay my prize. A trapezoidal plane of black stone, three feet on the bottom and little more than half that at the top, smooth and dark as obsidian but without the mirror shine. The sun had risen high by then, and in the light I could almost make out tiny flecks of green and gold in the material. I'd never seen a natural substance quite like it.

⌘

"Yes, yes, black stone, green dots, very exciting," Charles muttered, intent on his brother's words. "Were there carvings? Symbols, words, pictures, anything of the sort?"

Oh yes," RG smiled.

⌘

There was indeed. An inscription ran about edges and spiraled into the center. I'd never seen such a writing style, nor the tongue it was written in.

I had studied works in ancient Sumeria, Assyrian, Aramaic, old Hebrew script and Old Kingdom hieroglyphics, and a smattering of others. But the engraving was none of the above. It bore no likeness to Arabic, and was certainly nothing like the Latin alphabet. I could have almost detected a hint of the Oriental forms, perhaps more Japanese than Mandarin, but even that would be a stretch. The lines were too flowing, the curves and swooshes contorted. It reminded me of waves, of an ocean at high tide. A trick of the imagination, of course. We were hundreds of miles from any sea. There could have been no such inspiration for a purely inland society.

Regardless of their origin, I set about attempting to decipher the inscription with what few resources I had available. The hours skipped past, with little success. I was tempted to take a rubbing and return to civilization, perhaps even return home to this very library. But if I missed something, I would not be able to return for some time. And I worried that the porters would fail to keep quiet. News of a lost ruin in the jungle would've attracted any number of base cretins seeking treasure, and I had little in the way of measures to secure the site. I would crack the code, then and there, and keep at it until the limit of our provisions was reached.

While I worked, I dispatched the porters into the surrounding jungle, seeking water. No, not to drink, Charles. I know what I'd heard, and by all logic, there should have been a tributary or small lake of some kind, either feeding into or being fed by the source I'd heard. If found, it could have led us to a way underground. Truthfully, I wasn't counting on it. Such a route would have undoubtedly required a fair amount of underwater exploration, for which we were completely unprepared. And I was not about to sacrifice my minuscule pool of labor in a vain quest. I certainly wasn't about to carry the several trunks we brought on my back.

The day flew by, as it's wont to do when one is engrossed in something. No lake or waterway was found. And the inscription proved maddeningly unwilling to give up its secrets. By sunset, I was out of ideas, and had even less patience. Nowadays I might have let the translation sit for a *time whilst I ruminated on a solution. Back then, I was far less inclined to take things at a measured pace...or keep my temper in check. I've wondered since what the men must have thought, hearing the commotion I made in my tent. They made little fuss, of course. More broken wood meant there was less to carry back.*

As I did then, and have done since, I turned to outside sources of enlightenment to find my answers. What? Yes, Charles, that outside. Do you think I wander into the wooded areas of our estate to commune with the trees?! No, I speak of a greater 'outside.' Of realms you've only read of, or glimpsed in your deepest dreams. There are intellects in such places beyond what any mortal can comprehend. Unfortunately, many of those sorts of beings are, shall we say, disinclined to aid a mere human, and the debt incurred when seeking their help can be...cumbersome, at best. Over the years I've grown more disciplined, seeking out such help only as a last, desperate measure.

But we're not talking of my present, are we? Suffice it to say, I was far less cautious back then, and I heralded the great pale disk of Artemis that night with frenzied cries of supplication.

Don't give me that look, Charles. I didn't loose some demon into the wilds of Africa, and believe me, even if I had, the Dark Continent has demons enough of its own that mine would have been in good company. I called up neither hellion nor fiend that night. What I called forth was something...older than the boogeymen of the Christians. Something I don't care to elaborate on, save that it was quite handy in ferreting out knowledge lost to the ages. It demanded payment, as standard, and I gave it willingly, though at a postponed date. As I said, I wasn't about to carry my own luggage out of the wilderness. My proposal was accepted, and true to form, my vaporous associate delivered, in its usual fashion. The pain subsided, after a time, and I regained consciousness in due course. I was dismayed at seeing the dawn again, yet when I beheld the stone, and the inscription's meaning was clear as day, that rather made up for lost time.

☙❧

As RG mentioned that he could read the stone, Charles snapped to attention. "And what did it say? Come now, RG, give up the secret! You've sat here nearly an hour detailing your little venture. I need information, not a tour! "

The older man huffed in disapproval. "Impatient as always. Tell me, Charles, are you the type to skip to the end of a murder novel just to find out the culprit?"

"I no longer bother reading such fare. I've read enough to predict how any one of them ends. Now quit stalling. The inscription—"

"Yes, yes, the inscription." RG reminisced on that moment, relishing the intensity of his brother's interest. "I staggered to my feet that morning, not daring to take my eyes off the engraving. It was strange, the way the language seemed to flow and ebb, the rules of grammar shifting, rushing, the syntax and the phrasing utterly bizarre. Have you ever looked at something underwater, Charles? The distortion of perception caused by a fluid medium? That's as close as I could describe it to you. Even with full understanding, it was migraine-inducing to read. I'd already wiped the blood from my nose when I woke up, but that damnable writing nearly made me repeat the gesture."

"Unfortunate, RG, truly unfortunate." Charles had begun lean forward, his recording implements held up and ready. "The *name*, RG. Tell me the *name*!"

"Oh, you mean I ran my hands over the stone, drawing a finger down the seam between the halves. It was a fine indentation, nearly imperceptible. And there were no hinges of any kind, so to assume this *was* a door at all—"

Charles blinked. "Wait...hold on. What did you say?"

"The door, Charles? The engraving's instructions revealed it as a doorway. Honestly, man, if you're not going to listen—"

"No no! I'm listening." Charles shook his head to clear the cobwebs. *Must have tired myself earlier.* "So, going back a bit–"

"Yes, the lack of hinges. The inscription wasn't all that clear on just *how* the door was to open, only *that* it would open upon utterance of the name Not so much as a creak. I can't say I was at all surprised at the lack of sound. This was no haunted manse for tourists. But the darkness beyond was unnerving. Utterly soul-chilling. Like gazing into the heavens on a starless night." RG did not quite shudder, but the twitch at the corner of one eye was enough. "At any rate – something the matter? You seem confused."

"I...what?" Charles rubbed his eyes. *What the hell is wrong with me? Did I forget to eat today...again?* "I...what were we...never mind. The name? The First God's name opened the door, correct?"

RG let out an annoyed sigh. "Yes, Charles. That *was* what the writing said, more or less. As I told you, the language followed its own rules, with multiple interpretations of a single word commonplace. It would be as if I said 'the dog ran' and it could likewise mean 'the dog *flew*', though, I suppose, with enough poetic license."

"But...the name...what was the name?"

"*Really*, Charles. I'm honestly shocked you have such poor retention for details. Well, no matter. To put it plainly, the door read something to the effect that beyond the door lay neither *now* nor *was* nor *will be* – or some sort of temporal gibberish – and that it was the nest of 'I don't care what else it costs,' I told him. 'Get into the blasted hole!' I may have used more crude language than that, but such is the province of young, angry men. I'm not sure if it was the promise of greater payment or my fury which compelled that poor soul into the yawning maw. It was more than likely the latter. But crawl into it he did and–Charles? CHARLES!" RG snapped his fingers in annoyance. "Pay attention! I didn't wheel myself out here to watch you nap."

The younger of the pair felt himself snapping back to attention. "Wh…nap? I was napping? I don't nap!" *The most important story of my career and I can't follow the damn narrative. How is this old fool so boring?!* "Just keep going. Something about a maw…?"

☙❧

The door was connected to an incline, a steep one, but navigable. That first fellow managed to catch himself by clutching some kind of statue, we found. After preparing some torches I got a look at the thing. Ghastly artwork, even by standards of an occult nature. All flailing limbs and wings. Not sure if it was meant to portray one animal or a collection mashed into one, and why it was congealed into a human-esque form — but then, such was the nature of primitive mythological symbolism, as you know. I suspect it was supposed to depict I of course argued that we had plenty of daylight left, and so long as it shone through the portal above us we – CHARLES! If I find you dozing off again, I'm leaving! Honestly, man! Family is no excuse for such rudeness. Now, where was I? Ah, yes. The bottom of the ramp. As far as the torchlight revealed, it was a flat expanse stretching around us in all directions. I surmised we must have been a good hundred feet underground, given how the sounds of the jungle had fallen away. Oddly, the sound of water I'd first heard before the door opened was still present, but not at all any louder. At least now the other two could hear it. With nothing but empty darkness around us, we took the only logical route forward, slowly to make sure we didn't lose the light above. It continued on for some time. And there was nothing to mark our progress, save the illuminated doorway behind us. I was rather hoping for more statues, at least to break up the monotony. Even if it was just another bust of The writing on the pillar was the same, the language was as dead as the god its writer had worshiped. Or – not dead, perhaps. Once again, it said multiple things at once. 'Here it rests, our savior, our

sire, our god' I should have known something was amiss before we saw it. The ground had taken on an odd texture, nearly sponge-like. And the air had lost that earthy scent one would expect in a cave. Those cleaner odors had been replaced by a putrid, acrid stench, like rot mixed with something chemical. As repulsive as the smell was, it paled in noxiousness compared to the thing emitting it. The depictions I saw earlier hardly did it justice. I cried for the other man to stay away, but I was too late recognizing the danger, though I couldn't have saved the fellow even if I had. There was no retaking the flesh stolen by and I ran on, torch be damned, the fading light my only guide. I could feel that thing behind me, reaching, its tendrils writhing in the blackness, reaching for me, but I would not be another meal for I flung myself through the hole into fading daylight, rolling past the last porter. That poor fool, so startled by my appearance he had no chance to escape Luckily, the captain recognized me, and he ordered the men to pull me out of the water. I was half-crazed, according to him, and given what I can recall, I'm inclined to agree. I'm not even sure what my plan had been, other than to escape the clutches of The linguist of course had no idea what I was talking about. I even tried writing down the name, yet unfortunately the Latin alphabet was insufficient to translate. Returning home was not in the cards, so I returned to Bavaria. There were a few learned circles I had acquaintances in that might have heard of and with little else to do, I took my paramour up on her offer and —
Charles? Chaaaarles?

⊗

RG took a long look at his brother, shuddering in his chair with the stiffness of a seizure victim. The man's eyes showed nothing more than red-veined whiteness, and the foam at the corner of his mouth was flecked with scarlet drops, no doubt the consequence of a bitten tongue. The skin of the face had begun to take on the hue of a fresh bruise, while stran-gled sounds issued from the throat. The elder brother gave a thoughtful "hmmm", and held one hand over Charles's face. He whispered a string of words in an ancient tongue, snapped his fingers once, and the man's body relaxed immediately, slumping into the chain but not sliding off altogether. The chest began to rise and and fall with comforting regularity, and satisfied that his sibling wouldn't asphyxiate, RG rolled himself out of the library.

Upon exiting the room, he spied his sister striding down the hallway towards him. He swallowed his distaste for a confrontation, and swiveled about to face her. "Genevieve. Taking a rest from your plants, are we?"

⊱⊰

"As much as you're taking a break from your scrolls and beakers," she shot back with a degree more venom. RG twitched at her impertinence. Their brother held a proper degree of respect for his elder, but whatever reservations Genevieve had about addressing her betters, she had none when it came to him. "I'm looking for Charles." She rooted herself in front of him, arms crossed and face stern.

He did not quite glare upward, but his expression would have put granite to shame. "Well, I'm glad you've direction in life beyond your garden. Do tell me if you manage to locate the bookworm." RG pivoted his chair about, but only made it as far as facing the wall to his left before his sister commanded "Wait." Ordinarily he wouldn't have heeded such a declaration, but he wasn't about to get into a needless tussle with someone of Genevieve's caliber. That she was family bore little consequence next to her prowess.

She was peering into the library, and naturally had noticed the quivering form slumped in a chair. She turned back to RG, her voice betraying outrage and a sliver of curiosity. "What did you do to him?"

RG did not bother to hide the self-satisfied smirk on his face as he wheeled the rest of the way towards his laboratory.

"I only gave him what he asked for."

"And how long will this 'gift' of yours last? I need Charles's input on something, and I don't want the maid finding him like this. She's already skittish enough, no thanks to *you*."

He looked over his shoulder, a slightly patronizing cast to his grin. "You need not fret with your charms and salts. He should be right as rain in an hour or two." RG turned back around, and began rolling away. "Ideally, he'll be wiser when he comes around, especially in regards to what he asks for. Some things are simply not meant for the untested ear, or mind, to hear." Genevieve couldn't see the scowl return to her brother's face as he left, but she heard it in his voice as he muttered. "At the very least, he'll be more cautious about the names he employs, even behind closed doors."

Survival

Curtis Harrell

Curtis Harrell has a recurring dream where an invisible entity lurks in the back room of a house he hasn't lived in for forty years. His poetry, short fiction, and one-act plays have all been attempts to hold a conversation with whatever that thing is. Curtis has also recently had some of those works collected and published by Sley House Publishing under the title MELPOMENE'S GARDEN.

The sudden jangle of the servant bell startled her as she dozed on her low stool in the corner of the pantry, her mannish hands clasping each other on her lap. The dinner china had been removed to the kitchen hours ago, and she was tired now. She knew from many long days of experience that the command came from the library, a short staircase and a hallway away, and the softly polished walls of the wooden corridor returned the slough of her worn shoes on the marble floor as she obeyed the summoning ring. She stopped meekly at the threshold and observed Master Sley draining the last drops from a cut-lead decanter into a snifter held by a man she had never seen before.

"Ah! There she is, my petite brute," enunciated Sley with a smile, pleased with the alliterative t's on his tongue.

☙❦❧

"Charles!" admonished his guest, a fellow collector of the odd, the unexplained, the denizens that prowl the unknown, "please have some decency. She is but a young lady and your servant."

Charles Sley dismissed the reproach with a wave of the empty vessel.

"She understands not a word of our language, I fear. And I'm not certain if she is capable of spoken expression."

"Is she mute, then? Afflicted in some way?"

"Oh, no, my dear friend. She is something completely other than me and you."

She entered the room, retrieved a silver platter from a serving cart, and stood a respectable distance from Master Sley, her eyes down.

"Other?" replied the guest. "She could be my granddaughter, your niece."

"Never," said Sley. "Notice her short stature, under five foot, the wide girth of her hips and ribcage, the length and breadth of her nose, her large eyes, the thick musculature of her limbs."

"But her proportions are also harmonious in a primitive way. Her countenance, though large-featured, is sweet, her expression gentle."

"I am not saying that she is not handsome in her own way," said Charles. "I am saying that she belongs to another species. Her abnormal strength attests to that."

The guest regarded her, and then Sley, and then her again with a trained eye. Then he looked back at Charles.

"Surely you are mistaken," said the guest, "surely. There are no other species."

Charles Sley said, "Supposedly not now, but 40,000 years ago, we homo sapiens shared the earth with others similar to us. Think of horses and zebras. They share many traits, yet they are distinctly separate species. But despite the difference in species, they can breed."

"So she is not homo sapiens?"

"No," replied Sley, "what is your guess?"

"Martian, Venusian, Atlantean, I have no clue!"

"Come, man, consider the clues I just gave you. Look at her physique."

"Denisovan?"

"Neanderthal," replied Charles.

Chin in hand, the guest pondered this assertion, and he said, "But some studies suggest virtually all modern humans have some Neanderthal DNA."

"True. Most may have perhaps two percent, but not her."

She stood before the two men with the tray held before her, awaiting the empty decanter to be refilled. The weariness in her arms claimed all her attention.

"What," queried the guest, "ten percent, twenty, more?"

In the same way a card player might smile when he played a

handful of aces, Charles Sley smiled and leaned forward in his overstuffed chair.

"But not like horses and zebras."

"What are you saying?"

"One hundred percent."

Shards of expensive glass scattered across the floor when the snifter slipped from the guest's fingers and shattered.

She immediately knelt and gathered the broken pieces, piling them on the tray as the men looked at her in both dismay and wonder.

"She came here almost three years ago on an October night, late, after the time we would expect guests. My manservant answered the door, closed it, and then immediately summoned me. On the porch, when I opened the door, were two figures in the dim light, a man and a girl, both shrouded in rough frocks, their faces barely visible beneath their hoods. I could see he had a wild, thick beard, a huge, flattened nose, a preternaturally piercing light in his wide eyes. In a guttural voice, almost like a croak, he said three words. 'Keep her.' And then, with a long sibilance at the end of the syllable, 'Please.'"

She stopped gathering the last of the glittering flakes of crystal from the marble and looked up at Master Sley when he said this, though neither man noticed.

"I couldn't risk sending her DNA sample to a lab once I was suspicious of her background, so I conducted the test here. It was conclusive."

"But how?" asked the guest, "How could this happen? How could an extinct species survive, let alone conceal themselves for forty millennia?"

"Serendipity. Cosmic luck, perhaps. After all, people swear the Sasquatch roams the remote corners of our world," Sley responded.

The guest slumped back in his chair and eyed her with both jealousy and desire. When she finished her chore, Charles Sley took the tray from her and placed it on the sideboard. He yanked a bouquet of daisies, black-eyed Susans, buttercups, and violets from the vase on his end table and thrust them toward her.

"Here; it's been a long day for you, my sweet brute."

She took them, and retraced her path back to the pantry, where she changed out of her uniform. She held the flowers close to her as she left the mansion through the servants' entrance to step into the late evening, the hint of winter a subtle, low layer in the fall breeze. Once she was out of earshot of the mansion, on the sidewalk leading to the subway, she looked up at the moon and said, in a clear, articulate, and girlish voice, "But I have promises to keep, and miles to go before I sleep."

⬅⬞⬞➡

Past midnight now. The subway car rhythmically trundled through the cold tunnel. She huddled in her summer dress, her back to the cold window. She gently swayed, her chin resting on her chest, the thick bouquet of wildflowers clenched in her hand. The rocking made the memory come. The abundant scent of the flowers made the memory come, as did the cool air whistling into the car. She closed her eyes.

She remembered shadow, a dark glen, and, beyond the gloominess of the trees, a vast meadow, bright as brass. Light slanted in where she crouched, the light golden with pollen rising as shining points in the rays. She felt the proximity of others of her kind behind her, hidden in the tangle of the forest. She heard, behind her, the muffled grunting of a big male. From a berry thicket, an old female responded with the same utterance. That sound, that throat-driven word in her native, guttural tongue, was the name for the creatures that now clamored through the dry grass, leaping and chattering, gibbering with shrill voices. She watched as they waded the meadow with loose strides, yellow-headed, their bodies nude and sleek, browned by the sun. That frantic word had two meanings in her growling language: slender, and frightened. These lithe beasts were the Slender Ones, the Frightened Ones. They were also the Schemers. Sometimes their charred bones littered the firepit.

She opened her eyes. In the murky light of the subway car, she stared at the wildflowers bunched in her fist. She had never been outside of the city. What she knew of forests was scraps of conversation she had overheard on the subway, in crowds on the jammed sidewalks. She had seen them only in discarded magazines, a flash of green on a slick page as it fluttered in the gutter. This image had haunted her; this vision conjured up by the scent of flowers was nothing her eye had ever seen. It was not her mind's memory; it was her blood's memory.

◌◌◌

He slipped in through the steel doors just as the subway lurched forward, and she smelled the musty tang of gunpowder. He slowly lowered himself into the seat across from her, sitting so lightly that the muscles of his thighs bulged under the slick-worn fabric of his trousers. His eyes swept over the dozen sleepy riders as they huddled in their seats. They were, she thought, the eyes of a stray dog, one that fed on the overflow of alley dumpsters, an abandoned pet two sharp kicks away from biting someone.

The rows of lights in the subway car extinguished as they pressed into a long curve. In the clanking darkness she could hear him, his breath whistling in his narrow nostrils. She could smell the musk of body-warmed leather that was his belt, nestling the pistol in the top of his piss-stained pants. Even in the near-pitch darkness, she could discern the white of his face swiveling from the front of the car to the back.

Every detail—the cracked plastic fabric of the seats, the palm-polished gleam of the aluminum poles, the grinning dentist in the advertisement above the gunman's head, the dank walls they rushed past—was charged with his presence. She slowly breathed in these truths to quell her alarm. Survival depended on her calm. Her species depended on her timing, her judgement, her stealth. None of her fellow passengers were equal to his nervous and desperate energy, the viciously feckless nature of his potential—not the two grandmothers clutching their bags full of marked-down beef and withered lettuce, the four skinny students spitting whispers at each other in a hissing dispute, the half dozen middle-aged men in their rumpled suits, cloistered behind their newspapers. She kept her head bowed, the flowers concealing her discreet sideways glances, her scrupulous study of the man with the gun.

She sensed the whine of the wheels drop in pitch as the train approached the next stop. The man craned his neck above the upturned collar of his trench coat in impatience and anxiety. The opportunity he waited for eluded him—he would have to wait now for the next stretch of line. When the train stopped no one disembarked, but a child, a girl of perhaps seven years, boarded through the hissing doors and clambered onto the seat beside the gunman. By nature's miracle, her gut immediately recognized her, not personally, but her kind; she understood they were the same. In the improbable branching of fate, their eyes locked, and they practiced the eternal code that kept them safe. They quickly looked askance from one another though their nostrils confirmed each other's ancestral scent. The immaturity of the young one's features belied her heritage, her nose still upturned, her torso still that of a child. But a palpable resonance connected them through blood, through memory.

A quick jerk in its rhythmic journey propelled the subway car into the next tunnel. The blooming odor of the man's acrid sweat alerted her to his intentions. She let go her two-handed grasp of the bouquet and let one hand encircle the handrail beside her. The girl swung her legs. They both could hear the infinitesimal quickening of the gunman's pulse as the car gained velocity through the strobing passageway. The car sped faster; and faster beat the young thug's heart. In an ecstasy of apprehension, she lunged for the girl's hand across the aisle, but, at that same moment, the courage that the man ached for barged out in desperation, and he snatched the girl in a one-armed hug, raising her kicking legs high as he staggered in the swaying aisle.

"This is a robbery," he bawled, gun thrust aloft as the lights flickered out and darkness flooded the car.

She could see him staring uselessly into the blackness and once again grabbed the handrail on the seatback beside her. This time it came effortlessly free in her grasp. She approached the man in the prison of his blindness.

The pulling of the emergency brake sprawled the passengers out of their seats, and, in the pitch blackness, the report of the pistol lit the terrified face of the girl for a brutal second. A second shot flashed the astonished face of the gunman. In the earsplitting silence, everyone's head ringing from the concussion of the shots, they could barely discern the clanging of metal on metal, the shattering of glass, the creaky rending of steel being violently bent.

When the lights flickered back on one at a time, up and down the car, the passengers saw the gunman sitting unarmed and unharmed and bewildered on a bench. The subway door had been wrenched from its track, folded over, bent double to allow escape. She and the girl had vanished into the subterranean night, into time's long tunnel.

RG's Amazing Wonderful Flying Time Machine

In appreciation of: Kurt Vonnegut

Scot Walker

Scot Walker, who is too poor to afford the second "T" and drinks a lot of coffee to compensate, is celebrating his 70th year as a paid author. He began as a 10-year old when Santa gave him a kid-sized printing press and Scot composed, printed and sold twenty copies of his newspapers for a penny apiece. Subsequently he has seen over 450 of his poems, short stories, novels, non-fiction works, letters, plays, essays, videos, and reviews published and dozens of his plays produced in American and in Europe. Mr. Walker has won an L. Ron Hubbard Award for The Ruler of the Elves, a Flannery O'Connor Award for A Slow Bus Ride to a Shallow Grave; a Thomas Wolfe Short Story award for Earsounds; a New Century Writer Ray Bradbury Fellowship award for Watched; a Kernodle New Play award for Kenu Hear the Wild Birds Sing?; A McLaren Memorial Comedy Play Writing award for, Screeches from the Zoo; and he has twice won awards in the Writer's Digest Competitions, once in the Stage Play Category for Abide with Me, and again in short story competition for La Mer. In 2023, his poem, Earth's Repose, was published in Asia (India); Europe (England) and in the USA (North America) making him a Triple Crown Winner! He's a lifetime member of the Dramatists Guild and his plays have been performed throughout the USA and Europe. You can email him at scotwalker2004@yahoo.com or search the internet. Be sure to go to Smashwords—and look for his latest publication: Amazing Stories, which includes 80 of his award winning and published best.

☙❧

Chapter One

Our Amazing flying time machine had crashed somewhere near the Sonoran Desert and RG folded it up and put it in his pocket, winked once, mumbled the Anglo Saxon word "Cuma" and created a powder blue 2022 Porsche 911 convertible.

"Hop in boys," he said—'I'm taking a nap in the back seat. Be good . . . and drive safely." With that, he disappeared into a blanket-covered lump, snoring happily as the keys floated above his head for either Charles or I to grab.

And I thought: that's a no-brainer! Charles could barely drive a tricycle let alone this beauty, so I grabbed the keys, caressed the dashboard as only a man can, started the engine, and turned on my favorite 24/7 Johann Sebastian Bach radio station as we headed north. Trust me if I say the car was a blast but I mean exactly that—it blasted along that highway almost as quickly through time and space as RG's Amazing Wonderful Flying Time Machine propelled us though galaxies and universes more immense than a human mind - could ever comprehend!

Sixteen days. . . or six minutes. . . or an eternity before we took off in our Flying Time Machine, we were in Vegas and that's where my life began to resemble the "jingle-jangle-jumble" RG said from that time when he was the Imperial Wizard at Camelot. But now my throat was as dry as the Aral Sea and the seven rolls of of shiny new quarters I'd won in Vegas, banged against my balls and both they and I were glad Vegas was nothing more than a memory and it was if the town had vanished and Medea had arisen in her chariot and spewed forth enough smoke to set that evil town on fire—in a conflagrations that filled the sky with gunk, turning it from blue to gray to a Stygian blackness of smoke and flames merge-meshing into a miasma of seventeen hellish hues.

But that was then—when the Flying Time Machine made good on her promises to take us anywhere any time. Now, however, there was no way of telling what time it was, much less which direction north or south or any directions beside backwards, forwards and upside down still existed. RG was in the back seat—but he was of no help now that his snores drowned out the cracking of burning tree limbs and the honking Land Rovers filling the roads.

After a half hour of squinting through the grime covered windshield, which my buddy, Charles Sley, cleared with a mop dangling from his right arm as he leaned out thumping it against the windshield. I said nothing. My mouth, ears and nose were filled with ashes and dust, and I leaned forward, squinting to see through the smog and the rags of that damned dangling mop.

Yet,

Charles tried.

And tried again.

And all around us, the only sound louder than the thump, thump thumping of that miserable mop, were the horns blaring around us. Just one more thump, I thought, and that damned mop will blast through the windshield of our hundred-thousand-dollar Porsche.

Charles, however, was a "bookwormish" man and knew nothing about mops or cars or the rain. . . and it was best to let him have his leave.

〇≳≷〇

Happily the gunk and the fog and the stuff in the sky finally lifted and the Porsche, as if guided by the great wizard's magic, was still hugging the two-lane blacktop road that snaked into the distance like one of those Picasso roads Charles and I saw at the Musée Picasso in Paree. I didn't see roads or highways anywhere except in real life, but Charles saw them as the art he had seen in his 327 volumes of famous paintings. . . and, I guess, that's why he and RG got along so well because they both saw things others could barely dream.

Anyway, the road seemed to merge into the twisted pines along each side of us, before snaking up at a forty-five-degree angle toward some lumpy taupe-colored hills before disappearing. . . so, I surmised: before and after were the only cardinal directions. That was, after all, the mantra RG taught us when he propelled us back and forth through time, space and everything in between. One moment we existed before we existed and the next we seemed to be in a world so vast and so far away that only RG knew when or if we would return.

Suddenly, we heard what sounded like a chainsaw growling in the distance or perhaps it was a wolverine in heat. It was impossible to tell what it really was and what waited for us there—in the forest or hiding up in the lumpy hills, or perhaps it was just the rumbling of my empty stomach. . . or then again, maybe, just maybe it was that damned wolverine. I just wanted RG to wake up and transport us from this hellish place.

Trying to ignore the "wolverine," my primordial needs consumed me and I pulled over for a bush stop when a band of Roma crept out looking at me as if I was the strangest thing in their world. I assumed they were like all the others RG, Charles and I met on our journeys through time, gaping and gawking as though we were the anomalies—the queer ones—the outsiders—and not they! Honestly, I'm a church going Methodist, for Christ's sake, innovative, brilliantly articulate and totally self-sufficient so I just let the yokels wonder—and RG continued snoring, and Charles reclined his seat nearly bumping into RG, who snorted and snored happily!

As soon as I started to pee, Charles, popped out of the car, rummaged through the back seat and tossed a dozen water bottles, several sandwiches left over from our Friday night church barn-dance wing-ding, a half dozen packages of slightly gnawed beef jerkys, a crumpled bag of Lays and a half dozen Reese's peanut butter cups that I guarded with my soul into a cooler and I saw the look of hunger in the Roma men's eyes and hoped it was our left-overs they were after and not our asses.

Just then, Charles dragged the cooler and plopped it on the blankets that were sheltering the crimpled and curled RG fully awake.

RJ gave us his mesmerizing wizard grin and winked his brown left eye and stood before us as the wizard of half the entire universe and waited.

Chapter Two

Years later, on my deathbed at Mona McAlister's Mental Rehabilitation Home for Incurable Maniacs, three blocks from downtown Missoula, Montana, where the ants were eating the last of my New York cheesecake, I realized RG was right! He had always been right. As I had always been "left." He had the power to transform within seconds because now he was dressed in his favorite loose flowing toga and wore a Roman laurel leaf crown cocked jauntily over his right blue eye as he meandered in front of me or beside me, or over me. . . it was hard to tell because of the bruise over my left eye caused in that terrible midget wrestling exposition when my nurse, Billy Poe, assured me my heels dug into the yellow and green striped linoleum that was tarred to the floor. He and the rest of them, all claimed I needed socialization because of my illness—but Billy sat me right smack dab in the front row in between stinky Mrs. Dempsey and lanky Mr. Koonce and within minutes, midget Gail Saunders who attempted to drop kick her opponent, Happy Harold Prince, missed him and whacked the holy crap out of my left eye. I felt the splinters sliding into my iris—but I digress. . . RG will be there with me in the future, just as I was with him in Camelot, as his chimney boy. That's where I first noticed RG's walk. . . his damned right foot, left foot, fearlessly forward, toe in the ground, then next step heel up, slowly sliding it forward. . . over and over again. Repeat with left. Repeat with the right as his bottom wiggled alluringly, too alluringly for my boyish heart back then, I might add, as his thighs glistened in his God-awful sweat, and his armpits oozed with the scent of

Yorkshire pudding and fried kippers, co-mingled, in some ar-chaic mysterious way, with gobs of clover honey, rolling no—oozing out of his pit pores, with a stench that made the nurses want to run like lemmings to the nearest cliff and dive into the sea.

But all that is in the future. Or is it the past. It's impossible to tell with this man, this wizard, this magician, this mysterious magical RG.

My mind jumps too much after so many years as RG's left-hand man. He joked about that when he created the position. "You're all that's left, Scot," he said. . . so I guess that makes you my—

"Left hand man," we spoke simultaneously.

I smiled as broadly as RG grinned.

"And if," RG said, "I ever find a right-hand man, be assured only you will be left."

But let's get back to the 21st Century. I'm beginning to tell stories like RG does—starting thousands of years in the future and working backwards, tossing a few middles into the mix and then starting at the end again. . . .so let me breathe a mo-ment. Inhale. Exhale. Inhale. Exhale.

We're back to reality now. Present day and RG is naked, tell-ing me to wash his clothes, so I dumped his Yorkshire pudding kipper scented underwear onto the asphalt figuring he'd not be using them again and even though RG had tired of working wonders on our grime, dust and dirt and I figured we could be on our way in a heartbeat when two shimmering gold bars glistened underneath his tighty whities.

"I'm so tired of his damned magic."

"I don't want his magic anymore!"

We've had that discussion a dozen times and that's why we decided to work in this town in Nodsville, Middle Earth, by going door-to-door performing wonders in exchange for gold.

"Want a miracle in your life?" we'd ask when someone answered and before they could open their mouths, RG would wave his wand and mumble, "Kazaam! Your wish is our command!"

I know it sounds clunky but it worked, and clunky makes money. So in less than a week, we'd talked our way into the hearts, minds and souls of fifty-six thousand men, women and children who gave us their gold watches, earrings, necklaces and coins—RG's favorite was a gold Superman pin, a twelve year old handed him. Such is the power of magic and wizardry, I thought as we hired a few local boys to lug the nineteen bags of gold and a corralled a dozen girls to rip out all the crap that wasn't gold: things like the works in watches, silver bindings, and pearls, all of which we tossed into the truck and hauled up to the Joseph P. Morgan Reservoir just off SR-10, a few miles north of Castle Dale.

They made the most glorious plopping sound and their splashes resembled lost souls writhing in Dante's hell—which is not the real hell, though. . . nothing could be that glorious. Charles Sley joked he should have been a drummer as he hefted bag after bag and slung them like Hefty bags brimming in G-strings loaded with garbage, into the reservoir, listening to the boom-thunka-thunka, boom-thunka-thunka-thunk-thunk-thunk, boom! And Echo responded to what she thought was Narcissus's cry: boom-thunka-thunka, boom-thunka-thunka-thunk-thunk-thunk, boom! And as Echo's echo resounded from the canyon walls, it faded into three more boom-thunka-thunka, boom-thunka-thunka-thunk-thunk-thunk, boom! boom-thunka-thunka, boom-thunka-thunka-thunk-thunk-thunk, boom! boom-thunka-thunka, boom-thunka-thunka-thunk-thunk-thunk, booms!

Charles grinned the entire time and he tossed each bag one-by-one so he could get as many booms out of each as possible.

Charles, by the way, was the first guy I ever loved. He was as strong as an ox and dumb as one too, but he was sweet and kind, and always put everyone else first—except of course when he listened to echoes—then he was a man possessed, there is obviously narcissism in all of us, after all.

Charles's main skill was his ability to look at a piece of gold and know instinctively how pure it was without having to chew it down and gnaw it into bits like the novices do. He also knew how to refine and pour it into ingots that were 99.999%, just as pure as he was in heart and soul.

Charles and I had met, by the way, actually all three of us had met, at a Teens for Christ revival meeting sponsored by the Wheaton Bible Church in a tent with strewn sawdust a few inches deep and hard backless benches to perch on. We were all thirteen years old—well, Charles and I were thirteen. I'm not sure about RG. RG, the inquisitive, had visited every form of magic and voodoo and religious service, carny show and burlesque performance and that was his sole reason for attending our Teens for Christ revival back then. . . so he joined us, sitting there on that bench on August 24, 1957 as Pastor Kirk droned on and on about us being as pure as gold and the merciful children of God and after standing for three hours and singing Just As I Am without one Plea, and that Thy Blood was Shed for Me three dozen times—with all four verses—and me unable to think of any meaning whatsoever to the damned gibberish because all I wanted was to dash out of the tent to the john. Even the thought of those peanut butter cups in the Time Machine I had longed to eat before those damned fire ants devoured them, wasn't enough to drown out the chorus that rang from the lips of the hundred or so zealots around us. Then those benches seemed to have gotten harder and I nudged RG to see if he could soften them trying to let him know how sore two of our three asses were and that we were just about ready to do anything—including selling our souls to the hock shop man who did business out of his garage behind Wheeler's Auto Repair and Recap Specialists, when Pastor Kirk asked who wanted to come forward to be saved from eternal hell fire and damnation. I think I lost a couple of drops of pee in my tighty-whities from the heat in the tent as RG touched our thighs and winked and said, "If you want to learn real magic come on down—Kirk is standing in front of curtain number one, which do you choose?"

"There's only one curtain," I said.

"Really? Let's find out for sure."

My past, present and future meshed into one as we raced down that sawdust trail to the three shimmering curtains that we now saw plainly, and I glimpsed Charles's glorious wiggling ass, in and there is nothing else like it on this planet, so I have to admit I did stumble once or twice.

I guess you're asking how I met RG the first time here in Wheaton, Maryland when I already explained that I met RG thousands of years ago at the Magician Union's Job Fair, but I'm a kid, okay, a kid at heart anyway, and I don't always get my timeline straight, but if there's one thing RG ingrained in my soul, it's that all timelines are in motion—I bet you've had that feeling several times yourself, haven't you? You felt you were someplace before when you knew you weren't? You felt as if you were reliving something you'd never yet lived? That's the fluid timeline, folks. We've all experienced it. Most of us try to laugh it off or we ignore it—but you've felt it.

RG dug his right sneaker into that sawdust, then lifted his heel up then pressed his full sneak weight down, but Oh My

God! His ass is what Charles and I looked at, salivated over actually, as drool seeped from our hot boy lips.

If you know anything about RG, it's that his entire existence is magic. And he was now wearing the tightest pair of white see-through nylon shorts known to man and how his ass jiggled and wiggled. Jell-O had nothing on RG. Brother, how that ass jiggled, tight and smooth and beautiful to behold. And I looked at Charles and Charles looked at me and without saying a word, we followed RG down that aisle, wiggling our hot little asses, too.

And if you ever decide to get saved, or looked up admiringly at the three gigantic curtains with Bob Barker dressed in black slacks and a blue blazer with matching tie and pointing from one curtain to the other to the other, take a thick blanket with you because that sawdust crap can eat right straight through your kneecaps pretty damned fast and stick to your thighs and your legs and fester and itch like fire ants are doing the mambo in your Underoos. But RG didn't seem to care. I remember reading someplace at some time on my fluid timeline that RG had been persecuted throughout the ages. I don't know how because I didn't read much back then, other than Scrooge comic books, and yes, to dispel all myths, Uncle Scrooge was my favorite and I pictured myself floating in his mile long mile wide mile high vault filled with gold, and that for a boy who had barely begun puberty, was enough to make my you know what hard, but back to Charles and my take on RG. Charles and I had heard RG was maligned throughout history—that's why he just pops up from time to time. 1947 in Bimini at the Miss Caribbean Seafood Festival, 1978 in Rehoboth Beach Delaware at Dolly's Water Taffy Emporium, and 1996 in Vegas—at that glorious magic show he performed for over five years while the hot gay guys with the tigers were next door.

Yet, I could never get my head around RG or his magic and for me, back then, with my sawdust covered knees and my aching ankles, all I could wrap my head around was that one mile wide by one mile long by one mile high vault Scrooge McDuck had built and filled to the tippy-top with money. In my mind I stripped naked and floated on it as the gold washed my body crystal clean. . . So I sort of blocked out most of what Pastor Kirk said, and Charles and I even took our eyes off the curtains most of the time—although they seemed to come and go, which I guess depended most on if we were looking at them or not, and I still needed to pee and Charles did as well, but I think he started without me, and I still needed to brush off the dirt from my aching knees. And, damn it, on top of all that, it was only Monday night and Saturday was bath night and all the boys would laugh at me the next day in Mr. Fox's boys' physical education class, where the showers were broken because some damned ninth grader had filled the faucets with Superglue. Life was a bitch and a trap and my mind flicked from curtain to curtain to curtain to my inability to piss like a sailor.

But somehow the words came back to me, I guess you can only concentrate on pee so long before you give up and wait for the words that say amen and that means you can run like hell to the bathroom. So I listened to Pastor Kirk drone on and on as the fire ants danced from my naked legs to RG's to Charles's and back again, teaching all six legs to rumba and mambo and cha-cha-cha at the same time.

And then just when I thought I couldn't hold it anymore, Pastor Kirk had us rise and blessed us and the congregation sang some damned song or another—although not as long as the first one—and he presented us each with a red Bible and told us the Bible must be red and we all thought that was pretty cool. Then Pastor Kirk took out this expensive looking fountain pen—I think it was made of gold, maybe even gold Kirk had taken from Uncle Scrooge's money bin, but I knew Huey, Dewey and Louie must never find out or they'd quack us to death for sure, and Pastor Kirk wrote his name in big round thick fat girly handwriting that Charles said it reminded him of his girlfriend. And as Kirk went down the row, we wondered why he had to desecrate the Word of God by scribbling his name in our brand new, never opened, never read Bibles and I thought, I bet he did that so we won't resell them. So I looked at Charles and RG and gave them the old wink eye which meant, "we'll swear an oath when this ordeal is over and rip out the cover pages and sell them anyways." And then we shot like cannon balls to the toilets where we peed and peed for twenty minutes before we were half empty. And that's how Charles and I met RG but the best thing about RG is that after all these centuries, his ass seems to get hotter and hotter every time I look at it. But to tell you the truth, RG spends as much time looking at our fannies as well.

Chapter Three

I think I may have digressed again. I was talking about the gold bars hiding in RG's tighty-whities. Charles's face lit up in smiles when he saw the self-generating, fully charged solar powered flying machine that was able to take us to the nethermost points of the universe. It was one of my patented inventions.

Anywhere, poof, bang, pop, we're all back to the present and I barely have a headache but Charles turned red-faced again and almost lost his cookies—not the thin mint or peanut butter sandwich cookies or Samosas that the Girl Scouts sell, but those other nasty cookies because Charles's body hates time travel even though his soul (yes Pastor Kirk never really saved our damned souls partially because of his "Let me scribble my name in your brand new Bible" caper) loves the magic!

The three of us put our collective noggins together and figured we could make it all the way to Cuyahoga Falls. Charles suggested the place because he loved the sound of the words as they flowed out of his lips and I thought I like everything that flows out of Charles's lips so I sure as hell like the sound of Cuyahoga Falls, too. And so did RJ and even though none of knew where the hell Cuyahoga Falls was or even if there was a such a thing called Cuyahoga or even who might fall where, we figured we'd just have to journey, like we journeyed down that sawdust aisle together, and find out for ourselves.

Charles mentioned his Aunt Edna had a couple of falls in her life, so we'd better be careful, but that didn't dissuade any of the three of us from loving the sound: Cuyahoga. It might have been something Carol Burnett shouted in one of her Tarzan yells: Cu-yaaaaaaa-hoooooo-gaaaaaa. Cu-yaaaaaaa-hoooooo-gaaaaaa faaaaaa-lllls. And I let loose and cu-yaaaaaaaaaaa-hooooooooooo-gggggggggggggged so loud it echoed up and down that damned barren valley and Charles stared at me with a look that was halfway between the fear of God and the ecstasy of his girlfriend's inner thighs. Charles might have remembered those tenor-singing days in Mrs. Holcomb's tenth grade chorus at Wheaton High School, when our girlish boy voices filled the auditorium. . . or the times he and I sat in my backyard on Sheraton Street and sang loud enough for the neighbors to hear. Charles said he heard them applaud. I thought they were yelling so I'll accept Charles's memory, but let me tell you, if RG had not commandeered my time machine, Charles and I could have Cu-yaaaaaaa-hoooooo-gaaaaaaed those falls 'til the cows came home. But, even with the ancient wizard calling the shots, we kept on letting loose and cu-yaaaaaaaaaaa-hooooooooooo-gggggggggggggged our hot little asses to wherever in the hell we were headed.

RG gave us one of his wizardly old man looks, hanging his face down and look up at us over his glasses, a pose that always freaked us out, but we realized it was time for us to get a mosey on, that's a phrase we picked up from watching Roy Rogers, the Lone Ranger and Gene Autry. You know, when they weren't on horses, they just moseyed a lot. .So we started a-moseying, knowing the folks here in the valley would be waking up from their drunken slumber and realizing RG had shorted out all their damned batteries. We didn't have to look at him to know his power. When you pissed RG off, like this whole town did, he pissed on you.

The folks down there were the only ones who refused to hand over their gold watches, earrings and dinnerware, so RG's wand spat out the command and: off went their power—and for good measure, watered down their booze.

RG was a teetotaler: you probably remember that if you ever read the Collected Works of King Arthur and His Roundheads Who Turned the Tables on the Romans. . . Next to the Uncle Scrooge comic book that showed his mile high gold vault, it's the coolest book ever—although it's hard to find now. If you want to look for it, don't go online, check out the local thrift shops—it's usually back there in the boys underwear department or next to the stuffed foxes and skunks.

RG gave a nod and played with his beard. That was a sign that we were off for a flying adventure, off to Cu-yaaaaaaaaaaa-hooooooooooo-gggggggggggggg, off to see the wizard, off to follow the second star on the right, off on Scout and Silver to save the great white whale from Captain Ahab. Off to save the world.

You keep distracting me! Look in the boy's department at the Glenmont Ladies Home Auxiliary Thrift Shop under the boy's underwear and you'll find a copy of the King Arthur book that tells the truth about, like I'm saying.

We were talking about the gold bars, weren't we? I bet these will be better than Bitcoin because they're real and maybe we can ask RG to put his toe print on them to show ownership like they do on Gene Langley's show where Gene sews labels in kid's clothes so when they get washed the right kid puts the right socks and sneaks and stuff back on so we figured it would be real easy for RG to turn our gold into Bitcoins or nod his head or shake his left sandal or swish his hot ass and say his magic words and change them any which way he wanted.

And both me and Charles agreed, nodding our heads up and down, like those ducks you see on a peg board with strings and you shake the board a little and the duck heads peck up and down looking, I guess, for sawdust or something to eat.

Anyway, RG grabbed us both by our skulls and tapped our noggins together—not hard—just an embarrassing jolt to tell us to stop acting so childishly.

"Tell me again about the magic," Charles said.

"He was on Bimini," I said, as I watched Charles's head throb and his eyes roll back in his head as if he was in a trance, trying to picture himself as brave as RG, living alone, with nothing but his wand and spell book, eating coconuts and bananas for thousands of years, as he pulled away from us humans."

"Yes," I said, but we met him long before that, and again a

while ago in the tent revival meeting but each time RG came into our lives we blocked out our previous meetings, Charles on the other hand wasn't able to assimilate things so I just let his eyes roll back in his skull and painted a picture for him.

RG's can transcend time!

"Like Superman!" Charles shouted.

"Yes, like Superman!"

Charles paused for a long time and my legs hurt. Charles was a big man and the longer his head rested on my lap the more my body ached.

"Do you think all those years on the beach is what gave RG such a hot ass?"

"Yes," I said as RG appeared out of nowhere in my time machine.

"Load it up, boys; we're off for an adventure."

So we loaded up our Zero Cokes and Dr. Peppers, and all the food Charles had taken from the truck, along with several pairs of clean underwear that RG miraculously pulled out of the glove compartment. Then we struggled with the gold bars, until I turned on my anti-gravity machine (patent pending) and they wafted across the open field and gently landed in the gondola of our amazing flying time machine—which, like RG's heart and soul—was way bigger on the inside than it was on the outside.

RG nodded at me and I pushed the button and off we went—flying high into the late afternoon sky, waiting for the moon rise, the stars to come out and say howdy RG, Charles and Scot: I hope you have a glorious evening (and yes, stars talk, you just have to listen), as we wondered how much our gold bars would glisten and gleam in the dancing moonlight.

Within twenty minutes, Charles was fast asleep, purring like a calico kitten who'd lapped up a saucerful of half-and half and I faced the void and the gold alone, waiting for one or the other to gleam—to give me a sign—to let me know what our mission really was. Were we really existing and re-existing and co-existing with RG through vortex after vortex of time or was our relationship, like Dr. Leon Meadows, that freaky free-clinic psychiatrist and graduate of the Mississippi School of Agriculture, had suggested, just a figment of my demented mind? Well, let me tell you, I sure as hell let the good old doc know I was the sanest peanut in his peanut brittle can and you should have seen his face! And all I could do was hold my giggles and my pee as I imagined how undereducated the shrink was and hoped I'd look down on him one day in my solar flying machine with my gold bars glistening and my heart thumping and my cookies rocking and rolling in Tembo (named after Dumbo, the flying elephant's third born son) hand-painted elephant cookie jar, and yes, every time I lifted the lid, Tembo made a trumpeting call which only made me open it more and more each day, often just prying it up an inch or two, hoping other Swahili elephant cookie jars in the neighborhood would heed Tembo and bring a trunk load of cookies to my door. But it got old after a dozen visits to shrink Meadows with me and my elephant cookie jar sitting side by side in the doc's chartreuse Lazy-Boy recliner and he, wanting to find a way to split in a meaningful but boyish way, so I ordered the good doctor a box of multi-color Coral Gables rattlesnakes cookies that had been infused with real rattlesnake eggs by a wave of Merlin's magic wand, for which I thanked him immensely, but someone they got lost by UPS so . . . word to the wise, if you ever find an extra-large crate marked homemade peanut brittle and it's hissing, don't open it, just look up Doctor Leon P. Meadows and forward it pronto!

I looked at the GPS, I'd given up trying to figure out

the meaning of the stars, but as my WIFI connection
kept fading in and out, I dared give another Carol Burnett Tarzan yell. . . what the heck. I had nothing to lose:
Cu-yaaaaaaaaaaa-hoooooooooo-ggggggggggggg, but when
there was no response, and no elephants dropped cookies
from the sky, and no distant rattlesnakes hissed, and both RG
and Charles snored and tossed and turned, I still didn't know
where any of us were.

Finally, Charles and RG woke up, waddled over to the cooler and set up our midnight meal of six Mr. Ed sandwiches
(Italian ham, salami, Provolone cheese, bacon, tomatoes, on-
ions, lettuce , Italian dressing, and hot peppers), several Cokes,
a dozen Girl Scout Samoas, a quart of Popeyes Coleslaw, a
large pack of cold McDonald's French fries, three Starbuck's
apple pies, and a cluster of Concord grapes.

Nearly simultaneously, Charles and I reached for the bunch
of grapes. He got half. I got the other half and we bit into a
mouthful at the same instant. God, how could anything be so
sour? One by one I tossed them out of the flying time machine only to notice a murder of crows circling us, need I say
"ominously." I tossed a few to them, as did Charles and soon
all our grapes were gone—as were the majority of the murder.
And we watched them fall to the ground in small groups, cawing agonizingly with their tiny talons splayed out before them
(many of them actually flipping over and falling upside down
as I wondered if they were alive, would they have landed like a
cat, flipping over at the last moment and landing on all fours)
until they splattered onto Route 40 a thousand feet below us,
and all the while, we finished the sandwiches, cookies and fries,
eating and giggling boyishly as we changed our underwear and
tossed our dirty drawers over the side, laughing as they para-
chuted slowly down: my "Valentine's Day is for Lovers" box-

ers, Charles's "Kiss mylawyer" briefs, and RG's "This is the End" boxer shorts. They flickered down to the highway and landed on the heads of the freshly murdered murder of crows. What a way to go, I thought, buried so no one will find them, not even their crow mommies and daddies. RG, Charles and I made mournful little cawing sounds, so precise that even Carol Burnett would have been proud . . . or at least Tim Conway may have.

The full moon rose over the horizon – bathing us in its ethereal beauty and it was as if RG was hiding behind it, showering us with his magic, protecting us from the crows and the filthy underwear and the failed batteries in the Porsche we'd abandoned in that hellhole of a town bubbling over with slobbering drunks who did nothing more than shoot bullets into each others' legs for fun screaming "Gotcha!" And I thought, frontal lobotomies can't get much better! But as I thought that thought, RG dropped a Tootsie Roll Pop from somewhere (or created it or wished it or whatever) and while it was rolling over and over in our rock and rolling rollicking time machine, he reached down, touching his toes, as his gorgeous ass was squeezed and squished into his tight shorts and now not only Charles was drooling. . . but so was I. I know, I know, I've already described RG's ass, but some of you are breast men and others are leg men—it's all a matter of perspective and as RG said, "Judge not numb nuts, less thee also be judged." And how that Arthurian ass simmered and quivered and all I could think was why an artist—a real artist like Rembrandt or Da Vinci—not fake ones like Dali or Warhol, hadn't painted a portrait of that ass . . . or even his legs or breasts if artists were of that proclivity, or of RG's big oval Opal colored eyes, which often, like teeny tiny traffic lights when we were late getting from point A to point 19 to point infinity to point M, turned green. But RG's eyes were also ebon black sometimes, or hazel. . . or blue like Sinatra's or Newman's. And all the while, RG's quivering ass rose and fell, rose and fell, rose and. . . as his eyes changed color and his entire body glowed—or was it mine? Or were the winds merely playing mischief here in our time machine as they lifted us from cloud to cloud and back to point 19 or point M again?

Then I slipped and fell to the floor and looked up at his hairy as a simian's from one of those Planet of the Apes when Charlton Heston was naked far too long. RG, help me, my mind is so easily distracted. Can it be that you are an ape from a Carol Burnett Tarzan flick or a nephew of Charlton? I inhaled more deeply than normal. Yes, there is a Kurt Vonnegut Monkey House smell about RJ. A monkey house smell, for sure.

Without warning, Charles fell on the floor, rolling back and forth as if he was having a seizure as he looked up at RG and winked and when Charles stood back up he had a chocolate Tootsie Roll dangling from his lips like he was James Dean in Rebel Without a Cause, and I saw tears in his eyes that could barely contain the guffaws he and RG emitted and my mouth watered because those two rascals had scarfed the last of the Great Pyramid Tootsie Rolls—the ones we'd discovered in the King's Chamber back in 3,256 B.C.E.

Then Charles stood up as RG waved his wand up and down to show off Charles's brand new tighty-whities and both wizard and man stared at me in my ever tightening Batman underwear and both of them sang, "Hold tight!" as my size thirty-twos became size thirty became twenty-eights and I yelled. "I give! I give! This is worse than a wedgie!"

"Let's try boy size eighteen," RG said as the two rolled on the floor in delight and my balls . . . well, no matter how many time machines you fly in or how far you travel, you never want to picture me at that moment.

"Let's move on," RG said as my 32's sprang back into shape and I was able to join in the laughter. . . but I was nowhere near as silly or joyous or loud as the other two until RG slowed down our time machine and Charles gave me a hug and twisted my nipples and smiled and I looked down and saw what I thought was our town, our Carol Burnett town—but it wasn't cu-yaaaaaaaaaaa-hooooooooooo-ggggggggggggggg, it was Orlando . . . and I don't meet Bloom, it was the real Orlando, not the namesake. Below us were the Magic Kingdom, Pirate World, Space Adventure, and the newest attraction, El Dorado. "They're nothing at all like cu-yaaaaaaaaaaa-hooooooooooo-gg-gggggggggggg!" we all howled. "Damn it to hell!"

The flying machine landed gently at parking space 1,345 in lot number 19, about a half mile from all the attractions and I decided to wing it. Bad choice of words, after the murder of the murder of crows. I decided Charles and I would free-style and we'd toss a coin (which I always kept in the secret compartment of my high top sneakers) and the winner (he he) would get them both and the loser would check our solar batteries (which meant standing in the sun, focusing the solar collector in the right direction as the winner (me) went off for a quiet afternoon.

Well none of that happened because the flying time machine battery adjusted and recharged itself, even on overcast days, so it was never a matter of being without power in that glorious machine—just in cars and trucks where it only seemed to work every other Friday.

RG magically changed all our outfits so we could blend in as tourists in the Magic Kingdom, including extra pockets in our trouser legs in case we came upon some extraneous gold, which we didn't, but we did use them like snack packs as we went through the park.

It seemed like we'd never make it to the monorail or that marvelous ship that sailed across the lake, until RG magically transported us to the entrance right smack dab in front of the Crystal Palace as it stood there, glistening in the morning sun. "It's a gift shop," RG said, "or at least that's what everyone else thinks." He waved his wand and it became a junior high school cafeteria.

"Let's eat," he said and we ordered lunch but all they had were left over peanut butter and grape jelly sandwiches on whole wheat bread and RG said the lunch fare reminded him of those meals they served him while magically putting doing plumbing at the House for of Retired Knights and Dames of Camelot. Somehow, however, we got all that chunky peanut butter down and as I picked up my tray, I noticed a bar of gold under it—"one more," I thought as I shoved it in one of my deep leg pockets. Just right for gold, I thought.

Charles and I hurried off to catch as many rides as we could as RG checked out the Haunted House by correcting all the spooks and pitfalls.

Charles's favorites were the coasters. Mine was Fantasyland and our eyes were blinded. We were standing at the threshold of the three bears' house, you know the one Goldilocks ate all their damned porridge in and then sat in all their chairs and hid three bars of gold under the floorboards before falling asleep across all three beds.

"Damn," I thought, "there are three more gold bars right here under these beds and all Charles and I have to do is cre-ate a disturbance and we can slide them in our hidden pockets and meander out of here. So we heaved them up and into our pockets but within moments, we saw the flashing red light, heard the sirens, and sensed the mood of the crowd had changed. We slowed to a trot, then to a walk as we mingled among the Snow White, all seven dwarfs and the wicked witch as I pretended to be a gold mining dwarf, swaggering along with them, singing Hi Ho, and Charles fell into the same mood as we danced a tarantella together, wondering why anyone would want to spend more than a few moments watching two crazy gold miners dancing in the Disney streets and we sighed a brief sigh as three moppets came to join us and we danced, all of us now, as Charles and I taught the kids the moves to the tarantella and the gold bars we had hidden in our pants starting sliding until one by one they fell into the street.

I panicked, knowing the law would be after us faster than the cannibals chased Robinson Crusoe, but again, thank our lucky stars, nothing happened. The law did not come crashing down on us. Instead the moppets thought it was all part of the act, as did their parents, and soon I heard pockets jingling and coins tossed helter-skelter here and there until the street was shining with silver coins. Charles bent down and began picking up the quarters and dimes and I tried brushing him aside and whispering to him but the damned band was banging out another Hi Ho Hi Ho Hi Ho song and the dwarfs starting dancing a weird variation of the tarantella I'd taught the moppets and I don't think anyone could have heard me, even if I had had a fifty-foot megaphone. Just then Dumbo, or rather the two men dressed as Dumbo, ambled by in their elephant walk style and the crowd cheered and the band struck up the Dumbo music and I plugged my ears as Charles giggled along with the moppets and showed them his Elephant Walk dance that he'd learned at that Teens for Christ social when we all pretended to be jungle animals and drank Hawaiian punch and ate animal crackers and I guess it was the first time anyone had ever seen Snow White mount an elephant and ride like that procession in Aida down the Main Street USA in Disney World, but I can still hear the cheering and think one day, I'll head back to Disney and get myself a job as a dance instructor—and if worse comes to worse, I'll be able to watch the hottest asses in the south as they mambo and rumba and salsa from one end of Main Street to the other.

Both Charles and I stepped back, inching our way further from the crowd to the place where our gold bars had tumbled out onto the street and we hoisted them and shoved them back into our clothes again, feeling like Marco Polo, I guess, as we hid all the treasures of the world in our tight clothes.

Suddenly the skies opened and the streets, Snow White, Dumbo, the moppets and all seven dwarfs were drenched to the skin, but then, Charlie swooped down and picked up the rest of the quarters and dimes, which were now shimmering below three inches of water on the Main Street parade route. I kicked him. Honest to God, I kicked and told him to get his sorry butt and our gold moving back to the time machine, otherwise we'd be weighed down with God knows how many pounds of quarters and dims and stuck here in Florida, and, more than likely, sometimes my brain is more imaginative than it should be, end up as hired Disney paraders, dressed, more than likely, as we were now—as Snow and Company's assistant gold miners, and end our lives as dwarfs under the feet of the fifty-seven million annual tourists who trample those streets.

Just then my ears started popping and I saw the fireworks display—surprised that neither rain nor heat nor the Seven Dwarfs nor Dumbo, himself, could stop it and I figured that was the diversion Charles and I longed for so we oozed our way through the soggy streets as I pulled out my cell phone and did a quick GPS search to locate the exact location of our flying machine.

The sun was settling by the time we returned and we jumped into the gondola, slowly watched the gold bars work their way down our shrunken pants so the only way we could remove the gold bars was to wriggle out of our pants and watch the golden ingots seep slowly down our wet legs and let me tell you, the sound and sight of gold bars sliding down your leg might give you a hard-on, but that is definitely not the case. The gold cuts your leg hairs and tickles and it's so slow, it was like the old folks say, "slower than molasses in January." Well, I never really thought about that a lot until those twelve agonizing (and yes I timed it) minutes when those gold bars slid, no inched their way like yellow caterpillars, down my leg and finally landed with a slugging sound, like one of those fake coins crooks drop into vending machines, onto the metal floor of RG's magical flying time machine just in time for us to clear Sleeping Beauty's Castle and hurl up into the stratosphere . . . almost!

People say the thud was so loud police from towns within thirty miles responded, as did six fire departments, but all I could hear was the wailing, the screeching and the shrieks of children as they looked up at that broken steeple with childish tears that would have melted Scrooge's heart—not my hero, Uncle Scrooge, the duck, but the real one, you know, that nasty old man in the Christmas Carol.

Anyway, I'm pretty sure some of the gold bars hit Sleeping Beauty's Castle so hard that flecks of gold are still there if you want to borrow my patented gold detecting radar wand for $3,250 a day plus a $500,000 deposit. I'm sure it will be worth it for the right person, someone who can climb up a steep cas-tle wall and hang from the nethermost point of the turret with a six-ounce wand in his hand.

Happily, our fully charged battery flung us up and up and further away from the Disney World we had come to love as kids and which now, though partially wrecked, and with one of its steeples akimbo, would haunt us in our dreams forever.

Charles looked at me with hunger in his eyes. . . well in his tummy, actually, and I dug down into the lower part of the gondola and pulled out a bucket of Kentucky fried chicken. I hid it there the evening before our departure, hoping I'd have a quiet beach-like resort to enjoy it in, but here flying over Kentucky, I figured it was the best time to eat it. . . although I'm sure the colonel was busy elsewhere, we paid him homage by wafting chicken bones from the gondola down to the rooftop of a KFC on Route U.S. 23. We sure heard the ping, ping, ping and RG said we needed to get a life, otherwise we would chicken bone some poor old codger to death, you know the type of man I mean, the one who is afraid to go in a restaurant so he chops away in the Drive-Thru lane, munching loudly for half an hour before sucking the marrow out of the bones as a dozen irate motorists honk behind him. Charles and RG and I swore we heard the codger burp as he finished his soda, screeched the truck in gear and moved along. . . more than likely to Howard Johnsons, which, sad to say, doesn't have a drive-in-window but which will bring it out to his car because the manager is the old codger's great-grandson and knew when he bought the franchise he'd have to accommodate his great gramps.

A few minutes later, Charles gave me one of his childlike looks and I tossed him two chicken legs and picked up several wings for myself. Dark meat is always the best, I thought as I looked toward Charles for confirmation but all I got was a system of ummms and burps and an inexplicable belch just as RG took the breasts and turned them into chicken a la king.

We continued our flight across the country and if you've never flown in a time machine, you must know the world is not like what you see on those maps we grew up with as kids. Not at all. It's all splotchy and zigzaggy and it's impossible to identify anything. You'd think those folks who made those maps would have warned us about this like they warned us about not standing on the top rung of a ladder or not plugging hair driers in while you're in the shower—but oh no, they didn't tell us there would be clouds and glare all around us and that when we looked down we wouldn't see those map words identifying anything. And there were no solid colors—not really—just sometimes a big field of green stuff, but there were no purples, no oranges, and no striped lines either—other than the ones on highways which sure as heck needed a paint job. In fact, our only map help was by spotting the occasional message written on water towers: "Billy's Chantilly Meatballs" or "Prince Frederick Tires" or "Hagerstown Hooters," which I thought was a hoot because it was written so high up on those two big breast-like humps no one would ever be able to read it. But other than those, we had no real idea where we were, except for my phone, which, thankfully, gave us a real view of what we were passing as it spoke the names of the towns, which we couldn't detect, and the rivers, which looked like broken blue straws, and the highways, which weren't straight at all like they seem to be when we drove on them but sinuously winding up and down through the patches of green here and there.

When we got to Piscataway, Maryland we pissed over the side of the damned gondola. We pissed good and long and hard and laid down and went to sleep and I swear I don't know how long we were out but the sun was setting as we were pissing and by the time I woke up I had a hard on and, well, I took care of that. Charles didn't – or at least I don't think he did but

RG always took care of those matters during the night—usually a half dozen times or so, moaning and groaning so loud Charles and I could barely sleep.

Then we sailed through what I thought was shaving cream until I realized they were clouds. And then we saw nothing, just fog. That's what it looks like. Really. Just mountains and mountains of Burma Shave. Until we bumped into a mountain—I'm not sure what it was, but there were soldiers on it in Confederate uniforms and I swear I felt one of their sabers brushing against my ass. Charles must have, too, because he said ouch or oooo or something indecipherable and I reached down for the bucket of chicken with all the trimmings and grabbed a carton of very cold mashed potatoes with gravy and I swear they were the best thing I ate in my life and took out my phone and discovered we were flying over Stone Mountain Georgia and thought, it's a stone alright, maybe the Disney people can fix it when they're done repairing Sleeping Beauty's Castle.

And the three of us talked and talked about our adventures, well RG talked most. He seemed to be on a jag now that we'd bumped into so many things and he giggled and laughed and told us what it was living in Camelot in the good old days when knights were as merry as Robin Hood's men and how much he longed for it—but as many times as he returned in the time machine, it was never the same. So, he wanted to go back to Bimini for a while and enjoy the beach and the hot boys and the water and the seashells. And RG waved his hand and there were about six hundred shells in the gondola and he described each one as we sat there looking at the shells, sort of, and at his ass, mostly, and then into his ever changing eyes— flicking from blue to brown to chartreuse to stripped and as the gondola began to descend, I searched for a cell phone signal and discovered we were nearing the Mississippi—not the state—the river, and I wished we could go low enough to see one of those riverboats—you know the ones I'm talking about—the ones we see in all those great musicals like Show Boat and Disney World, but by then RG had waved his hands again and his shells whisked themselves off to Never-land or wherever they went so I took over the conversation and told RG about the model showboat I put together from a kit when I was fourteen—it must have had 5,000 plastic pieces and each one needed to be painted and glued somewhere and the instructions must have been written perfectly because that ship, which I christened The Scotty W., was awesome, I mean honest injun', can I say that? Or am I dating myself? No if I was dating myself I'd be the last person on earth, wouldn't I? But I'm not, because Charles is here and so is RG so I'll delete the word 'injun' from this story before it's published and if I forget. Mea culpa, all right? Anyway, the Scotty W. had a tragic ending—because on New Year's Eve, my dog, Lassie, attacked it while I was sleeping. I'm not sure what she thought it was, but she tore it from stem to stern and that night I was sleeping so soundly I didn't hear a thing except something that sounded like a boy crunching on potato chips, which made me hungry and I woke up with my mouth gnawing on the bedpost and spit it out and never told anybody, so don't read this part okay? That's where we need an editor's blue pencil or someone with a pair of scissors.

I decided to go down to see what had become of our car and that backwater of a town we had escaped, but I brought us down too fast and our ears popped. I looked over at Charles who was turning purple and hurried over to him, hugging him, wondering if he needed mouth-to-mouth. It had been a long time since we had done that, but he held me and cuddled me and I knew no matter what we, us, me, him, our love would survive forever.

RG smiled at both of us and for a moment I thought he was going to come close and snuggle with us, but he didn't. He seemed too happy watching us being happy. And RG just stood there in his Valentine Day boxers and Bimini is for Lovers T-shirt pointing toward the west, toward the setting sun and then to the five bars of gold we'd found and reminded us of the crows who had died and told us he'd perform magic and restore the crows to life.

We decided then and there to dump the five bars of gold and the extra battery that had been charging all day down to the men in the crowd below us. This time nothing killed anybody. The gold bars just landed in a row five or ten feet away from each other and the battery landed even more gently because RG helped lower everything to the ground and the three of us well-fed underwear clad men looked down on that town, at the bars, at the battery, at the living flying crows, and at the men who were racing toward the golden bars. And RG pulled out the charm he had made of our 2024 Porsche 911 Convertible and lowered it to the ground where it grew and grew and grew right back to its original shape. And then we felt ourselves floating down, down, down and watched as RG and the time machine disappeared. Then Charles and I walked to the Porsche, where we discovered two T-shirts with the words Bimini is for Lovers and two plane tickets for that happy island.

The note attached said, "You thought I left you, I'm just making some early preparations for your visit. It's going to be a lollapalooza so bring some extra Kentucky fried chicken—the islanders here never mastered the recipe like the old colonel did.

Jonathan

Zachary Stillings

Zackary L. Stillings lives in Columbus, Ohio, with his partner and Boston Terrier. He is an attorney by day, but spends his free time growing hot peppers, playing Dungeons & Dragons, and exploring the city's breweries. He is an avid horror fan, and loves uncertain endings and morally ambiguous characters. For more of Zack's writing, follow him on Instagram @zlswrites.

CRSO

Ice clinks in crystal glasses as the small group moves throughout Sley House. The group's conversation ebbs and flows as they walk, from the cigar room to the study, the dining room to the library, to the ballroom, and then, finally, to the brightly lit salon. Genevieve strides to the dry bar in the corner, her footsteps staccato clicks on the cherrywood floors.

"A refill, anyone?" she asks before gesturing around the

space they had just entered, an expansive, wood-paneled room lined with books, aesthetically designed around a large, peculiar plant. "The salon. We might have our next drink here, if there are no objections." She gives them a wry grin before turning about to pull several liquor bottles from their shelves.

"I'll have another," a young woman says enthusiastically, "the gin you used in the first was simply magical." Her glass is empty, with not even an ice cube remaining as she hands it to Genevieve.

"We make it here at the house—our own aromatic blend." Genevieve holds up an unmarked glass bottle containing a pale, golden liquid. "The secret is the Angelica," she says, pouring several shots of it into a shaker. "We've bred quite a flavorful strain here in the nursery. Add some juniper, carda-mom, cassia bark, lemon peel, and coriander, and you get a lovely, herbaceous gin." She turns to look at the group. "Any-one else?"

The other woman nods appreciatively, before handing her empty glass to Genevieve with a curtseyed "thank you." The man, however, is no longer listening to his host. He is, instead, inspecting the room's centerpiece. The first woman—blonde, with round eyes and milky-pale skin—clears her throat, giving airs of propriety, the practiced politesse of one who knows how to draw attention to rudeness without being rude oneself. He looks up.

"Ms. Sley," he says, barely startled. "What is it, exactly?"

She laughs, a curt, one-note scoff. "That, dear Winston, is quite the story," she says. "And it is one that shall require a few more of these, I dare say. Shall I make you one?"

He looks towards her, and then the other women, a brief sense of unease passing over his face. "Of course, of course," he says. "And then, I would love to know that story."

The three look to Genevieve, who has begun to pour drinks gently into their glasses, before each, in turn, faces the flora that has so captivated Winston.

Before them lies the most peculiar vegetation that any of them have ever seen. The pot in which it is planted is a centerpiece in and of itself. Clear crystal, it is shaped as a large, shallow bowl, nearly six feet in diameter, and yet only two feet deep. Through the crystal, it is possible to see more than just dirt. A lighter color—white, tan, yellowing—is visible in places, made pearlescent by the crystal that holds it.

But for all the pot's intricacies, the bush itself—if, in fact, it is a bush—is somehow even more spectacular. It maintains the green color of most plants, though its stems, leaves, and trunks are intermittently tinged with a deep red, except for the largest of its appendages, which, upon close examination, grows through or about, or from or around a solid, pale-white substance. The plant has form, and it—as few plants do—appears to have a planned structure. The three visitors to the house look on, the plant's red and cream and green combining to both attract and assault their eyes, the plant's appearance both beautiful and putrescent.

The blonde woman approaches the pot, moving intently towards one of several large flowers that decorate its external reaches. They are a deep, pale, purplish blue, a color unexpected, but also fully concordant with the plant's aesthetic. The woman approaches it, reaching out her finger to touch the solid white stamen protruding from the center of the flower, and a frisson of unease causes her to shiver.

"I wouldn't touch that, Eugenia," Genevieve says, passing out drinks to the first two before handing Eugenia her own. "At least not yet." Genevieve takes an intent sip of her drink, before taking a seat directly in front of her centerpiece, where she is framed in the evening sunlight streaming in from the stained-glass windows that cover the center of the salon. "Why don't you have a seat," she says, settling into her chair. She reaches into the drawer of the end table next to her, pulling out an envelope, from which she removes several sheets of stationery.

"It all began with a letter," she says, and she begins to read.

⚜

Dearest Genevieve,

It has been far too long since I have written, though in truth, I have thought of you often and fondly over these past years, particularly when, as has become my habit, I walk through the rose garden, which is now full of the cultivars that you created. It is most pleasant just before dark, when, as I am certain you will recall, the last vestiges of sunlight stream through the western archway, lighting a golden path through the dusk. It is then that I walk the paths, when the peach roses are alight with the sun's last glimmers, and the air in the garden is fragrant with their blossoms, just until the night itself takes over, and all that is left are the great hulking outlines of the bushes in the moonlight.

It gives me peace, it does. When I go to the garden, I have on numerous occasions silently thanked you for your part in designing it, how your great knowledge of horticulture contributed to the only place I have true solitude on this earth. You see, I have been much occupied with my travails of late, both personal and professional. You are fortunate not to have any children, Genevieve! My daughter is a young woman now, as yet unmarried, though I fear she was recently smitten by one unworthy of her gaze. And while I am certain that her virtue remains intact, and that her affections for this man have come to an end, I still fear for her future, and for the reckless choices I feel she will make. Perhaps someday you shall meet her, and understand the insouciance of her nature, which gives me such concerns. She chose a course of study identical to your own, in fact, and I believe the two of you would have much to discuss should your paths ever cross.

Of course, my concerns over my flighty young woman would not be enough to put me in my current distressed state, were it not for the ever-changing requirements that my superiors have placed upon me. When I began my work, you will recall, I had great success in synthesizing new compounds, compounds which, you will also recall, are now used in factories in all industrial centers of our great land. But success—for better or for worse, dear Genevieve—eventually requires more and more success, until at some point, one has reached the limits of one's capabilities.

When I walk through the garden, there are times when I fear that is what has become of me. That my chemical endeavors have reached the limits of my intellect, that I am no longer the man I was, the man able to singlehandedly increase humanity's productivity through the combination of disparate elements. The new requirements they have placed upon me— lubricants to eliminate friction, the transmutation of carbons into other substances, fertilizers to make the most barren land fertile—they now seem to me to be more alchemy than chemistry.

I digress. Certainly, you were the more intelligent of the two of us, choosing as you did to study the natural world, to study that which we know can take place in the wilds, such that there is a finite universe of what is possible, of what is naturally occurring. It is, in a roundabout way, why I am contacting you now.

You see, I have observed what can only be described as a natural anomaly on the estate; I can think of no other word sufficient to describe it. There is, I fear, no explanation that my mind can conjure for its existence, there at the boundary of my holdings, near the river's edge. It is a plant, I must surmise, a bush of some sort, perhaps. Though it is a bush that possesses what my untrained eye can only describe as a skeletal structure. My groundskeepers found it some months ago, and, having dismissed it as an invasive species, attempted to cut it down, though its main stem— trunk, even—resisted the shears to such a point that they were ruined in the attempt to destroy it.

I say skeletal because, as it will become clear if you are to accept my invitation, there is also a corporeal sense to the thing, as though it is not merely a plant, but also, in some sense, a body. Indeed, upon the attempt to cut it down, it emitted a thin, iron-rich sap the color of sapphires, a sap which then dulled to a deep maroon before hardening on the stem. It was, if you will not think me silly for saying it, as though the plant were bleeding.

I myself have gone to examine it on multiple occasions, now, and the more that my thoughts dwell on it, the more discomforted I am. It is, I fear, becoming a fixation for my mind, and its existence on my property has caused a cloud of unease to sit, uncomfortably, over all my waking thoughts. It is for this reason that I write: I must be rid of it, Genevieve.

I would like to invite you to come to the estate, to view this—dare I even say, abomination—and, if providence will smile upon me, relieve me of its presence. You can kill it, you can take it, you can study it, you can do whatever you feel is appropriate to do with it. The only thing I ask, dear Genevieve, is that you relieve me of it. I will make rooms available to you, should you choose to accept, and will make myself available to you at any time you wish. It is my most sincere hope that our years of friendship have not diminished our affections for one another, notwithstanding the distance that has grown between us, and that I will have the great pleasure of viewing your countenance again.

Very truly yours,

E

☙❦❧

Genevieve folds up the papers, placing them back into the envelope, before placing the envelope back in a drawer.

"And so, I went," she says.

The visitors look at Genevieve expectantly, as though she would now continue the story. But, she pauses.

"So," she says, looking not at the three guests, but instead at the plant in the middle of the room. "What is it?"

Helen, a short, large, dark-haired woman with horn-rimmed glasses and a round face, chuckles nervously. "But, we're supposed to be the ones mentored by you, Ms. Sley," she said, "and we are only in our third year of study."

"Surely," Genevieve says, "you must at least have a guess. Winston, Eugenia—anything from either of you?"

Winston squints an eye, looking perplexingly at the plant, before he stands to approach it, standing with his back to Genevieve. He makes a loud "hm," noise, pulling off his glasses, wiping them, and replacing them, before touching one of the plant's leaves, ever so gently.

It recoils. The leaf rolls onto itself, returning to the shape of a shoot, as though it had never grown to unroll itself at all. Several other leaves on the branch begin to roll as well, now appearing more as small verdant spears than leaves. Winston steps back with a gasp of surprise, as the final leaf rolls into itself, and the branch as a whole recoils, a snake preparing to strike. Winston takes another step back, as the branch springs forward as though to skewer him, falling but several inches short of his chest.

Winston lets out a shriek, before re-composing himself to face the women.

"It is not a plant at all," Eugenia says, still seated. She takes a drink of the gin, finishing her glass. "Or, it is at least not fully a plant. It is," she pauses, "a hybrid, I would have to imagine. Of what, I cannot be certain, but it has certain, shall we say, elements, that I have never seen described as belonging to flora before."

Genevieve raises an eyebrow. "What about *Mimosa pudica*, the 'sensitive plants?'" she says. "They, too, exhibit movement.

And while you are correct that it may have strange elements for a plant, it is clearly not an animal, clearly not a fungus. What say you to that?"

Winston and Helen remain silent, leaning forward in their chairs, the ice in their glasses tinkling as though to signal the anticipation of the moment.

"A species of sensitive plant, then? That could possibly explain the movement in the leaves, but," she pauses, thinking, before she says, "but that movement in the sensitive plant is defensive. This bush did not seem to be acting defensively. It was almost as though the leaves were" she pauses again, before taking another breath, "sharpened, in a way. As though the plant was hunting that which touched it."

Winston leans closer. "You're saying that I was almost attacked by a plant?"

"Not exactly, though it cannot be ruled out," Eugenia says, "I mean only to say that its movements differed from the defensive posture taken by sensitive plants. And a sensitive plant continues to recoil onto itself. This plant's movement, particularly its final movement towards Winston, there, would almost require musculature, of some sort. It is that which I find the most puzzling. And, it is that which leads me to believe that it must be some sort of hybrid."

Genevieve nods.

"So, that is my final answer. It is a hybrid—the plant portion of its genes perhaps related the sensitive plant family, though somehow mixed with the underlying biology of an animal." Eugenia turns her face from the plant, now looking squarely at Genevieve. "Is that correct?"

"A good guess," she responds. "Anything more from either of you?" she asks, looking first to Helen, and then to Winston. They both shake their heads.

"It is a decent hypothesis," Helen states, "though it sounds rather supernatural to my ear, after all, who has heard of such a thing in the natural world? A plant-animal hybrid?" She chuckles nervously.

Genevieve smiles, giving nothing away. "You three are at the top of the class at the University—it is, of course, why I offered to mentor you all through the end of your studies. So consider this a mentorship lesson. This E, this person who wrote that letter, was wrong. The natural world is full of mystery, and full of the unknown. Sometimes," she looks at them each in turn, her voice becoming quieter, yet firmer, "when looking at natural mysteries, you must also be open to supernatural explanations."

She stands, her glass empty. "Would anyone like another beverage before we continue?"

Genevieve refills their drinks, they retake their seats, and she continues the story.

☙❧

"Genevieve!" Edward called from the doorway, as she stepped out of the carriage that had brought her from the city. The estate was exactly as she had remembered from their time as University classmates. The palatial stone home was far from the main road, and even in a sturdy carriage, it was a five-minute ride on the Stones' driveway before one could even see the home. In front of the home were numerous fountains and decorative shrubs, and Genevieve had passed at least three dark-skinned servants tending to the living sculptures as she approached.

"Edward!" she yelled, "I'll be right up!" She reached back into the carriage to grab her luggage, only to find that another servant had already grabbed it. "Oh, I can take that myself," she said, reaching for the trunk.

"No ma'am," the man said, his Caribbean accent clear even in those scant two words. "Mr. Stone would have my hide, he would!" He laughed, despite the implication of his words. "This will be in your room when you need it, ma'am," he said, before trotting off with her belongings.

His comment disturbed her. Surely he could not have meant it literally. Edward Stone was of old stock, certainly, and was of the very sort of person whose life benefit the most from the status quo. And yet, the Edward Stone she knew as a young man would surely not raise a hand to his staff. She put the comment in her mind for later examination, once she had more evidence, more experience with Edward Stone, the adult.

Genevieve picked up the edges of the dress she had worn, to avoid the dust, and climbed the twelve stairs to the Stones' front door. Edward stood before a female member of his staff, a white bonnet covering her head, her eyes gazing towards Edward's shoes.

"Genevieve, how wonderful it is to see you!" he said, reaching out for a hug.

Genevieve hated hugs. It was not as though she did not enjoy human contact. To the contrary, she loved physical closeness when it was done on her terms. But hugs—particularly from those she did not know well—were a physical imposition of the highest order. They were a momentary surrender of her ownership of herself, as though she was required to give access to herself, if only momentarily, to another for the sole purpose of social cohesion.

When his arms wrapped around her, she kept hers at her side. And when he squeezed, she took her right hand, and patted him on the back three times.

Edward released her.

"We have so much to catch up on," he said, "though I regret

it will have to wait until this evening. I just received word of an emergency at the lab that I must attend to, but rest assured I will be here for dinner."

"Of course," Genevieve said, "you were always so dedicated to your experiments."

He chuckled. "Some things never change, do they? But speaking of things that never change—perhaps this would be a great time for you to examine my own little natural mystery!"

"That is the reason I'm here, of course, though you must know it is lovely to see you," Genevieve replied. "Perhaps one of your groundskeepers could point me in the right direction if it would not be too much of a bother. Your letter had mentioned that one had already tried to cut the plant down, if I recall?"

"Yes, yes," he said, turning to the woman behind him. She was short, far shorter than Genevieve, and had a pleasant, soft aura about her. "Paula," Edward directed towards her, "could you please show Ms. Sley to her room?"

She mumbled a soft, "Yessir," to him, her eyes only then rising to meet Genevieve's.

"And then once she is ready, please ask Jethro and Orville to show her to that strange plant at the rear of the estate. They'll know which one."

"Yessir," she said, her eyes again going towards his shoes.

"Paula here will have you settled in no time, and will be happy to get you whatever you need while I'm away. Paula and her family have been with us for years, now. She'll take good care of you, I'm certain."

Genevieve and Edward bid each other adieu, before Genevieve continued into the *Maison Pierre*, as the Stones referred to their manse. Paula led her through a massive foyer, and up a curved stone staircase, carpeted in lush crimson. The second floor was no less grand than the first, adorned on both sides with exquisite oil paintings, both pastorals and portraitures. The portraits all had similar appearances: all white, all blonde, all male, all possessing the strong jawline and Roman nose that had always made Edward so recognizable.

"Edward had said you'd been here for years," Genevieve said, smiling at Paula. "How long have you been here?" The woman looked up at her then, as they approached what she presumed would be her room, where her luggage was placed neatly outside the door. To its left, another portrait hung, this time, a young woman, perhaps in her late teens or early twenties, blonde, with round eyes and milky-pale skin. She, too, favored Edward.

"'Bout ten years, ma'am," she said, opening the door and gesturing Genevieve inside. "Master Stone advertised back in the islands years ago for help, and a whole group of us came, lookin' for work, lookin' to be here on the mainland. I brought my whole family," she said, her island accent now crystal clear. She stood back, then, gesturing to the room.

A four-post bed dominated the room, highlighted by drapes of a luxurious emerald velvet. The bed itself was also princely, topped with a small mountain of decorative silk and velvet pillows and topped by a golden down comforter. Oil studies of various plant species hung on the walls, giving her the impression that she had been placed in this particular room quite intentionally.

"This is beautiful, Paula," she said warmly, hoping to perk the woman up a bit.

"Thank you, ma'am," she replied, "the restroom is right over there, and you are welcome to visit anywhere you wish in the home. I will let you change, ma'am, and you can just meet us downstairs."

"No need," Genevieve replied, beginning to open her suitcase. "I will just be a minute to get ready, really," she said, pulling out a pair of pants and a button up shirt. "It's still a chilly morning out there, but this should be enough!" she said, heading towards the other side of a changing screen in the corner of the room.

"So, Paula," she continued, beginning the process of taking off her dress, "what does the rest of your family do here? You had mentioned they all came with you?"
Paula took a few seconds before responding. "Yes, ma'am. My husband, Earl, he works with the animals, and as a general handyman around the estate here. And my son, my son left us. He's back home."

"Oh that's lovely," Genevieve responded. "I will have to meet your Earl." She pulled on her pants. "How does you son enjoy your home country?"

And now Paula did take some time to respond. "I do not know," she said, "I have not heard from him in some months, going on a year."

Genevieve struggled with a response. "Well, young men can be fickle," she said, "and I am certain that the mail is anything but regular with that distance between us. I am sure he is loving it there. And if he does not enjoy it, then he has you and Earl to return to, after all."

She finished buttoning her shirt, and came out from behind the screen preparing to pull on a pair of leather boots.

"I am certain you're right, ma'am. He's a good boy. It's probably just the post being slow." Her exterior softened then, as though for a moment she allowed Paula the person to speak, more than Paula the maid. It did not last long. "If you are ready, then, ma'am we can head right out to meet Jethro and Orville."

Paula led Genevieve to the foyer, after which Jethro and Orville led her to the stables, a hundred yards or so towards the river from the *Maison Pierre*. They wore the rough-hewn clothes of those accustomed to working outside, their hands both thick and calloused.

"This way, ma'am," Jethro said, as they entered the outbuilding. "We have a mare in here for you for the trip out." He was tall and plump, with a long face and kind eyes. "It's a bit of a trek out there, otherwise."

"Especially in all the muck, what with the rain we've had recently," added Orville. He looked to be the older of the two, with a shaved head and the same island accent that the other servants possessed. "Woulda' gotten those boots nice and muddy, ma'am!"

The scents of hay, and moisture and manure and feed, and *natural things* filled her nostrils when she entered. Horses, unseen in their pens, snorted and pranced in anticipation of time in the pasture. Orville remained with Genevieve while Jethro fetched the horses, the first of which—a roan mare they called Willow—they led to Genevieve.

She approached her head cautiously, reaching out to gently stroke the smooth fur between Willow's eyes, before moving her hand to touch the mare's cheek tenderly. "Good girl," she said sweetly, "we'll get along just fine." She moved her hand to the horse's shoulders, caressing them, cooing to Willow softly. And then, with Jethro giving her a boost, she mounted the mare, patting her muscular neck, forming a bond.

The others mounted their horses, and the trio left the stables for a half-hour trip through the estate's fields and marshes towards the river.

Genevieve could sense the plant before she saw it. It began

with a subtle change in the color of the dirt around her. From the stables through the fields, the dirt had been moist, almost muddy, dark as night with a loamy smell that permeated her senses. Her mare's hoofs sank deep into it, pulling out with a hearty *squish* with every movement, making it such that each of her senses felt, in some odd way, activated by the life it emanated. Until it stopped.

The ground grew harder, inexplicably. In the distance, Genevieve could see the river, which should at this distance be making the earth more moist—not less. And yet, it grew harder with each step that her mare took. At the same time, the healthy, black earth gave way to clay, first turning to a lighter brown, followed by a gray color more reminiscent of shale than farmland. And as the cracks in the soil grew more pronounced, it became clear that the area, too, could support less and less life. The wild grasses that were ubiquitous through the early parts of her journey became more and more scarce, their appearances further apart, their height dwindling until, as they approached the river, there was naught but the dying earth around their horses' feet.

It was not simply that the land had changed, though. The very air itself was changed, charged with some invisible, unnerving electricity. Genevieve was reminded of the way a party could become when two attendees come to blows, the air bristling with conflict, the static paralyzing all those who bear witness.

She felt the disquiet as she dismounted, approaching the plant cautiously, its solitude already noteworthy. Neither Jethro nor Orville got off their horses.

"We'll be right here, ma'am," Jethro said. "The horses, they get spooked if they get too close, y'understand." He tried to laugh after that statement, but the laughter died on his lips, its mirth sucked out by the strange energy that emanated from the plant.

She approached it cautiously. The leaves were in places the most verdant of greens, with crimson veins coursing throughout its structure. Towards the stalk were blotchy, indiscernible shapes of a putrid purple, buds, perhaps, but attached not to a stem as a normal flower, but rather to the skeletal frame of the plant.

It felt as no plant she had ever felt before. It felt isolated. It felt malnourished. It felt, in the most peculiar way, *angry*.

She touched one of the leaves. And then, the plant moved. First a twitch of the branch, followed by wholesale movement of the branch, followed by activity in several branches, and then the movement of the skeletal frame that undergirded the entire body. One of the buds burst, then, a sickening squelching noise erupting from it as red, sticky sap exploded towards Genevieve.

The mare squealed, and bolted. Genevieve recoiled. And in her mind, she heard a distinct voice, bearing a distinct accent, wielding a distinct malevolence. *Edward.*

⚜

Jethro eventually corralled the mare, and the three returned to the *Maison Pierre*. A gray haze had descended on the manse when they arrived, giving the stone structure a hard, unwelcoming air. The trio dismounted from the horses, and Genevieve gave her mare a fond caress before returning to the home.

Paula met her, and coughed politely as Genevieve opened the door.

"Of course," Genevieve said, "thank you for the reminder. I've already seen how hard you work here and certainly would not want to make that more difficult for you by tracking in this muck!" She removed her boots, placing them on a mat just to the side of the foyer she entered.

"It's not a worry ma'am," Paula replied, "though I certainly appreciate it. You know how the men can be—the master would have tracked the mud in without a second thought, only noticin' after the memory of it bein' him was gone from his brain." She chuckled.

"He's an interesting man," Genevieve replied, walking now into the main area of the home. "I knew Edward the boy, but Edward the man is someone still a stranger to me." Paula made a non-committal guttural noise that told Genevieve precisely nothing. She continued. "He seems congenial enough, though, don't you think?"
Paula looked at her, surprised. "Ma'am, those who Mr. Stone brings here do not tend to think much of what we servants think." She paused, and Genevieve let the silence force her to speak again. "His daughter, though," she said, "she's a good one, she is."

"Oh?" Genevieve replied. The two were now making their way up the stairs, towards Genevieve's room. "I do not believe I've had the pleasure of her acquaintance."

"She was good to my Jonathan, ma'am. Treated 'im no different than anyone her father invited over, rich or poor or white or black. A good girl. A good woman."

Genevieve smiled at her. "I should hope to make her acquaintance one day," she said. "Her father speaks so highly of her. A botanist, too, I understand—I would have much to discuss with her, I am certain."

Paula nodded, as they approached Genevieve's room. "That's her there, ma'am," she said, pointing to the portrait outside the room.

Genevieve studied her face. She looked kind, friendly. Attractive features like her father, without the hardness that made her wary of him, despite his genial comportment. "If she was close to your son," she said, "perhaps she has heard from him."

Paula laughed. "I doubt that, ma'am," she said, "she left for University this past year, and my boy left soon after. Had a meeting with Master Stone, he did, and then he left, back to the islands." She shook her head.

"I'm sure you'll hear from him soon," Genevieve replied, reassuring her again. "Is there any particular way I should dress this evening?" she asked. "I am always terribly unsure of how to put myself together for these situations." She opened the door, leading Paula into the room with her.

Paula smiled at her. "We only have one thing we're allowed to wear, I'm afraid, so I wouldn't know how to counsel you there." She winked. "But," she said, her eyes looking towards a dress that Genevieve had laid on the couch while she had been getting ready for her excursion to the strange plant, "that looks suitable to me."

"Thank you, Paula. I'll be down shortly."

⌘

The dinner was magnificent. Paula, Genevieve learned, was not only a pleasant governess and homemaker, but also, it turns out, an incredible chef. Edward had remembered Genevieve's appreciation for the exotic, it seemed, and had asked Paula to coordinate a dinner full of the flavors of the islands from which she and the other household attendants had come.

She arrived to the table, welcomed by fried plantains served with a mango-coconut sauce spiced with the slightest heat of scotch bonnet peppers. Cinnamon and nutmeg danced on her palate, which she cleansed with a passionfruit-coconut puree spiked with spiced rum. From there, she was given a stew of red beans and rice, cooked with sweet spices and savory beef bones. Aside it, the servants plated chicken flavored with both sweet and piquant spices. The effect was beautiful: an initial sweet taste hit her senses, followed by the savory flavor of brick oven chicken, and then followed with the most deliciously painful hit of capsaicin that she had ever experienced. Her mouth watered, her face began to sweat, and she reached for the milky rum drink to sooth the burn.

The conversation ebbed and flowed through dinner, as Stone and Sley relieved their University days surrounded by the aromas that wafted from Stone's servants' native cuisine. After the main course, the two split a slice of mango cheesecake, the cheesecake portion tinged with the ultra-sweet fruit, then drizzled with a mango compote before being sprinkled in coconut shards. It was intoxicating and mesmerizing, these flavors that were rarer than unicorns among the country's polite society.

"So," Edward said, having exhausted his rolodex of high-society gossip, "what do you think of my little infestation?"

"Infestation?" Genevieve laughed, aided by the copious amounts of sweet rum she had imbibed through the course of the evening. "You mean your plant? It is a gift, I think. A true horticultural mystery."

"Is it now?" Edward responded. "I simply want it gone. Its kind does not belong here, not like that, not around places like this. It is a wild thing, and it must be gone."

"Its kind," Genevieve questioned. "Whatever could you mean? I have never seen a thing like it, myself."
"Forget it," he said. "Only that my family will be better once it is gone."

"Then I shall arrange for it to be brought back to Sley House," she said. "I can probably have Charles here within the week to remove it. I will be certain to let you know what we learn, of course." The liquor was beginning to impact her, she knew, but she did her best to retain all that he said then, trying to discern the mystery of this exotic plant. She gazed at him expectantly, as he stared at an empty glass.

Edward held it up, and a servant came over, refilling it with the rum-sweet milky liquid that had intoxicated them all evening. After a long pause, he spoke again, softly, staring only at his glass. "Tell me, Genevieve. Did it speak to you?"

⋈

Genevieve smiles at the students, expectantly.

"So," Winston cuts in, his body poised at the edge of his seat, his eyes flitting between Genevieve and the plant, lest it attempt another attack against him, "what did you tell him?"

"What do you think I told him?" she says, a wry smile cracking her lips.

"You lied to him, I think," Eugenia replies, now walking confidently towards the plant. "You told him he was mad, you told him only a fool would say such a thing, and you told him that you would find a natural, scientific reason for how this… being…" she indicated the plant, "could exist." She reaches out to the plant, caressing a leaf, and then a stem.

It accepts her touch. It embraces her touch. It seems to *desire* her touch, as though a plant could desire anything other than sunlight and water. "Of course you didn't say 'being,' since that would have given it away." She looks to Genevieve, now, continuing. "You probably said 'plant,' or 'bush,' or even 'flora,' yes?"

Genevieve warms, knowing that Eugenia now knows what she knows. "Exactly the case, Ms. Stone. I asked my brother Charles to take some men out to dig the plant up, making sure to retain all of the original root system, making certain that none of the original body, none of the original bones, were left behind." She shakes her head. "And oh, what my brother Charles had to tell." She stands, approaching the bar, now pouring a draught of brownish liquid directly into her own glass.

"What ever could you mean?" asks Helen, looking back towards her, her brow furrowed in confusion.
"It is, quite simply, a tragedy," Genevieve responds. "We have in this country an aristocracy. It is no secret; there is no debate. We ourselves, in this home, at this moment, we are all part of it. Think of your own life, Helen. Your father, a member of parliament, a traditionalist, a large landholder. You are at the University by your own talents, that much is clear, but you are also there by virtue of his name. What would he do, if you were to seek companionship among those less fortunate? A man, even? A man who does not look like you, a man who does not speak like you, a man who would give you children that bear neither his resemblance nor his name?"

Helen begins to speak, but can only muster a barely audible, "I…"

"And you, Winston," Genevieve did not stop to worry about Helen. "Scion of the president of the city's largest bank. What would your parents do if you were to take up with a servant? What would your parents do if she were to take up with your child? They would, of course, send her away. Unless—of course—the servant with which you'd prefer to have a relationship was unable to bear a child. If he could, perhaps, discuss your indiscretions with others your parents might see at parties, at public functions. What then, do you think they would do to him? It is truly my hope you never find out, dear boy. None of us here would say a word, though—I do promise you that."

He looks at her, stunned. "How did you," he stammers.

"I'm not, you know," he tries to finish his sentence.

"No need to defend yourself. I ask only what if. This night is not about you, though I am certain the three of you will have plenty to discuss when it is over."

She then turned to Eugenia, whose hand now held a branch from the strange plant in the middle of the room. "In any event, Winston and Helen, no matter what you both *guess* your parents would do is of no matter." She strides to Eugenia, placing her hand reassuringly on her shoulder. "Ms. Stone, she *knows*, now."

Eugenia turns toward her. "Tell me everything."

Genevieve returns to her seat, takes a sip of her scotch, and begins to speak.

☙❦☙

"I knew the plant had been, at some point, a person, from the moment I heard it speak the name 'Edward.' It was in my head of course, but it was as real as you speaking to me now. It is, as you can see, unnatural, a hybrid the likes of which the University's botany department—nor, shall I assume, any botany department in the world—had ever seen. It was incredibly sad, while also incredibly fascinating.

"I did not tell you the entire truth, earlier. The plant, it—he—did not sense me as a threat. He did not only say your father's name, Eugenia. He said your father had done this. That your father had murdered him.

"Of course, I did not believe it at the time, or at least, I viewed the statement with the type of skepticism one should reserve for all supernatural events. I determined I would perform tests, that I would perform experiments, that I would determine the precise scientific nature of what had created this being."

Genevieve pauses, catching her breath. Winston stands,

pouring himself a drink, one finger, and then two, then three, not saying a word. Eugenia stands sentinel, a branch of the plant now draped over her shoulder.

"And then I spoke with Paula. The coincidences were too much. Edward's recent studies on fringe chemistry, on compounds that he did not understand, on fertilizers even, intended to compound the growth of god knows what types of flora. Then you had Paula's son's disappearance, and his apparent closeness with Edward's daughter. And of course, Edward's letter to me, discussing the recent end of his daughter's undesirable romantic relationship, it all made too much sense."

Genevieve walks to the plant, touching it gently, whispering to it, as though asking it for permission.

"But it was when Charles brought it back that we fully understood. My brother—you all do not know him, of course, but he is more in touch with these types of supernatural occurrences than am I. He can hear things, discern things, know things, that would largely be impossible even for a believer such as myself. He is, in short, able to understand a deeper message than I, myself, could discern.

"And it was he that confirmed my fears."

A solitary tear falls down Eugenia's face.

"Ms. Stone," Genevieve says, now looking directly at Eugenia. "You left for University some months ago. I understand from Charles—and, I might add, my understanding is confirmed by Paula, the governess you are certainly familiar with—that her son was brought to tea with your father, after which he disappeared.

"Of course, while your father led the household to believe that Jonathan had returned to the islands, he had in fact given him a failed chemistry experiment. A fertilizer, we understand, that had theretofore killed any plant with which it came in contact."

Eugenia shakes her head, tears now streaming from both her eyes. Helen rises, placing her hand on Eugenia's.

"But Jonathan was not a plant," Eugenia says, stifling her sobs.

"He is not," Genevieve responds. "Your father buried him after dark, miles from the estate, believing it to be the end of him.

"But it was not. He is alive, still. What is in front of you is alive. What is in front of you is Jonathan."

Eugenia shakes her head, her hand holding the nearest branch to her affectionately. "I had told him, before I left, that we should tell father about us," she says. "That I did not care about our stations, that I did not care about our backgrounds, that I loved him, that he is a good person, and that he is my person, that he is my heart." She draws a deep breath. "And then I thought he had left, because he did not believe in us, that he did not share my affections."

Her tears begin anew. "And until this moment, I believed he had abandoned me." She turns to the plant, caressing its stem, touching the exposed skeletal structure that had, at one point, been human.

"I'm sorry, Jonathan," she says. "I'm so sorry." She runs her finger up and down the main stalk of the plant, which makes way for her hand, accepting her touch.

CʒℰƆ

Minutes pass. Genevieve pulls Winston and Helen aside, entreating them to support Eugenia, to care for her in the coming days as her close friends, her peers. She pours a final cocktail for Eugenia, rubbing her back before handing it to her. "I have two more things to tell you," she says.

"What has happened is monstrous," she says, "but I will

happily keep care of Jonathan as long as you wish. We here—my brothers and I—understand his needs, and he shall never want for anything. Though you are, of course, more than welcome to visit any time you so wish."

Eugenia looks back at her, nodding her head, appreciation in her expression.

"And should you ever wish—whether it be in a year or ten years—we will assist you in facilitating his removal from Sley House to a location of your choosing, and will, of course, teach you precisely what he needs, and how to care for him."

The blonde-haired girl with big round eyes and the distinctive Stone cheekbones nods her head.

"It is," Genevieve adds, "all on whatever timeline you so choose. We are happy to retain him here, and he has, so far, appeared happy to be here."

And then, the first noise emanated from the plant, a creaking groan, combined with the natural chime of wind swishing through leaves. A sound that was, unmistakably, happy.

"I have also developed this," Genevieve says, holding out a vial to Eugenia. "It is what I believe your father used to make Jonathan this way. Between Charles' understanding of Jonathan, and Paula's investigations of your father's greenhouse, this is the substance that I believe he used to poison your love.

"I leave you with this, and with this alone. I will never again mention this substance again. What you do with it is yours. And it is…"

The group each—all of them, Winston, Helen, Genevieve, and most strongly, Eugenia—heard loudly, and clearly, a solitary voice in their minds:

"*Yours alone, Eugenia.*"

Hierarchy

K.M. West

K.M. West writes stories for people who want to believe in magic and love having their hearts broken.

A second-generation Filipina-American, she works through writing to piece together a sense of culture from one that's been rewritten, obscured, occluded, and in some cases, fed to crocodiles. West's stories mix dread and unease with a sense of discovery, leaning heavily on the myths of her childhood and worries of the modern world. The nightmares in her writing reflect personal experiences with things otherwise unseen.

West writes as often as she can around being a spouse and mother of three, an IT professional, a small business owner, a graphic designer, and chronic text ignorer. Her debut novel, Wild Things Will Roam, has been lauded as 'a dystopian horror with soul' and is available anywhere books are sold.

જાછ

The woman kneels, staring up at me with her face fixed in that space between realization and pleasure. Black hair trails down over her naked shoulders, a lavender knot of entrails poised haphazardly across her lap. She has discovered a secret, the cost of which is evisceration.

"She's a *manananggal*," Charles Sley announces from where he's perched in the doorway. "A cryptid from the Philippines, she's transforming in that portrait. Any moment now, the top half of her body will abandon the lower region and she'll fly through the night on her vampiric escapades to suck the souls from unborn babes."

My knuckle strikes the wooden border. "Not if she's trapped here in this frame."

Charles doesn't laugh. "Now you sound like my brother."

Around her hang other examples of the esoteric and arcane, beasts and beauties both, smattered with newspaper clippings of the other Sley ventures. Highlights that would be tactless in the grand entryway of such a home, but serve as appropriate reminders of just how powerful the Sleys are to those who work here in staff's quarters—the entrance I was instructed to come through.

To swap my Carhartt for my finest suit jacket and then be directed around back was the initial slap. The self-loathing came when I dusted myself off before entering, out of instinct. Still, each picture frame proves Charles Sley as something of a king maker. Celebrity enterprises, publishing giants, start-up endeavors, all meteoric in their rise when backed by this archangel. That my goal is to be on this wall stirs in me both excitement and horror.

"You'll pardon this greeting, the front hall is under construction," he says, attempting to invalidate my frustration/dismissal/irritation/rage, as though I can't see through his tactics.

"Come, let's take our discussion to the library."

"Have you ever met one?" I ask, following. My periphery absorbs the fine mahogany carpentry of his labyrinth—also from the Philippines, if I'm not mistaken—but I fix my mask into something neutral. To be impressed would just give him *more* power.

"What, a *manananggal*?" He scoffs, and for the first time, I'm uncertain of him.

How blind he is.

"I knew a girl once." I take my seat in his leather winged-back chair as casually as I can manage, crossing my legs. He doesn't bother to hide the impression this has made.

'I knew a girl' is the understatement of a lifetime. I *loved* a girl. Still do.

Mr. Sley says nothing as he takes a seat opposite me. If he's compelling me to speak, if this is some kind of power play, I'm not buying in.

Finally, he breaks. "So, what's your pitch? Let me hear the value proposition."

It takes everything to keep from laughing at him. "You're the one who requested *me*."

"Right, I know what *I* want; I'm asking what you want."

"That's not what you asked."

Irritation flickers through him, a tense energy that changes nothing about his outward appearance. Still, the whole room can feel it. "Let me be more clear, then. What do you want?"

He's not willing to pay for what I want; I know this already. "My own TV show. At least five seasons. Book deal. The whole package."

He doesn't even pause to consider. "One season, twelve episodes, on *FreeFear*. You get, say, fifty thousand viewers and we'll talk about a second season."

"Nothing about what I do is horror," I lie, because the horror of it is too much to articulate. I won't entertain my name associated with some trite supernaturalist tricks. "I want on *Reveal*, and I want five seasons. And a book."

"One season. Get forty thousand viewers and we'll sign for three instead of two. And an interview on the *LitBits* podcast."

I shift to the edge of my seat. "It's been nice talking with you."

"What's the driver? You want fame? Money?"

"Exposure."

He smiles, thinking he's heard *Power*. He doesn't listen. If he did, he would hear the walls of this home screaming. "You're a bit of an everyman, wouldn't you say?"

I'm stung by this accusation. "*Every* man, yes. Including you."

"No one is like me."

"Except the other Sley siblings?"

"Especially not."

"Our interests vary," he says, completely unaware of the thirteen statuesque gods who loom like pillars behind him. If he thinks there is a line between his brother's worship of occult, his sister's pagan practices, or his fascination with ancient gods, he is sorely naive. Of course, that *is* why I'm here, to see what he cannot.

"You all share an interest in the macabre, don't you? Not to mention, a house…"

"There, the line stops." His facade slips away a little, separated from himself. For an instant, I can see a little boy, abandoned into the hungry jaws of this library.

"Oh, you and RG have more in common than you'd like, I bet."

He's offended by my use of the familiar, unsure how I

would know his brother by name to begin with.

I do my research.

"Unlike my brother, I consider myself a purveyor of the—"

He's going to say *'arts,'* but what he means is *'artists.'* He's a collector—no, a *warden*, bending them to his will, lusting to hold power over them. A quick glance around his library shows Islamic first editions and forgotten Hebrew texts, but also busts carved by Greek sculptors, masks stolen from Ghana, and silks appropriated from China. His obvious fascination with the Egyptians nears tastelessness. He's a man with no culture, so instead he stitches one together into some Frankensteinian atrocity.

"—and I've learned that, with this sort of thing—" he's talking about my TV show, "—it's important that people relate to you. You're not some nut job, you're an ordinary man like them who happens to have these… gifts. We want to play up your ruggedness. They need to be able to put themselves in your shoes."

"That's exactly what I want."

That's what we want, the gods hiss.

"As for what I want, you're familiar with Maslow's hierarchy?"

I nod.

"I'm in the position that I can, at any moment, have all of my needs met, except one: Self-actualization."

"And you're not interested in having to simply survive."

His smile twists its way free from his thin, gray lips. "But you—"

"I'm an expert in surviving. Yeah."

"It's a risk I'm not willing to take with myself—just at my age, you know—but someone young and scrappy like you…"

I don't have the heart to tell this writhing old man of his

misconceptions. He thinks he's studying gods. They're watching back. Closer now.

(We all are).

Charles Sley is so closed off to anything but himself that he can't even feel them. Can't remember that everything has a spirit, not just rich, lonesome children who spend whole lifetimes latched to the teat of their father's wealth. He cannot reap reward without sacrifice, but men like him never learn this lesson. Not in this life. "I get it," I say instead. "You're Dorian Gray, I'm the picture."

"I wouldn't put it quite like that—"

"But it's true, let's not dance around it. So what you want is a chance to convene with… whom? A loved one? Your father?"

That elicits a visible reaction. "No," he contends, measured. "I want to speak with Ra."

Of the thirteen behind him, all vanish but the sun god. We make eye contact. I stand, removing my list of demands from my coat pocket—including the TV series—and place it on the table next to him. "I'll be back this evening. Drink lots of water and be prepared."

☙❧

I'm already weary from my travels the first time I see her face. Her laugh reaches me first, loud and pronounced over the roar of the bar. I lift my gaze from my drink and find, in the mirror, a petite woman doubled over in the throes of delight. Her joy captivates me, her lack of fear.

When she looks up, I see the dark circles of pain below equally black eyes. She's clearly someone who has known death, felt the all-consuming loss of those she loves, and yet chosen to embody pleasure. It's she who comes to me.

"Tough day," she says first in Tagalog, then translates. She orders two more, then informs the bartender that I'm paying.

Her wit is a triumph. Her hair is black as the ancient oceans. Her skin stretches taut and wondrous like the ranges of the Earth's mountains. The whole thing feels like some cheap echo of Solomon's song, and yet I suddenly find truth in such parables. Me, a man who is no one at all, has caught the eye of the most beautiful creature to ever live.

She belongs to another, the first night we meet, which is a poor man's poetic way of saying she's married. Jealousy has always escaped me, until here, until now. I would excuse myself, but I find rapture in her presence. I can't let her go.

Flirtation, at first: we dance around the spark. When I leave that night, we part as friends. But in my work, in my travels, I find no distraction. I'm transfixed, transformed. Soft as a rose, she has turned me into a beast.

Beatriz.

It's not the next visit, nor the next hundred. In truth, years pass between us: me, transient, resting only in her company; her, lost and lonely, dead among the living. When, at last, our lips finally meet, it is a salvation to us both.

She swears to me that only my kiss can save her. I've never been more at peace than when I hold her in my arms. Never more at peace, at least, until she first lays our son against my chest.

CREAD

I use the front door this time, ignoring the insistence otherwise from the valet. It's a sprawling foyer, anchored by marble floors and crowned with golden cherubs in the moldings. A woman looks down at me from the top of the stairs, though whether she's the famed Sley sister, Genevieve, or the ghost of someone else, I can't tell. It all bleeds together at night.

I make my way into the Great Room without invitation, and

spot Charles smoking on the Italian leather sofa. Surprised, he ushers me to the opposite seat before speaking. What follows is a quick volley from him to me and back again.

"You're early," he serves.

"My demands were clear," I return. "Where is the camera?"

"I'm not comfortable filming this encounter. We'll shoot the series with other clients, not me."

"Then there will be no encounter."

"Then I'll find another medium."

"Perfect." I barely shift weight to my heels before he's changed his mind.

"One camera, only. My team edits the footage."

I hesitate for show, then nod. My quick glance at the unlit fireplace brings a light flush to his cheeks, which he tries to conceal with a sip from his scotch.

(*Have we caught him with his pants down?*)

My eyes trace the silhouettes beyond the ceiling overhead. "Who else is in the house?"

The fireplace is bothering him—he's staring at it as he speaks—and I wonder if he's going to light it himself or commit to the cold on principle. It's not my comfort he's worried about, but the fear of appearing a bad host invokes the ghastly apparition of the innkeeper of Sodom and Gomorrah, even if Charles can't see him. A bad omen, that one. "RG never leaves. Gen may be here somewhere. I've reduced the staff for the night: two in the kitchen plus the one who should have met you outside."

"Seven."

"Well, yes, if you include yourself."

"Why wouldn't I?"

He doesn't try to hide how little he thinks of me because he hasn't even realized it. I'd be mad, except he's told me exactly what I had hoped to hear. I make my way to the overstuffed beast they call a chair—it's inherited the feud between the three men responsible for crafting it and as such, keeps the sitter pushed forward. I'll calibrate around it.

"I do have one question for you, Charles, before we begin."

He nods, enjoying my use of *his* familiar name even less.

"Why me? Why not one of RG's occultists?"

His laugh is a wry insult to the spirits around him. "I don't believe, necessarily, in all his symbols and cosmic brouhaha. I'm not looking for a magician to pull a rabbit from a hat, if you will. I'm looking for someone with a little more credibility in the matter of… contact. You came recommended through my own, independent sources."

Besides commenting on my rugged youth, this is the first true compliment he's paid. Even if it lacks flattery, I accept.

"I'm just here to show—'*Reveal*,' if you will—" I wink, "what has been occluded through generations of blind eyes. Now, offer me a glass and tell me what exactly it is you seek to find."

The compounded insult of his lackluster hosting is enough to stir him from his seat to ring the bell for the waitstaff. A doll of a woman enters and I'm instantly sorry for her; she's marked for sacrifice. When she hands me my glass, our hands touch. Etched across her porcelain face is the fear—the knowing, as I like to call it—that something horrible awaits her. Still, she lights the fire because what else does one do in the face of death? There's comfort in the ritual.

"The camera, if you will," Sley notes, an aside tossed over his shoulder. A solemn nod takes her to the shelf beside the fire, where she slides open the wall to reveal one of his lenses. He stares directly into the camera, attempting to dislodge his discomfort at feeling so exposed. "Do you need anything else?

Objects or anything?"

"No, no, nothing like that required for me. Is this your first time sitting?"

"It is."

"I just need your intention for our discussion with Ra, then we can begin."

He shifts in the heat. "I simply want to try to make contact."

"Nothing is so simple. I'm your bridge, Charles. I can't make a case on your behalf if I don't know all of your intentions."

He eyeballs the camera again.

I inform him, sternly, just how he is wasting my time. He doesn't appreciate the reprimand, but realizes he's in his own way.

"I want to know everything, I want to see into his eye and understand where he comes from, what his true origin was."

(She is my origin).

(We are a cycle).

(There is no beginning).

(No end).

"And?"

"That's all."

I look around the room, rolling my eyes with all of our journey companions. "What do you plan to do with that information?"

"Learn from it."

An impatient rage explodes within me.

(You're doing this to yourself,) they say.

(Your stubbornness).

(Your foolishness).

"My ego," I whisper.

"What was that?"

I try one final time, readying myself to abandon this foolish course. So close to my goals, and yet… I'm consenting to this treatment, to all of Sley's smoke. I'm doing this to myself. One last time, I ask, "What do you plan to do with the information?"

He hesitates again. "I want to be like the Pharaohs, a living god in my own right."

Men and gods. A tale as old as time. "Are you not already? As you said, the resources are available to you—"

"Does this look like the home of a god?"

Gods live at a subatomic level, where nothing exists. "No, I suppose it doesn't."

"I am not here to be judged by you. You want exposure, you want your damned seasons on a stupid Sley network, you want a *book*, then deliver. Let me meet Ra."

Anger. He's primed for the devil's deal. Laughter erupts from the walls.

"Do you want to see him? For yourself?"

"No, I don't have the gift. That's why *you're* here."

I offer a quick *tsk*, an introduction to the condescension he's so kindly bestowed upon me. "It's less of a gift than a resonance," I sniff my scotch, stretching time. "The reason so many of your hauntings pop up during the industrial revolution is resonance. The eyeball vibrates at a certain frequency, the same one that shifts cliffsides and causes that sense of unease. It screams, *danger!* It also happens to be the same hertz that machinery gives off."

"What's this to do with the eye?"

"*Ra's* eye, you might say. When its frequency is matched, the eye vibrates, and suddenly shapes and shadows begin to slip through," my fingertips wave. Sley's skeptical, but he wants it to be true. The little boy glistening inside him wants desperately to believe me. "My eye is shaped differently than yours, that's all. If you want to see, you simply need to hum the right note to vibrate your eyes."

"Ra's eye," he whispers, digesting this offering of his greatest dreams.

(We've got him now).

"As Above, So Below." I sip. The words taste rich, honey-like. Better in another language, but still flavorful in their own right. Southern, this time. As I toast him, everything goes black.

The first part is focusing—I'll hypnotize myself into seeing the greater world. Deep descent into relaxation, accounting for the forward shift of the damned chair. Together, Charles and I hum, shifting our bodies ever so slightly through what used to be called, 'the veil.' Solid matter is an illusion, a hologram of the energy that's constantly oscillating at the lower wavelengths. If you can extend beyond the physical body, your consciousness can transcend the holographic matrix and see anywhere in time and space. Anywhere, anytime. It seems, on the surface, like quite a burden to sort through, except *(we'll tell you a secret)* that all of it is constant. Everywhere. All at once.

The room around me shakes, I'm sure. Ra is present, foreboding, towering over the poor Charles Sley whose eyes have widened with the realization that the sun is blinding. Charles Sley, who has been melted by his scotch and his fireplace and the warmth of his kitchen maid with her healthy breasts that bounce all the way into lyrics of a song somewhere years from now. Charles Sley, blinded before but who now sees all the men harvested from distant islands to trim his walls, whose shamans were fed to the crocodiles and reborn into gods. Charles Sley, whose library shelves cry out in misery at being bound by wicked men who thought ideas were something owned instead of nurtured and set free. Charles Sley, who knew not what lay at his feet, or who he met at his door.

I, on the other hand, have descended far and away from Charles Sley. My consciousness sails past Genevieve, bathing in a blood-soaked clawfoot tub, to my target: RG.

It's a vault he's built, this house, and trapped the whole lot of them inside. I wonder if they even know why? Of course not, or they would never have let me pass the threshold, not even through the servant's door.

"Who let you in?" he demands once he detects my presence, posturing. It's all he can do, in the face of me. I run my frigid, haunting finger up his cracked and broken spine, a parting gift from our last encounter.

"You'd have done well to tell them why you built your walls so thick. Who broke your heart, who broke your body. Why can't your magic fix these legs, RG?"

His eyes dart around the cavern of his room, searching, for I am unseen. "Was it Gen? Did she, too, mistake you for a lover?"

Oh, he is hurt now. He's aged gravely since we last spoke, twisted and gnarled in his wheelchair. *'RG never leaves,'* Charles had said. He assumed his brother *couldn't,* not that he'd made a deliberate choice not to. A protective choice. "You prefer this to death?"

His gaze is steely, a cold fury beneath. "I prefer to punish you."

"An interesting way to do it…"

"She's safe here. If I must endure this way forever, then endure I shall, so long as she is safe."

I burn with the heat of ten thousand Ras. I shake the earth with my rage, such that the entire house shudders. "She is trapped here!"

"She is *saved.* Beatriz need never become the monster you tried to make her."

"She loved me."

"She loved *our son*, and when you took him from her—"

"He is *my* son," I hiss.

"Death has no son."

My breath catches in my chest; the shock pins me back into my body. In an instant, I see the Great Room again through my physical eyes.

Beneath the watchful gaze of his camera's lens, the younger Sley brother is rigid, scarcely breathing. His eyes seep blood, dripping red down the hollows of his cheeks and into his well-manicured mustache. I'd have spared him this, had he considered my reverence at all. But such is the natural consequence of the man who flies too close to the sun.

His voice emerges, faint. "Who are you?"

"Oh, Charles… the sweet, library-bound boy," I stroke his frozen cheek with a mother's gentle touch. "As one might say, *I am become Death.*"

I raise my body from the sofa to seek RG. Weaving through the corridors of Sley House on foot, I pass generations of enslaved souls, hung frozen in time along the walls. A gathering of spirits loose themselves from their prisons to make mayhem behind me, each a brick in the wall that RG had built to keep me out. Now that I am here, I am all-devouring, and I am the origin of those things that are yet to be.

When I find him, the bastard's rolled across the Calacatta marble of his chamber to enshrine himself within the boundaries of some cliche sigil.

"An expensive design choice," I mutter as the steel door seals behind me.

"I could say the same for you." His eyes have widened to

see me in the flesh. A terror to know that I can place my hands upon his skin.

"Your brother called it, *'rugged and young.'*"

"So it was Charles who let you in?"

"His hubris, yes."

He hides his heartbreak, though not well. Did Charles know of his brother's love? I doubt it; RG only knows the cold, emptiness of his own pursuits.

"No worse than lust," he growls.

"*Love,*" I spit back.

"It isn't love to take a mother's child."

"He is *my* son."

He's gritting his dentures too hard, they may crack. Would that I could reach through his boundaries and crack the entire skull. "He was *mine,*" he argues. "She was my *wife*. And you corrupted her."

"You abandoned her, RG I was consistent in my care, in my *love* for her!"

"Is it love that would twist the mind of a terminally-ill woman? That would convince her to kill her baby—" his voice strangles here; I almost feel something for him, "—kill *my* baby, so that they might be united in *death*."

"I AM DEATH," I roar. "There is no hierarchy for me! I am the beginning, the end, and all of time. I am the gateway from this illusion of mass and misery and into the truth. Beatriz knew this! She visited me again and again—she wanted to join me there!"

RG smirks. "Is that why she became the *manananggal?* Why, when she woke from her fever dream to find his limp, tiny body, she snapped? Why she took the knife to her belly, that she might become the creature who could siphon the souls of unborn children to save our boy?"

From her portrait, Beatriz kneels, staring up at me, begging me to save her.

"The child is safe with me. He's always been safe with me. But he needs his mother."

"She's safe here with me."

"She is your prisoner, RG Sley. She has always been entombed by you, by your absence, your wealth, your beliefs," I want to suck the marrow from his bones, obliterate him into nothing and reuse him for nothing. I want to wipe him from time and space, to be the god of tribulation unleashed… but then, I see him. I see his metal chair, its wheels contained within this tapestry etched to keep me out, and I realize… "You've cornered yourself," I whisper, cupping my hands to my mouth. "You may escape me for a time but you can only live—perpetually—without food, without water, without companionship. These barriers you made, they have meaning for now, until I decide to free the power of all the spirits you keep pinned to these grounds. Then, even this circle can't save you. You are *my* prisoner, RG Sley."

I do not wait to see the terror of his realization; there will be time for that. Time exists, always, and I can visit and revisit this moment again and again and again until I've had my fill of it, until I'm ready to destroy his entire world.

But now, I have someone I need to see.

☙❧

It takes her a moment to acclimate to the soft, white skin of the kitchen maid. Weakened before, the tuberculosis had ravaged her lungs, bringing her to my door. She inhales a full, deep breath and then another. Her hands meet her stomach, over the womb where she carried our boy, over the place where she'd opened herself in order to bring him back to the land of the living.

"He need not live here," I say. "But he can. We all can, for a time, if that's what you want."

Beatriz nods. "Tough day," she laughs.

I kiss her forehead, careful to avoid the kiss of death.

◈

"Mr. Sley, what's it like knowing you've single-handedly shifted the cultural lens toward broad acceptance of the occult?"

Charles smiles, his mustache twirling. "I can't take all the credit. I stumbled into this, actually. After my first exposure to the Egyptian god, Ra, through my dear friend, here," he pats my shoulder, "my entire worldview was changed. What you see in that first episode, that's what truly opened my eyes. Convinced me that this was the *real* deal."

I smile at him, seeing not the graying husk of Charles Sley but the beaming face of my son, who lives within. Together, we turn and face the camera.

Click.

Another article to hang in the halls of Sley House.

Reliquary of Madness

Jeremy Billingsley

Editor-in-chief of Sley House, he's worked so closely with the Sley Siblings, he might as well be one of them. Billingsley's short fiction has appeared in numerous anthologies, and his novels are exclusively published by Sley House Publishing. A Mind Full of Scorpions *is out now, and his next novel,* Under the Churchyard in the Chamber of Bone, *comes out this year. He lives in Northwest Arkansas with his family.*

ᘓᘔ

Coming this Halloween. Sley House Publishing in conjunction with Beast Apart Studios. THE RELIQUARY OF MADNESS! *Lost arcane objects said to not just be cursed, but* EVIL. *The ritual murder of an innocent. Unleashing Hell itself. You will lose your mind. You will lose your soul. From award-winning auteur Trevon Gladney comes the must-see film of the year. Experience the nightmare! Experience the hor-ror! Experience the insanity!* THE RELIQUARY OF MADNESS!

COMING SOON!

❈

The diner's drab yellow walls had browned with the layers of grease that had accumulated over the years. The same zombies seemed to populate the establishment no matter the hour of the day. That I could recognize them only spoke to how frequently I'd sat at this booth. Like the waitress, for instance. She must be pulling a double-, or even a triple-shift, because the makeup on her face seemed more powdery than it had this morning, her lipstick smeared, the eyeliner runny. Or Joe there at the counter. Was that the same cup of coffee he'd been sipping on eight hours ago? Joe with his disheveled coat and pants, his once-white dress shirt untucked, his tie loosened and his stare vacant and haunted. The stubble on his cheek a bit longer and grayer than it had been yesterday.

I come to this diner because I know what to expect here, and because my apartment and office are located three floors above. I know the waitress because she is here, like me, all the time. I know her name, unlike the fella at the counter whom I named Joe, but her name, and really his, doesn't matter.

The girl across from me this late night was young, her hair two-toned and short, her green eyes shifty and nervous. She was pale like she wore too much cake, and she bit her nails, chipped with paint. If something focused her attention out the window, I wasn't sure what it could be, as it was too dark and rainy to see anything.

"I want to hire you," she said again. This was the third time she'd said it, like she was working up the courage to say more.

I usually meet new clients in my office/apartment, but when

the client is a woman, I've found they tend to prefer someplace public until they can get to know me better.

I sipped my coffee and raised my eyes to the waitress. She caught my gaze at the cash register behind the counter, turned and grabbed the pot, and brought it over.

"Brew it yourself, Dolores?" I asked.

"Best in the city," she said.

"Doubt that."

She cracked a smile, our traditional exchange over with.

"I want–" the girl started again.

"What's the job?" I asked, cutting her off. We'd be here a long damn time if I waited for her to complete a thought.

She raised her eyes to me. They were sunk deep into dark circles of sleeplessness and wide and red. "My brother's gone missing," she said.

I nodded. Progress, finally. "Tell me about him."

This is more for me to assess the client and not the mark. It gives me a chance to see how honest they'll be with me.

"He plays guitar. House band down at the Lucky Tom. He's …" She trailed off, the words she might have spoken gone the way of her gaze, out the window to the black, rain-soaked streets. "He's a junkie. He's a good guitarist. Might be better if he laid off the smack."

"When's the last time you saw him?" I asked.

The girl, Susan she'd introduced herself as, offered me her gaze again. "Three days ago. Usually don't go more than two without hearing from him. I gave him another day just to be sure, but I knew something was wrong. I just knew it!"

I sipped my coffee. My stomach rumbled from underneath the booth, so I raised a finger. Dolores slapped the metal pass-through at the serving window. "Number three," she called. Grease popping, and maybe under it all the smell of sweat or

B.O., and the fat bald man in the white apron whose face and broad shoulders were all I'd ever seen since frequenting this place spat out something she understood but I'd yet to decipher.

"Your brother owe anyone money?"

She laughed derisively and rolled her eyes. "He owes everyone something, Mr. Phillips. Owes me damn near three grand." There was a meanness in her eyes that vanished after a moment, replaced with worry and fear. "But I don't think it was anyone he owed."

"Just call me Straker," I said. "I believe you. Sometimes intuition is all we got to go on, and if your gut says he's missing, then he probably is. I read people, Susan. Read them well. I think you're being mostly upfront with me. I'll still check out his haunts. Talk to the people he knew, maybe even his drug dealer. Maybe they know what happened. Probably they don't, but in such cases, it could turn up something. At the least, doing so has never hurt."

Hearing this, whatever weight she carried seemed to lighten a little. She forced a smile of relief.

"But I have to ask," I continued. "You got any other reason to believe this wasn't a case of him owing the wrong person?"

She fished a crumpled piece of paper out of her coat pocket and slid it across the table. I unfolded it to read a telephone number and an email address.

"This number has called me nearly nightly. A voice I don't recognize asks me where the vinyl is, and then where my brother is. When I try to call it back, a recording says the number is no longer in service, but it always calls back."

"And the email?"

"Same. They email two sentences. Where's the vinyl? Where's my brother? I try to email them back and I get a failure to deliver notice. The emails come nearly every morning."

"Vinyl?" I asked, frowning at this. "Like siding?"

"Or a record," she said. That did make more sense, given his profession.

"You got a key to his place?"

She shook her head. "No, but he and some of his band-mates share a loft about a block away from the Lucky Tom."

Dolores sat a plate down in front of me. I asked Susan if she wanted anything, and she shook her head. The cheeseburger's bun wore a sheen of grease, and the fries were soggy yet burned. How that broad-shouldered short-order managed to accomplish this on the regular never failed to astound me.

When Dolores left, Susan snatched a few fries off my plate and resumed her gaze out the window. "It's weird, Mr. Phi… Straker. Three days of phone calls and emails and the oddest dreams when I sleep. And I can't shake the feeling I'm being watched or followed. The past three days, I swear I've seen the same man in a bright red suit following me. I even thought he followed me tonight."

I swallowed and wiped grease from my lips with a cheap paper napkin that disintegrated almost on contact. I asked for a description and all she said was he was big, with bright blondish-red hair and a jaw like a boxer.

"He has black eyes," she said, and shivered. "Always has a scowl on his face."

The weight of the .357 in my shoulder holster reminded me the dude wouldn't be a problem if he wanted to follow me.

"There is the matter of my fee."

She pulled up a purse as drab and worn as the clothes she wore, and just like her clothes, the brand was something off-rack and inexpensive to begin with. She fished out of a billfold five crisp one-hundred-dollar bills. These she didn't chance messing up on the tabletop but held out to me.

"This is all I have, and I only have this much because my landlord agreed to give me an extension on this month's rent. Please, Mr. Phillips. I don't have a lot, but I do need help finding my brother."

I plucked three of the five bills from her hand and waved the rest away. I usually charged four times what she was offering for a job like this. "Go pay your rent," I said.

She didn't balk and she didn't protest, but crammed the remaining bills back in her purse before I had a chance to change my mind. I waved Dolores over and had her pack up the remainder of my dinner, ordered another burger and fries for Susan to take with her, and paid for it all with a ten from my billfold. When the bags were brought to us, I saw Susan to the door, and stood with her on the stoop as the rain came down in sheets all around us. The city streets shined black. Streetlights did little to illuminate the rows of buildings in either direction. A car here and there cruised past, but nothing out of place for this part of town and this time of night. I certainly didn't see any man in a red suit.

"You want me to walk you home?" I asked.

She considered it for a minute then stepped out into the rain, shaking her head. She looked back once, and I nodded to her. Then I watched her cross the street, step down the block, and turn the corner.

⚜

The Lucky Tom sits on the other side of town in a neighborhood just a little worse than my own. Frequented mostly by made men, their girlfriends or wives, and low-level thugs, it's a multi-story building with the main club being downstairs and the upstairs reserved for a few offices and rooms decked out with beds for the tame johns and kinkier fare for those who like it dirty. The stage features dancers and musicians, the house band playing a mix of jazz and rock, some swing. Occasionally my job had taken me there, and other times it was loneliness or boredom.

The following night, I made my way to the Lucky Tom and paid the door fee, ordered a scotch and soda and watched the band. They were dressed in white tuxedos. They were a five piece and had a guitarist, but I noticed that his suit didn't fit as well as the others and if there was an issue with time or being in step, it was this man who'd flubbed up the cadence. During their next break, I approached the trumpet player who seemed like the band leader.

"Your sub isn't keeping time," I said.

"Fucking can't keep a B-string to save his life. Broke three first set."

"Where's your regular player?"

The bartender brought him a Dark n' Stormy and he downed it one gulp. Bleary eyes and a sneer checked me out.

"And just who the fuck are you?"

I fished a business card out of my shirt pocket and gave him just enough time to read over it. "Straker Phillips, PI," I said, when he'd stared at it blankly for a minute. "Susan hired me to find—"

He thrust the card back at me. "Man, we don't know where he went."

I put a meaty paw on the stringy shoulder and made the trumpet player face me. "She's real worried about him," I said. "I'm not leaving here empty-handed."

"You got real brass ones laying your hand on me in this place."

"You think Mattione or his goons give one good fuck about a two-bit brass-player like you? I stepped over three better trumpet players on my way here tonight, wasting away in the gutters."

He jerked away from me with a look like a dog who'd been kicked too many times. "Man, all I know is he wouldn't shut up for the past week about a job he'd been hired for. Said it was gonna change his life."

"Did he say what that job was?"

"No," he said. "Just that his ship had come in. He'd clear his debts and be able to take care of his little sister. Then he up and vanished three days ago without any kind of word or warning and left us in the lurch. Good fucking riddance."

"That little girl is really upset," I said, grabbing his shoulder again and pulling him close. The ice cubes from his drink scattered across the bar top, and the bartender, who'd been wiping down a glass tumbler, shot a look over my shoulder.

"I don't know, man!" the trumpeter squealed. "Fuck! He left us without shelling out his part of the rent."

"Maybe you'll let me see his room?"

He fished an apartment key out of his pants pocket and thrust it at me.

"What's the trouble?" came the voice from behind.

"Don't steal nothing," the trumpeter said, turning his back to me.

"I'll bring it right back," I said, turning, coming face to chest with one of the bouncers. He was big and bald, his head freshly shaved. His tux, black, fit better than any worn by the band, and despite the low light of the club, shades covered his eyes so that I couldn't tell where he looked. I'm not a small man, or a weak man, myself, but I knew when I'd met my match.

"No trouble here," I said. Stepping around the wall of a man, I made my way out the club and down the street to the loft.

The door opened to darkness and the smell of weed and the burnt chemical odor of meth. Fumbling the wall to my right, I found the switch and flicked on the overhead, getting the joke immediately. There was nothing here to steal. The place was a shambles with the quality of the apartment aspiring to the state of being condemned; what furnishings filled the place were nothing to covet. The cushions of the couch were such that I saw from the doorway two different springs jutting out. A layer of filth and rot covered everything like fine dust. There was a record player but no TV, scattered piles of detritus occupying various corners not otherwise taken by a stained mattress, two sleeping bags, and a recliner stuck in the recline position. The fridge in the kitchen kicked out warm air and smelled of stale milk and the bright sulfur of raw eggs long since expired. A cut of cheddar was spotted green with mold. I closed it, poked my head into the bathroom and two bedrooms, then returned to the record player. More to the point, I knelt and began examining the records stored beneath it. Nothing stood out.

From behind me, the door opened. I turned to see another member of the band, a Black man who'd been tickling the ivories during the set. He didn't appear as strung out as the trumpeter.

"You the PI?" he asked, his hand on the door as he stood partially in the building, as if he planned to bolt depending on the answer I had to give. I stood and nodded.

I crossed easily, held the trumpeter's key out, and dropped it into the pianist's hand. "You'll return it to him okay?"

"Yeah. Listen, you need to know about Fred."

Susan's brother.

"He always been a little weird, man, but since getting this job…"

When he didn't continue, I asked, "Weird how?"

"Like, he really wanted to study music. Man, he did us a solid joining our band, but I'm pretty sure it was out of desperation. You know he studied. Like official?"

"He's a pro."

The pianist nodded. "Like, he knows about theory and shit. Wrote half our songs. But he always … especially he gets a little smack in the veins, or you get him high enough on reefer, and he'll talk about the Devil's Tritone or go on about Robert Johnson or some shit."

"The blues player?"

"I first met the cat, and I thought, sure, he play guitar, so maybe he just idolized RJ, but naw, he obsessed with that whole story."

"Did he tell you what he'd been hired for? Or by who?"

The pianist shook his head. "Not directly, but the way he carried on, I assumed it had to do with some of the weird shit he liked to talk about. Like the monks who throat sang and supposedly channeled Satan, or Hell's chord, a supposed eighth chord believed impossible to achieve in music."

I nodded and thanked him, then walked back out into the city. Alone with my thoughts, I considered this new information. Not normally a drinker, I took the time to clear my head before returning home. I walked in sometime after midnight, flicking on the lights and the television as a matter of habit, thankful for the noise. I'd turned on a late news broadcast by what I thought was coincidence, but as it turned out, it was by design.

"To return to our breaking story," the anchor continued, "the body was fished out of the channel just after 10pm. To recap, body of musician Fred…"

I turned. They had a picture to go with the story. In the pic, he wore the same white suit his bandmates had been wearing earlier that night. It seems the guitarist had been found, after all.

⊗

The day had started off foggy and cool, the cemetery quiet as though even the dead wanted to sleep in. The fog had settled to the ground by the time the services began. I kept my distance, standing near a gnarled old oak while the preacher droned on. In the distance I noticed a black car. Luxury. Shiny as though just polished. An older man and woman stood by the hood. They and I weren't the only intruders. A large man in a red suit stood down the hill, partially concealed by the mausoleum.

Thankfully Susan nor the bandmates saw the others, but once I saw her lift her eyes to me, and I nodded. After the service, the black car pulled away and I lost sight of the large man. The guests filed out a little at a time until Susan alone was left standing over her brother's coffin. The workers had begun the job of lowering it by the time I reached her. Instead of a consolatory hand, I offered her the bills she'd allowed me to take initially. She took them without looking up and stuffed them into the clutch she carried. Her funerary finest, the clutch a matching accessory, looked worn and drab and ill fitting, and the purse was just as ratty. I could have used the money, but it was obvious she needed it more.

"Thank you for all your help." When these words came, they were flat and unaccompanied by her eyes, which seemed glued to her brother's coffin. I put a hand on her shoulder.

"I'm not satisfied," I said. "I want to find out who did this."

She sniffed, produced a handkerchief, wiped her eyes and then her nose. "The police arrested his dealer."

I shook my head, not that she could see it. Something wasn't right, and this wasn't over. My gut told me that. "That doesn't sit with me," I said. "Are you okay if I keep nosing around?"

She offered me a little nod.

I waited a few minutes. The men had picked up their shovels and the pile of dirt looked terrible in its finality. She shouldn't have to watch this, but I also knew that if I tried to lead her away, she'd refuse. I'd seen enough bereaved clients to know when someone has to look. Has to see it to the end.

For me, this case gnawed at me. Never mind the recurring nightmare I'd been having. The unanswered questions plagued me. What had he been hired to find, and by whom? I couldn't shake the feeling that something much more sinister was at play here. Perhaps it was the atmosphere. Around us the wind had picked up and clouds had rolled in, much as in my nightmare. The oaks stripped of their leaves waved their gnarled limbs much as the ones in my nightmare had. Only there, I stood at an empty intersection in the middle of some rural flat land, the paths dirt and gravel, the clouds dark, lightning flashing around. In my nightmare, I held a guitar. I remembered then what the pianist had told me and asked her about her brother's fascination with the darker side of music.

The laugh she issued was in the manner of one who only had their memories left, and those memories that remained only brought smiles.

"I remember when he picked up the guitar. How fascinated he was by it. He bought books and visited clubs. Tried to find anyone and anything who could teach him to play it. Then, one day, we were in our teens, he asked me for some money. Said he heard about a place just outside the city. He wasn't much of a guitar player, then, but said he needed to go meet someone there. Ridgefield, I think it was."

I knew Ridgefield. Not much out there, even to this day.

Flatlands and trees. And crossroads.

"Anyway, he came back a couple of days later, and he could play the hell out of that thing. I never saw anything like it. It was like he was a different person. So, he played, and he got real good, but he was also haunted. Got into drinking. Then the reefer. Then harder stuff. Like he was trying to forget something. But he was also going to the library. Boy had never stepped foot in a library before that. But he went and he'd come home and talk about the craziest things."

"Devil's Tritone and Robert Johnson?"

She nodded.

The rain began. It came down hard without any warning. No fat drops to portend a coming storm. It's like the clouds just opened up and within seconds, we were soaked. Still, it was the lightning flashing that drew us to the mausoleum for cover. A protective arm around her, I guided Susan to cover and felt a swell of pity for the men whose job was to shovel in the dirt which was quickly turning into a muddy soup.

"You alright?" I asked.

She nodded. We stood there, safe under the canopy, watching even the workers withdraw to their old pickup when the flashing increased, and the thunder rolled over the hills. The storm was so much like what I experienced in my nightmare; I couldn't shake it. This new news, that her brother's journey to guitar mastery mirrored the famous blues man's story, took hold of me and wouldn't let go. This had something to do with not just why he was hired, but also his murder.

Movement in the polished black plates of the mausoleum markers caught my eye, and I saw him, the brother, when I looked over. I don't make a habit of seeing dead people, so seeing him, and seeing him offer me a little nod unsettled me, sure, but it also suggested I was on to something.

CR∞SO

After I got her home, I caught a train downtown. Just off fifth stood the eight-story building housing the city's paper, a century old rag printing news usually only fit to line a bird cage on paper that might suffice if you're out of the roll in the bathroom, but that didn't mean it was totally useless. More to the point, that didn't mean that everyone who worked there was totally useless.

Beck O'Donnel wrote the gossip column, *Ask Beck*, and usually offered dating advice or dished on which celebrities were dating whom, and I always thought this was a waste of her true talent. This day, she was sitting behind her desk, legs stretched out over her desktop as she reclined in her chair, engrossed in a paperback.

"Slow news day?" I asked, letting myself in, the smell of coffee and her perfume greeting me.

"Straker Phillips, as I live and breathe," she said, her tone unsurprised as though she expected me. She didn't even lower the book. "What can I do you for?"

" 'Bout a buck fifty, Beck," I said and plopped down in the chair across from her. She sat up, returning her gams under the desk, dog-eared the paperback and set it aside. She was pretty, angular features, wore thick plastic black frames that only added to her allure. With or without a smile, today it was without and her steely gaze told me I was intruding, her prettiness wasn't affected. Despite our banter, I'd never worked up the gumption to ask her out officially though she was the one woman who I knew could make an honest man out of me.

"I'm looking into that musician's murder," I said. I'd taken off my fedora and twirled it in my hand.

"I thought his drug dealer did it."

I shook my head. "I think he was into something. Sister told me he'd been hired for a job, and given what he was into, I think it was something related to an old blues musician, Robert Johnson."

She sat back, contemplative, fingers steepled together under her nose. "Hmm," she said, her gray eyes fixed on me, and that was it for a time. I knew better than to interrupt her.

"What was he into?"

"The darker history of music."

She nodded, stood, and crossed to her coffee pot, two-thirds filled. She poured two cups and handed me one. It was a ceramic cup and large with the words "Tell me when it's print-ed," scrawled across like some inside joke I didn't get.

She sat on the edge of her desk, directly in front of me, and crossed her legs.

"Might there have been a mention of an old vinyl record?"

"Yeah," I said, and sipped the swill just slightly less bitter than the joe I got at the diner on the regular.

"You know about the story of him going to the crossroads, right?" she asked.

I nodded.

"Story goes, right before he was killed by either the woman he was shacking up with or her jealous husband, he recorded a piece on his guitar. Vinyl recording was still pretty young in those days, but those close to him said the music set down was not just haunting, it was evil. It contained notes, tones, and chords most can't play on the guitar, and a few old-timers pres-ent even said it conjured something. Or started to. Story goes, every time it's played, the devil that gave Johnson his ability gets closer to coming back to our world. Play it enough, and the demon might just return to this world permanently."

I nodded. "That's quite the story."

She shrugged, stood, and returned to the chair behind the

desk. "If you believe that sort of thing. I personally believe that there might have been such a recording, but its power isn't supernatural, but capitalist."

I frowned at this. Took another sip.

"Johnson was a legend, but there isn't a lot of surviving recordings out there of him. Someone has an original vinyl featuring him playing, could fetch a pretty penny."

"So, someone hired this old boy to find and bring them this vinyl, thinking it would be valuable," I said. "And something went wrong …" I trailed off, content with the inference.

Beck wasn't. "And they killed him."

"Question is, who could have hired him, or would have hired him, to find this lost vinyl record?"

We sat silent for another minute, until Beck drained her cup and turned to the set of drawers directly behind her, next to the window that showed only the rain and several windows of the neighboring high rise. She rifled through the papers quickly, her back to me, turning with a flourish to set a file on her desk and slide it over.

"I've been putting it together for the society pages, but it reads more like an expose," she said. I took it and opened it. Three siblings, their pictures paperclipped to the front page, were the subject of this file.

"Sley Siblings," I read. "Genevieve, Charles. RG."

"They're rich, reclusive, influential, and they'd not only be interested in such a record, they'd also have the means to retrieve it."

"Who are they?" I asked. I felt ashamed. I'd been working as a PI in this city for five years, a cop ten years before that, and had lived my whole life here. I thought I knew every major player in this town, but I'd never heard of these three. Never got even a whiff of them in all my dealings with cops, reporters, low-life scum, dregs, or druggies.

"Wealthy socialites," she said. As she proceeded to tell me about them, all she'd learned, legitimate stories and the rumors, I found myself hypnotized by their gazes. It was obvious that RG was the eldest, and something had happened to him, because the portrait showed him in a wheelchair. The other two weren't spring chickens, but they weren't quite as old as their brother. All three wore the same gaze that said they weren't to be trifled with, and I felt only the slightest bit unnerved, as if even from the photographs they were staring right through me.

One word Beck muttered drew me out of my mesmerism. "Occult."

I looked across to her, eyebrows raised. She nodded, and a slight grin had crept to her lips.

"Rumor is," she continued, "they are into some dark stuff. Take this with a grain of salt, but rumor is they amassed their fortune by being involved in some very dark dealings."

It was all coming together. Beck, though, was not content to leave it to inference.

"If anyone had hired the musician to find something as dark as you're thinking, my money is on the Sley Siblings."

I downed my cup of joe and handed the cup to her as I stood, returning the fedora to my head. "Got an address for these siblings?" I asked. She nodded to the file, and I picked it up.

"Take it but bring it back to me. All you need is in there."

I thanked her and turned to leave, but she called my name.

"Yeah?" I asked.

In that quick moment I had my back to her, she'd fished keys from somewhere, and pitched them across the room right at my face like a major league fastball. I caught them with a jingle.

"You ain't going to reach their house by a train or cab, Straker. You'll have to drive. I expect you'll return my car in the same condition you find it."

I smiled. "Yes ma'am."

"You owe me, Phillips," she said, grinning also.

"Yes ma'am."

"Dinner, perhaps?" and cocked an eyebrow.

I blushed a bit, then nodded. "Yes ma'am."

I turned once more to leave.

"Straker," she called after me. When I turned around, I saw real concern on her face. More than that, I saw fear. "Be careful," she said.

⚬⚬⚬

I drove south, passing through a couple of rough neighborhoods to get to the expressway, which I stayed on for nearly a half hour before taking the exit into an affluent suburb. From there I headed east to access the gated community where even larger homes stood, some with yards as big as city parks. To the back of this collection of homes a single road led out into the country, the trees pressing in from all sides, the road narrowing and the shoulder thinning to nothing. The drive had become claustrophobic, and I'm not usually one to suffer from such things.

I crossed several hills and streams, then found the expanse of their estate as Beck's car crested another tree-covered hilltop. The house was a multistory Gothic horror, dilapidated and needing repair, but standing strong and tall and dark over the landscape. I shuddered as a cool wind enveloped me.

I'd parked in the circle drive just in front of the portico so I could take in the whole of the edifice. The windows were long and dark. In all my years, I wondered, how could I have not heard of such a place. It was like it appeared out of a nightmare. Maybe the same nightmare that had shown me the crossroads.

The wide arching steps led up to a porch and I knocked at the door. It opened almost immediately, answered by a short, diminutive man with an upturned nose and thinning hair, his belly protruding from the butler's uniform as another barrier to entry. His eyes appeared closed, but his head moved as if he were examining me fedora to loafer.

"Right this way, Mr. Phillips," he said then.

I started. Had they been expecting me? Had Beck called and told them I was coming?

"How'd you know my name?" I asked, but he made no attempt to comment further, just turned and led me into the house. I followed, pausing to take in the immense foyer and the deep, dark shadows. Overhead came the only sound I could discern. The creak and spin of an old wheel. This made me think of RG Sley's picture, seated in the wheelchair, and I shivered uncontrollably. Somehow the idea of that man in this house was more unsettling than the house being empty.

The servant ushered me into a side room, a parlor with a couch and fireplace, a few ornamental pieces. The fire was warm and crackled and the room felt cozy, despite the high, nearly twelve-foot ceiling.

"Someone will be with you shortly, Mr. Phillips," the servant said, and shut the door.

I heard the lock engage. Crossing the room, I tried the door, only to confirm my suspicions. He'd locked me in.

I banged on the door. "Hey!" I shouted. "Hey! Let me—"

Behind me, a sound like sliding, and I turned to see a maid enter through a hidden pocket door, carrying a tray.

"Scotch and soda, Mr. Phillips," she said. "While you wait."

I thanked her, nonplussed, and took the drink, though I had no intention of drinking it.

She returned to the pocket door and touched a spot on the wall; the door slid open. "Ms. Sley will be with you shortly," she called before the wall consumed her.

Holding the drink hip high, I looked around the room. The two latticed windows were tall and looked out over a courtyard. The décor of the parlor was tasteful. Wood-carved trim offered a sense of elegance, and the room was clean and in order. On one wall, tapestries were hung. I'm no expert, but these appeared old and very valuable. On another had been hung a shield with a crest: a cross with a cracked simplex encircled with five points jutting out behind it. I stared at that for how long I don't know, until the parlor door unlocked and opened.

Genevieve Sley looked just like her picture. She seemed to glide as she walked, her face stern but beautiful. Though her hair was silver, her face remained uncreased even as she wore a frown of disapproval. She regarded me for a moment, a glass of red wine in her hand, arms folded. She sipped slowly, staring, then took another step in.

"To what do we owe the pleasure, Mr. Phillips," she said. She offered no hand to shake, and there seemed to be no pleasure to be had, given her countenance.

"Did Beck call and say I was coming?" I asked.

She frowned at this. "I know no such name." Another sip of wine, and she looked at my untouched drink. "You haven't touched your drink. It isn't poisoned, I assure you."

I saw this challenge for what it was, raised the glass to my lips, and sipped.

"So how did you know I was—"

She raised a well-manicured hand to shush me. "We make it

our business to know everyone in our employ."

"I'm not in your employ," I said.

Now she cracked a smile. "Not yet."

Whirling, she stepped away from me to one of the windows. "You're fortunate, Mr. Phillips. RG himself wanted to meet you. Charles and I thought this might be better."

"Does that mean you want to hire me?" I sidled up next to her, took another sip, and followed her gaze out the window. Across the courtyard was visible another wing of the house and in between, a dead elm caught in throes of agony, it appeared, a concrete bench over a sea of dead yellow grass. Of course, it was too late in the year for the elm or grass to be seen otherwise, but I wondered if even in spring and summer, this flora stayed dead.

"We do. We know you've been working for the young lady to find out what happened to her brother. Permit me the chance to explain some things."

I waited, sipping again at my drink. Genevieve Sley was in no hurry, however, and took several minutes to collect her thoughts.

"We hired the musician, as well as a writer and a painter to procure for us several rare items not yet in our collection. The exact natures of those items are not important…"

"One was a vinyl recording of Robert Johnson supposedly playing music given to him by the devil," I said.

Again, the flicker of a smile. "Not *the* devil, I'm afraid. *A* devil, though, yes."

I took another sip and felt the ice fall against my lips, what liquid crossing my tongue cold but weak compared to the rest of the drink. The maid appeared over my other shoulder, causing me to jump a little as I'd heard no one enter, and took my empty tumbler, replacing it with a full one.

"Plants don't die the same way we do," Genevieve said, still staring out the window. "In fact, it takes quite a lot to kill them. And even after, some do not lose their potency. The elm and the grass might appear dead, Mr. Phillips, but they are still quite powerful. Still quite … aware."

I took a drink, wondering if she had been reading my mind, and I could have sworn I saw another flicker of a smile cross her lips.

"Flora can," she continued, "provide innumerable resources for us, to be sure. But they can be quite the predators. Strange to think of something rooted in place and apparently stationary its whole existence as a predator, but the tricks they can play on fauna, the way flora can manipulate *sentient* beings speaks to the uniqueness of nature."

"What does this have—"

"Do not interrupt, Mr. Phillips. Not when someone is trying to educate you. Now, the exact nature of the other two items is not important, suffice it to say that one is a rare and out of print tome and one is a set of antique paint brushes."

"Should I assume that the story behind these two items is just as unique as the record?"

"If you must."

She reached into her pant's pocket and pulled out a slip of paper. "Here are the names and addresses for the painter and the writer. Although, I'm fairly certain you will not find the painter at his address, as that is why we wish to hire you."

"I don't understand."

"The painter has absconded with your previous client and our three items. We are convinced he wishes to sell them on the black market in an attempt to fetch a higher fee than what we were to pay. Greed, I'm afraid, drives many men. Our pay was generous, as you see when you hear my offer, but understanding the rarity of these procurements, I'm sure the painter felt he could earn a great deal more."

"You think he killed Susan's brother and stole the book, record, and brushes."

"I think he's working in concert with the young woman, and I'm afraid you've been duped, Mr. Phillips. Nevertheless, we will pay you a thousand dollars a day plus expenses to return to us our possessions and discover their location so that the police might make the appropriate arrest."

From the breast pocket of her shirt, she produced another folded piece of paper. This one unfurled to reveal a check. The memo read retainer and she'd already covered a week's worth of the pay. I pocketed the check and finished my drink. When I turned to offer the empty tumbler to the maid, however, I found I was alone with the Sley sibling once more. I'd again not heard the pocket door nor sensed that she'd left.

Genevieve held out her hand. "I'll take your glass, Mr. Phillips." She did so, holding it as if my very touch had infested it with a virus. "I do not need to remind you of discretion. Or perhaps I do. A man living in the tenement you occupy might not be familiar with such an idea, but we Sleys thrive on it."

"I can be discreet," I said through gritted teeth, thinking about the check in my breast pocket.

⊂⊃

Later, after I'd returned Beck's car and she'd dropped me off at my apartment, I sat staring at the check. I felt slimy working for the Sleys, but those zeroes held my attention and reminded me that with a long enough shower, most slime could be washed off.

The other piece of paper I looked at also, reading the names of the writer and the painter. I stood, unhooking my shoulder holster and setting my .357 on the tabletop, unbuttoning my shirt. That's when I saw him. He was skinny with long, scraggly hair down to his shoulders and an angry, defiant expression on his beard-splotched face. And he was see-through, the door to my bedroom very clearly visible through his chest. That was when I realized I probably wouldn't find the painter at all. Alive, at least.

⊂⊃⧲⊂⊃

"A magical ring?" I asked, disbelieving.

It was too early in the morning for me to be occupying a barstool at the Lucky Tom, but it was the only place the writer would meet me. Their coffee was on par with the diner's, but it was too early for anything stiffer. For me, at least. The writer was working on his third pint and seemed in no desire to slow down just yet.

He nodded. "Given to him by the Archangel Michael. All the noncanonical text says is that he used that ring to control the demons and make them build the temple in Jerusalem."

"But you think some spell was used as well."

He nodded and downed the pint, then let the glass fall heavy on the bar top and waved a hand at the bartender who'd been sitting back, watching us. Though they were technically open, we were the only patrons.

"Yeah, or controlling words, or something."

"And those words were written in this codex?"

"Yeah, but not just that. You ever hear of the Voynich Manuscript?"

When I said I hadn't, he explained that it was another ancient text, a grimoire, if you will, that no one had ever been able to decipher. This book he'd been hired to find contained the code to decipher it.

"If it's real," I said, "then that would be a powerful book."

"Goddamn Sleys. Did you see their reliquary?"

"Genevieve didn't give me a tour."

He shook his head and downed half the fresh pint, smacking his lips. "Trust me when I say these aren't even the strangest items in their possession."

"What do they want them for?"

He shrugged, but his stare was vacant. Haunted. The stare told me his shrug was a lie. He swallowed hard as if he were about to say something then chewed it back down. "They hired me," he said, paused in reflection, then took another sip of beer. "They hired me not just to find the book, but to help them. Said they're branching out. Media. Publishing. Arts. I found the painter and the musician. If I hadn't, maybe that guitarist would still be alive."

I wanted to tell him he shouldn't do that to himself, but in a way, he was correct, and it wasn't really my place to absolve anyone of their guilt, real or imagined. I finished my coffee.

"Call you a cab?" I asked him.

Still staring at his own reflection in the mirror behind the bar, he gave the briefest of head shakes, raised his hand so the bartender was ready for another, then decided to polish off what little remained in his glass. I dropped a ten on the counter to cover our drinks then walked out.

The city's transit authority was crooked, and the lines were notoriously unreliable, so it took me longer than expected to cross three neighborhoods on my way to the west side. I found Susan's apartment easily enough, buzzed to be let in, then took the elevator in the lobby that sounded as if its gears hadn't been cleaned since the day it was installed. The gate creaked an exhausted whine as I closed it, and the whole compartment jolted to life, straining to lift me to her floor. I stepped down the hall, avoiding odd brown stains and noting the discolored walls and peeling plaster, eyes locked on the ajar door at the end of the hall, not realizing until I neared that it was my destination.

"Susan," I called out, drawing my .357 and knocking lightly while pushing the door open.

No answer.

"Susan?"

The apartment was silent. I stood in the entry hall with just a hint of the kitchen in the distance. To my left, a door. I eased it open and peeked inside. Bathroom, from the looks of it. I flicked on the light. The shower curtain had been pulled across, but it was nearly transparent. I pulled the door closed a bit and inched a little further, taking it all in. She kept a clean home. Sparsely furnished and what she did have looked cheap, but it was all well cared for. A door mostly closed just past the kitchen and to the right, the living area stretched out. That whole wall was glass with a sliding door, a balcony just beyond.

A few pieces of mail were strewn across a small dining table. Next to her phone I saw a note scribbled on a pad. The painter's name and his phone number.

I picked it up and studied it, then crammed it in my coat pocket, just as I was alerted to a sound from behind. I turned and started to call her name. I saw instead the large man from the funeral, the one she was afraid of, dressed all in red. His fist was raised and coming at my face like a freight train. I didn't even have time to raise my gun.

CONCERNS

Beck tossed me another ice pack, shaking her head, grinning a little. This was the first thing I noticed as my vision unblurred. I tried to shake off the concussion and recognized the tell-tale signs of my own apartment. But how the hell I'd ended up back here would have to be a mystery for another day.

"Eye swole like your nose," she said, smirking.

Now she knew good damn well I boxed for a time. So how the hell had this joker gotten the drop on me? It happens to everyone might seem like a cliché, but it is true. Fact is, anyone can be off just a smidge, and in those moments, people can get the drop on 'em. Big man got the drop on me. I promised myself, though, it'd be the only time that happened.

"What brings ya?" I probably sounded curt but at the moment, my face and skull throbbing in intervals of stab and a duller, darker pain, that was the best I had to offer this conversation.

Her brows knitted together. "Really?! You don't remember calling me from that pay phone on 34th and Sycamore?"

Turning on a heel, she bent over the bar where I ate most my meals and spun to a flourish, producing another tiny stack of papers. Her other hand adjusted her glasses, and her mouth decided it was time for a smirk.

Class was in session.

"The vinyl was recorded in Mississippi shortly before Johnson's death. The brushes are made of a particular wood only found in the Middle East and a particular breed of horse only found in China. They are rumored to be five hundred years old. They have been owned by several notable artists and, if the stories are to be believed, whatever they paint will come to life. Finally, the book."

She raised her eyebrows and her smile broadened.

"The book?"

"It's got the papers saying tests were done to authenticate it. It made an appearance at Sothersby's … that's where the Sleys purchased it, in fact. News article buried deep in a regional paper traces the path of the book through the years." She fluffed the pages in her hand and arched her eyebrows over her glasses, her head tilted so. "Many … many … years."

"That goofy ass writer was right?" I asked.

"It's old," she said, nodding.

"So, what do a haunted recording, cursed paint brushes, and a demonic book have in common?" I asked, standing. I pulled the ice pack from my eye and stared at the cold bundle in my hand.

"I'm glad you asked," Beck said, winking and again shuffling the papers. "Ever heard of Trevon Gladney?"

I'd seen his movies. He'd been popular a few years ago, an auteur with a hauntingly cinematic vision. But recently he'd vanished from Hollywood. While I'd heard of him, I wasn't the biggest fan in the world, or a fan at all, really. His work was too abstract for me. So, the reason for that vanishing wasn't apparent to me.

"Trouble," Beck said, when I asked why he hadn't had a film lately. "Allegations he can't shake. Some involve a young starlet. Very young. And cocaine. He's had his lawyers fighting these accusations in court, but the studio that had been his biggest financier and distributor dropped him, all the same. Word on the street is, he's found a backer for something completely off the wall."

"Have to be if it involves these objects."

"And the Sley Siblings."

My eyes narrowed. Here it was.

"They don't have the kind of family money that can solely and successfully back a film, but they have enough to make a healthy contribution. Seems they are very interested in what Trevon Gladney has for a vision."

It was my turn to crack a grin. "Too bad Mr. Gladney is all the way in Hollywood."

Her hips shook and her grin twitched playfully. "Or he's here," and slipped me a folded piece of paper.

The Willingham is a swanky place downtown, opened since the turn of the last century, replete with its own stories of parties and ghosts, love and hate. Unlike the dives in my neck of the woods, this place charges by the night, takes reservations, features fine crystal and the plastered walls are papered, not patchy. If I'd left right then, I could make it to the doormen in two trains and about forty-five minutes.

"He takes his meals promptly at six," she said. "Or so rumor has it."

Forty-five minutes was cutting it close, but I tossed her the ice pack and bolted for my trench coat and fedora.

⚞⚟

I spotted him as he'd been featured on the national rags, sure. His mug was pretty famous for anyone with an eye open. But of the ragtag group filing into the hotel's restaurant from the lobby, he was the most nervous: a talkative little man with a potbelly and receding curly red thick hair, his hands articulating every syllable his quavering tongue flapped.

I watched his party slip just out of range of the hostess, who stood frozen behind her podium, smiling at me like an idiot. I passed her without acknowledging and snatched up an empty chair from a four-sided table with only three patrons behind three place settings. This I plopped down between Trevon and the bodyguard to his left: big and broad.

The bodyguard grunted.

"Straker Phillips, PI. I'm helping a young girl find out what happened to her brother."

Trevon faced his group and forced a smile. I could give two fucks if he was nervous.

"He was a musician," I said.

His eyes widened as he focused on me, and now he raised his right hand over the table to wave off any fear of their meal being disrupted.

"Can we talk in private?"

"No," I said, matching his dramatic whisper.

He regarded me for a second, looking from brow to chin, then broadened his smile and waved his hands with a flourish. He produced a voice meant for an auditorium when he said: "The Sleys have put up a hefty sum as collateral for a loan to finance my next venture, Mr. Phillips. One that will so shock and awe the populace, the world will never be the same."

"Sounds," I wanted to say something about delusions of grandeur, but I needed more answers. This joker might know where the objects were, and where the painter and, more importantly, Susan had gone off to. "Ambitious."

"Oh, no," he said, his broad smile broadening impossibly wider. "It is so much more than that. You know, I know a lot about slander. People have said the most awful things about me. I had a friend once, during the war, who was victim to the same kind of vicious rumor. He was, as most who knew his name, a self-proclaimed magician, but because he didn't fall into the Christian ideal, many claimed him evil. Can you believe that? Are you a Christian child, Mr. Phillips?"

I shook my head. I'd never really come down either way on the subject.

"Well, they sure crucified him, just as they've tried to crucify me. Said he performed spells to bring about the apocalypse! Hmph! Can you believe it? Do you know who wants to bring about the apocalypse, Mr. Phillips? Those goddamn Bible thumpers. They think their god will return to rescue them. They don't have a clue what will truly happen."

"Did he perform those spells he's accused of?" I asked.

"Oh yes!" he said, a gleam in his eye. He looked around. Everyone at his table sat rapt by his story. "Oh yes indeed, but not for the reasons they think. You see, my dear friend – Aleister's his name – knew what would really happen, and knew those forces were getting stronger. Have you ever wondered, Mr. Phillips, why we no longer have magic in the world? Why people no longer believe in demons and ghosts and the things that go bump in the night? Why rational adult humans consider such things fairy tales for little kids and the uneducated?"

"Because science has proved it's a lot of bunk," I said.

He laughed and shook his head, derisively. "Oh dear. Oh no. It is because the door was sealed…"

He let these last words hang in the air, his eyes gleaming.

I picked up the inference. "By your friend."

"Yes. He knew what the apocalypse would bring, and he did the world a favor it did not deserve."

I sat back, regarding him. I was still struggling to see the point of all of this.

The waiter came and took the group's order. When he looked to me, I waved a hand to pass. I didn't need all eyes on me to tell me I was only welcome so long as I could get the answers I sought. Another server brought a tray of drinks, just enough for everyone but me.

Gladney took a sip of his Merlot and flashed me a toothy grin, his pearly whites stained temporarily pink from the wine. "I believe, detective, I've told you all I care to. If you cannot infer the rest, then I'm afraid you are not the man to find that poor young woman in time."

He flashed another look to his bodyguard, who stood and loomed quite impressively over me. Now more people in the restaurant took notice. Some of them looked nervous. I tucked my hands into my trench coat as I stood, nodded to the women at the table, regarded the men, then Gladney, then the bodyguard, whose nostrils flared and who did not blink.

"Thank you for your time," I said, and left the hotel.

I chose the surface streets back to my place, needing the time and footwork to think. If I read between the lines, then Gladney wanted these artifacts and who knows what others to perform a spell to reverse what his friend did, and if he were to be believed, then unleashing magic and the supernatural would not be good for this world. The question was, how much did the Sleys know about Gladney's intentions, and how much did the people they hired know? The answer came from the writer's demeanor at the bar. I was convinced he knew more than he was letting on, and now I was certain of it. I wasn't quite sure what else they would need, but something in my gut told me Susan might be in danger, so what I had to do was clear. I had to secure those items and keep them out of reach of Gladney and the Sleys, and I had to find Susan.

It was after dark when I reached my apartment. Before I got the door opened, I could hear my phone ringing. I was able to answer it in time to find my old partner on the line.

"Straker," he said, his voice carrying that sound like he was smiling. "Ready to get some payback?"

"Didn't think the police force condoned such actions," I said, knowing that was utter horseshit. They just didn't condone such actions for any civilians. Police got revenge all the time.

"I found him," my old partner said. "The man in red."

⚭

I grabbed a quick sandwich from the diner while I waited for Jake, my old buddy from the force, to show up, and downed it on our way to an even seedier side of town. Town like this has more seedy sides than good ones. We landed at a spot called the Busty Cowgirl, a strip joint whose clientele were the exact opposite of what I'd encountered at the swanky hotel just a few hours earlier. He asked me if I was packing and I nodded, but I didn't want to resort to a gunfight unless I had to. I owed this sumvabitch a right cross for getting the drop on me like he did. It was raining again, coming down hard, and lightning flashed between the skyscrapers. One blast exploded overhead as we approached the bouncer at the front door.

Dude held a hand up to stop us, and Jake drew his badge. Bouncer moved aside.

There was no sign of the man in red when we entered, so I crossed to the bar and asked the bartender. He pretended he was either deaf or dumb, don't know which and don't care. I caught the arm of a passing cocktail waitress who was prettier than the girl on the stage.

"Looking for a big man," I said. "Crooked nose. Orange hair. Looks mean."

She looked up at me with the eyes of a rabbit, timid and wide and scared. "Is he wearing a red suit?"

I raised my eyebrows to Jake at this. I hadn't thought to ask about that because I'd assumed the bastard would change his clothes, dirty asshole.

She nodded toward the back, to the left of the stage. The sign over the black curtain read "VIP room."

I thanked her and dropped a five on her tray, then Jake and I made our way between the tables and seating, waving off dancers. Jake flashed his badge at a few disgruntled patrons upset we'd temporarily obstructed their view. Finally, at the curtain, we played a game of "Rock, Paper, Scissors" to see who'd go in first, and I won. Jake always went for paper.

I pushed the curtain back and squeezed my eyes shut, hoping they'd adjust. Luckily, it wasn't as dark as I'd assumed. Purple lamps were scattered about, and the room smelled of old jizz and old bourbon. I could just make out the red collar and his thick curls. The girl straddling him moaned and bounced, her eyes closed. As we neared her motion slowed and she opened her eyes, regarding us. I placed a palm on his shoulder.

"Lap dance is over," I said.

Red muttered a curse and looked over his shoulder first at me, then at Jake. The girl was up, adjusting herself as he was zipping up.

"No one comes in here," I called out as she hustled out of the room.

"Police business," Jake added.

Big man stood. "You son of a bitch," he said, balling his fists.

This time, I was the one to get the drop. I stepped into a right cross that caught him in the jaw, then offered an uppercut that made him double over with a whoof. He tried to throw a punch but I was faster, finishing him by driving my fist down, catching his temple. The stars he must have seen. He warbled a bit then sank to his ass. He towered over me a good four inches, and outweighed me by at least fifty pounds of muscle, but I weren't no slouch and a few well-placed punches can level the playing field. I'd known that since my boxing days.

Jake cuffed him and we each caught him under the arm, tossing him back up on the couch. He looked from one of us to the other with a sour look, like he was a punk kid whose fun we'd spoiled.

"Who do you work for?" I asked.

He spit at me in defiance. I worked a quick jab that broke his nose again, spraying a fine mist of blood. "Jesus!" he muttered nasally.

"Didn't know he was hiring," I said.

"Man asked you a question," Jake said.

"The Sleys," the man in red said. "Hired me to watch after

the girl. Didn't trust her or her brother. They don't trust many people. Definitely not you, detective."

"Where is she?" I asked.

He shook his head. "I don't know. Lost her a few days ago. Been looking myself. She got some property of theirs."

"Is that all they want her for?" I asked, still considering Gladney and that gnawing feeling in my gut.

He looked up at me and then to Jake. "Don't know. I don't get paid to ask questions."

I knelt so we were eye level. "I think you know a lot more than that. I think—"

But before I could finish, two gunshots rang out from behind us. I felt the bullet flit through my coat and another whiz past my ear. One caught the man in red in his chest and the other got him between the eyes. Jake and I both spun on our heels, but all either of us saw was the billowing curtain leading back to the main floor. We sprinted through in time to see a shadowy figure darting past the bouncer, out the door to the rain-soaked city. We gave chase, but whoever the shooter was had already rounded one of the multitude of corners that led deep into the city by the time we exited.

"Dammit," I said.

Jake shook his head. "I'll call it in."

❦

It was nearly dawn before I returned to my apartment. The cops treated the scene like a gangland slaying and as if Jake and I were on the take. I could hear Jake's captain rip him a new one for letting me tag along. I never much liked the limey bastard anyway – thought he kissed too much ass to get those bars – but I wasn't about to say anything as Jake was in enough hot water as it were. When all was said and done, Jake pulled me aside and suggested I lay low.

"Can't," I said, and explained how I still needed to find the girl and the artifacts.

Jake shook his head. "Captain got a call. Sley's found out what went down here. They are not paying you anymore money. You're off the case."

"But–!"

"It's a police matter, old buddy," Jake said, hand on my shoulder. I had no choice. I tucked tail and turned home, meandering through the rain on the long trek back to my apartment. He'd offered me a ride, but I knew I wouldn't be much company, so I refused and pulled my fedora down over my eyes, slumped my shoulders and made my way through the dirty, grimy city.

The people here are selfish and mean; for a long time that had been enough for me. There was a dog-eat-dog mentality that I'd gravitated toward my whole life. The world was a cold, wet, dangerous place, this city had taught me, and no one was going to look out for you. I'd lived a whole lifetime believing this. But then Susan and the Sleys and this whole crazy mess entered my life, and I found my world was topsy-turvy. Fired or not, I cared about what happened to this girl, and I was genuinely concerned about what the Sleys were up to. I wasn't ready to believe in the hokum of magic and the supernatural, but I was sure they were up to something and the world at large could suffer. I also realized that if I pursued this thing, my life could change. My reputation would probably take a hit. Fine. I didn't give two shits what other folk thought of me. But I might not make it out of this alive. I could, if I pursued this case, wind up on a slab like that red-clad giant, and that didn't sit so well with me. I kind of liked breathing, difficult as it was right now with my busted nose. So I was nearly at the notion that I would drop the whole thing. I'd use the money the Sleys paid to get me caught up on a few bills and be on the lookout for another case. The whole mess had just about been decided, until I got home. Outside my apartment, Susan sat on the floor of the hall. She'd been crying.

I shook off my fedora and then, returning it to my head, did the same with my trench coat, shaking the rain off before folding it over my arm. She stood, wiping her eyes.

"You have to help me, Mr. Phillips," she said. "I'm being hunted."

Damn it all, anyway.

CRED

The storm didn't seem to be letting up. I fixed her some tea as the rain pelted the windows and the roof. I clicked on only a single lamp light and hung up my fedora and coat, removed my suit jacket and, after considering removing my shoulder holster, I thought better and kept it on.

"The painter is dead," she said, and said his name as if it should matter anymore. To her it did, for her lips trembled.

"I know," I responded, pouring our tea as the kettle whistled.

"I've hidden the artifacts."

"You should have told me you were in cahoots with him," I said.

"I couldn't. You don't know what they're up to. It's … monstrous. There's this director, see—"

"Trevor Gladney," I said, nodding.

"Then you know what he's up to?"

"Something about casting a spell to reverse what his buddy did years ago, bring magic and the supernatural back into our world."

"It'll be the extinction of the human race," she said. "If the Sleys get their hands on the artifacts—"

"Your brother knew about this too?"

She nodded. "We all did. The painter, the writer, my brother, and me. The Sleys seem to trust the writer, but when we figured out what they were up to, we had to do something."

"And when your brother went missing," I said, sipping my tea.

"I knew they got him. I was hoping you could help. You've got a reputation, Mr. Phillips."

"Listen, Susan. I'm afraid your life could be in danger. I want you to stay here with me. No funny business—"

She shook her head, a humorless smile plastered on her lips. "I'm not safe here. I'm not safe anywhere. You gotta smoke?"

I pulled a couple of Lucky's and lit them with a match strike on my thumb, just like my granddad taught me. I wasn't much of a smoker, but I kept a pack handy for those clients who were. People came to see me, usually their nerves were shot, and a smoke would help steady them some. I handed her one cigarette and took a small puff of the other.

"I got friends at the police force," I said, then corrected myself. "I've got a friend at the police force. He can make a call. Get you in police custody."

"That won't stop the Sleys, or their hired goon."

"Goon?"

"The man in red. He's … unstoppable. Who do you think killed my brother and the painter?"

I cracked a smile and puffed on my own smoke, then tapped it out. Anymore than a few puffs and I'd be thrown into a coughing fit. "No worries, then. The man in red is dead. Saw two bullets pumped into him myself. One through the heart and the other between the eyes."

She considered this for a second. Outside the rain pounding on the windows, I heard the far-off ding of the elevator as it reached my floor. A smile spread across her face as she dropped her eyes, and when she lifted them, she was laughing. I smiled too to join her, until I heard just how maniacal that laughter was. Her eyes were wild, and tears flowed from them. Through her laughter and her tears, tamping out her own cig, she glared at me. "You think that is enough to kill him?"

Her words fell on me as dumb and fruitless as the rain, and I didn't have time to let them soak in. A knock came to my door, hard and forceful, rattling the hinges themselves. And then the door exploded inward. With a growl, the man in red stepped into my apartment, the bullet hole between his eyes a bloodless black unblinking eye searching us out.

Instinct kicked in even as rational thought went numb trying to process his resurrection. I drew my .357 and fired three times as he turned towards us, hitting him center mass in the chest. Blood and clothing and bits of tissue fountained from his chest, and he tumbled backward. I leapt over him, snatching my coat and fedora, taking her hand and dragging her out of the apartment. We hadn't made it far when he was already struggling to rise.

"Shit," I muttered. He wobbled as he stood, then fixed his eyes on us and staggered out of my apartment, thundering down the hall with fists bunched, feet stomping hard enough to rattle the floors with every step. I'd hit the elevator button, but the compartment was rising too slowly, so we made a beeline for the stairs. I pushed her until she nearly toppled over, down and down, winding down the staircase. I could hear him above, taking the stairs, leaping and hitting the landing, then taking a few more. Christ if he wasn't about to catch us. We made it to the street and darted into the diner, ducking behind the counter much to Dolores' surprise. The big man entered, looked around, then backed out into the street. Dolores tapped my shoulder when the coast was clear, offering me little more than a reproachful look.

"Friend of yours?" she asked.

"You know me," I said, straightening, my knees and back creaking a little more than I cared for, "I sure know how to pick 'em." I helped Susan up.

"Was I imagining things or did he have holes—"

"Hey Dolores," I said, interrupting her thoughts. "How 'bout a couple of coffees?"

"Sure thing, doll face," she said and turned her back on us.

⚭

I used the payphone to call a cab to the diner, then directed the cabbie to an old safehouse Jake and I had used before. It wasn't much to look at. Off the interstate and dusty from disuse, not much in the way of furniture. It wouldn't be easy to find, and it was easy to see who was coming, and that's why we used it. Jake arrived not long after, looking as though I'd interrupted his sleep. He gave the girl a cursory glance then punched my shoulder.

"I thought I told you to lay low. Let the police handle it."

I shook my head. "No good. She found me at my apartment. Besides, our friend in the red suit isn't as dead as we thought."

He gaped at me. "I was going to call you first thing in the morning to tell you someone had stolen his body out of the morgue. You saying he's alive?"

"I don't know how, and he was still sporting that fresh hole between his eyes. I put three slugs in him myself back at my apartment. Mope just shook it off and charged after us."

"How the hell–?"

Susan answered for us. "The Sleys' reliquary holds a lot of reputedly mystical objects. They've traveled the world searching for these things."

"And you think they found something to raise the dead?" I asked her.

"My brother toured the reliquary once," she said. "Said they had some objects from the Caribbean. Stuff like a Voodoo witch doctor might have."

"You're saying he's a zombie?" Jake asked.

Susan shrugged. "I don't know, but with what they have their hands in, I wouldn't be surprised to see a vampire leap out at us next."

"So, what's the plan?" Jake asked me.

"You get a guard detail on her. Don't let her out of your sight. I'm going to grab a few things from my apartment, then I'll give you a call."

"What if that behemoth is there waiting for you?"

"I don't think he will be," I said. "But if he is, I'll find something. Chainsaw, maybe. Something will keep him down."

"Take care of yourself," Jake said, and I nodded.

Before I could climb in the car, Jake called out to me. "Oh, by the way, I meant to tell you Gladney's gone missing now also."

I frowned at this, something I was sure he couldn't see through the curtain of nightfall and rain. That the director was now missing did little to ease my mind about the direction this case was turning.

I'd instructed the cab to keep the meter running, and I didn't like where the tab sat when I climbed back into the back seat, so I told him to floor it back to my place. Once there, I paid and made my way inside, this time taking the elevator up. Before the compartment opened with a ding, I had my gun drawn, and was expecting the worst. What I got was silence. I expected the cops to be there, for my neighbors to have called when they heard the gunshots, but I saw nothing. Heard nothing. No one was there. My door stood wide open and dark just beyond the threshold, but the entire hall was empty.

Cautiously I walked inside. Nothing seemed out of place, and there was no sign of the man in the red suit. I flicked on a couple of lamps and still checked around, but the apartment was empty. My notes on the case were still on my desk. Maybe he didn't come…

Phillips takes Susan to a safe house after they escape the MiR

What in hell? It was like I blinked and in that second, I was back at the safehouse, and some voice was speaking over me. Telling me what was happening as it happ– *Jake arrives to protect her.*

There was a static sound, like electricity, when it happened, when the world shifted from one scene to another, and the colors went all neon and wonky and hissed like a snake. That's not exactly what happened, but that's the best I can remember, because the next thing I knew, I was–

⊙₰⊙

–tied to a chair in a large loft, and near as I could tell, somewhere in the warehouse district. My head pounded, throbbed with each of the neon colors that existed now not in my mind but on a piece of canvas on an easel in front of me. It was still nightfall and the rain still fell, beating a chaotic rhythm against the glass. Not too far off, a ship's foghorn blew. How the hell had I arrived all the way across the city at the port authority, I wondered.

I focused then on the painting, and the artist, using the brushes much like a maestro might use his baton to keep the orchestra in time, except where the baton generated music, the brushes spread the oily paint across the canvas in a thick, dark, monstrosity of a painting. I'd never seen anything like that thing, its many arms and few eyes, its gaping, bloodied maw. It was reaching with a clawed hand as if toward the painter, who stood with arms crossed, studying each stroke before and after performing it.

"Do you like it, Monsieur Straker?" the painter asked. The glance he cast to me over his shoulder told me he was the guy I was looking for. I'd thought he was dead, but then again, I thought that about the man dressed in red.

"Straker's my first name," I said, struggling against the knots. "It's Monsieur Phillips."

He considered me again. With his back turn, the image he'd painted waivered a little, as if caught in a wave. "Do you think it'll matter much in a few minutes?"

"Been looking for you," I said. "You got a lot to answer for."

He walked over to me and straddled my lap, his face not just bloody but half the flesh had peeled away in flakes and what remained was pallid and smelled of fish and saltwater. His dead eyes oozed something gooey but clear. While he could see me, his eyes didn't appear to look at anything.

"What is art? What is the purpose of art? How should we consider the craft of the artist if that has been ascribed to the medium through years of study, or is art anything we want it to be? If we monetize the artist's product, should we not monetize the study of the craft? Should we not have in place some criteria by which we grade and value the art? Should we not then teach that criteria as craft? These are the consumerist questions capitalism thrusts upon us like a bitch pup with too large a litter. Take this one! I can't answer for myself!"

"Who should have the answer?" I asked. My hands and fingers were still kneading at the knots. I was still in my trench coat, which was in my favor, as it provided a layer of bulk that kept the ropes from securing too tightly. I could tell from the weight of my shoulder holster that he'd forgotten to remove my gun.

"Indeed!" he squealed. "Who should have the answer?"

"A man ought to be compensated for his labor," I said. "Be he a farmer, a scientist, a bricklayer, or an artist."

He snarled at me, and a cockroach crawled out from between his ragged, dead lips, and scurried up to his ear. "Or a detective."

"Say," I said, needing just another minute. "You lost that French accent." Truth was, he'd lost it after the initial greeting, but like I said, I needed only another minute or so.

Behind him, the painting shuddered. The arm he'd painted, outstretched, broke free from the canvas bonds and stretched into the room. The creature's eyes went wild with the first signs of life.

My mouth fell open, unable to respond. My heart thudded in my chest. He stood and backed away. "You won't beat them, you know. You'll die."

Now it was pulling itself out of the canvas, as though the strip of fabric stretched across the easel was a window separating our world from its world, and it found passage through that window. "Dear God," I muttered. I shook, the ropes fell to the ground, and I stood, drawing my gun.

"Think this is bad," the painter said, "You ought to see what else is in their reliquary."

I fired three shots, then reloaded. His head exploded and he sank to the floor as if he were undersea. The thing continued to crawl forth, but the gunshots alerted it to me, and it turned its fierce, yellow, dead gaze upon me with a snarl, baring impossibly sharp and innumerable teeth. One great giant claw swiped at me, and I had just enough sense to duck, and then

I fired another two shots at the canvas. This only helped to dislodge it, and it was crawling for me. Crawling, I say, because he hadn't yet painted its legs, but it was crawling and crawling fast, and I could hear the painter still laughing, even without a head, and it was wild and maniacal and I had to wonder if it wasn't my own laughter I heard, my mind snapping. I found a heavy iron door, threw back the bar bolting it shut, and exited the great loft into a stairwell. The thing thudded against the door, and the reverberation shook me off my feet, sent me tumbling down the stairs end over end. I dropped my gun and heard it clatter away into the shadows, and then I heard a ringing.

I felt twisted in my coat, only to realize as I raised my head and heard that the ringing was my own telephone, that I was twisted not in my coat but in my bed sheets. Jesus, was it a dream?

CRSO

It was Jake on the line. He'd just received more word that knocked me for a loop.

"The painter's dead," he said. "Jesus, you sound like shit, Straker."

I tried to wipe the cotton feeling from my mouth. My apartment still swirled around me. Wherever I was with the painter, I felt like a part of me was still there.

"They found him at a warehouse loft," I said, my words a drunken jumble of barely audible mutterings reverberating out of a scratched up and desert-dry throat. I needed some water, but the fucking cord wouldn't stretch to the kitchen, and this was too important.

"No," he said, the confusion in his voice ringing clear. "Waterfront. Drowned. Been a while, too. Corpse was bloated. Fish had been eating on it."

So, it had been a dream, then. But it had felt so real. Even now, I could feel the rope burns on my wrists from where I'd been tied to the chair.

"Any idea what did him in?" I asked.

"Coroner's looking at him now," Jake said.

"How are you both doing?"

"She's sleeping. Patrol can't get out yet, so I'm keeping an eye out, but no sign of your undead guy."

I said I'd check in later and hung up, then clicked on a few lights. This made me aware of a dull pounding behind the eyes. Phrenological bruises corresponded with those thuds, suggesting I'd actually taken a tumble down some stairs. After downing a few glasses of sewer-flavored water from the tap, I began the task of inventorying the items I was sure I'd returned with. There was my trench coat and fedora, strewn over the back of the couch. My suit coat hung on the coat rack by the door. My shoulder holster lay empty on the table. In the dream, I'd dropped the Magnum as I fell down the stairs.

I called Beck, downed a few aspirin with another glass of water, then began a more detailed search. By the time she'd arrived at my place, I'd overturned the couch and the mattress, but there was no sign of my gun. I could feel the heat rising in my temples.

She entered, handing me a sandwich. "You sounded like shit on the phone," she said.

I curtly went about filling her in on the night's events. When I'd finished, she helped me right the sofa and return its cushions, and then we sat together, her arm around me, patting my back.

"We'll find your gun," she said.

"I was drugged, Beck. Had to be."

"I took the liberty of calling Pete down in research," she said. When I raised my eyebrows, she shook her head. "Don't worry, I didn't give him your name or any particulars. But he said it sounded like it could be one of several plant toxins. They're easy to disguise and can cause the hallucination you experienced and the loss of consciousness."

"Great," I mumbled. "Someone dropped a daisy in my tea."

"I think we can narrow it down a bit more than that," Beck said. "You ever hear of Tritan Pharmaceuticals?" I had. They were big here in the city, employing a number of workers and fashioning a lot of prescription medicine, both in use and experimental. "A plant toxin like this would more than likely be stored at a place like that, more than likely in their R&R department."

"It's a place to start," I said. Something clicked in the back of my mind, but as I was still fuzzy, all I saw was something blurry and half formed. Still, that I could have been poisoned by a plant toxin felt especially important.

⳩

Breaking into Tritan was easy enough. The night guard was a fat old codger we'd awakened from what I'm sure was an unauthorized nap who was all too willing to buy the story we were from the FDA, and soon enough we found ourselves in the records department. Beck found the inventory list and we moved to R&R two floors up. A half hour later, and we'd discovered our first lead.

"*Salvia divinorum*," I said. A hallucinogenic from Mexico currently being tested here at Tritan.

"Inventory levels are off," she said. "And look here," she added, flipping to another page. "They were experimenting with it in cocktails. Someone wanted it ingested for a delayed effect."

"How long a delay?" I asked, my mind clicking a bit faster now.

She shook her head, skimming the paragraphs. "Hours. I don't know. Why?"

We'd been hunkered over a desk, reading through the file under the lone light of a desk lamp. Now I straightened and tapped my lips with my index finger. "Let's head down to HR. I want to see who sits on the board of Tritan."

HR was locked, but that only presented a minor problem, as I was able to jimmy access and soon enough, we were poring through more files. It didn't take long to confirm my suspicions once we found the executive folder.

"Right here, on the board," I said. "Genevieve Sley."

"Hold on," Beck said, and pulled out the sign-in log from R&R. "Look who signed out a batch of Salvia just a day before you went to the Sley mansion."

The initials read: GS. "Says she checked the batch back in a few hours later," I said.

Beck shrugged. "That could be doctored. And that's so close to the missing amount."

I frowned at this. "So, Genevieve Sley checks out the amount needed to dump into my tumbler when I come to visit, knowing it'll kick in a bit later? How'd she know I was going to visit her?"

"Maybe she's psychic," Beck said, wearing a half grin. Meant for a joke, I know, but still my stomach rumbled at the thought just enough to make me queasy. *They're trying to bring back the supernatural.*

"We need to go. I need to get ahold of Jake and get Susan to tell me where she stashed those objects."

"Then what?"

"When I get the objects, I'll visit Ms. Sley myself and get to the bottom of this."

❧❦❧

It was almost dawn when I found myself down at the wharf. The smell of fish and diesel mingled sourly, waves lapped against the docks, the water black as oil in the predawn light. I found the storage building and the individual unit easily enough, picked the lock while Beck stood watch, then entered.

Empty.

There was nothing except a wharf rat sniffing around for crumbs and a few cobwebs. The lock hadn't been messed with, so I couldn't help but think I'd been hoodwinked.

Beck started to say something but grew quiet. I'd been focused on the storage unit so this didn't register to me immediately, but when I turned around to leave I realized why. The man in red stood behind her, holding her by the throat, grinning at me like the goddamn Cheshire cat.

I reached for my gun, and he laughed, producing it with his free hand. "Drop something?" he asked.

"You let her go," I said. "This is between you and me."

"You don't get it," he said. "They've already won. They've stacked the cards in their favor, so neither you nor your trollop here have any chance. Hell, you don't even know what's real and what's imagined anymore. Like if I told you that you really did fall down those stairs running out of that warehouse, and that's where I found your gun, you'd think it was crazy, 'cause you've about convinced yourself it was a dream. But it wasn't a dream, Straker Phillips."

"Drop the gun and let the girl go," I said.

"Or what?" he said.

I charged him. It was all I had. He raised my .357 and tried to cock the hammer, but what he didn't realize was you had to cock it a special way or the hammer would catch, and the gun wouldn't fire. This was a feature I'd tinkered with until I had it just right, back when I'd first gotten the gun from my father, for just such an occasion. Like I said, anyone can get the drop on anyone at any time. Big man here got the drop on me once and thought he had again. Turns out, I was the one with the advantage.

When the gun wouldn't fire, I went in for a haymaker as Beck elbowed him in the gut. Both actions caused him to drop the gun and sent him reeling against the door to another unit. I worked the body with a few more punches until he went to his knees. From behind me, I heard the gun cock. Beck knew about the trick with the hammer.

I stood back as the man in red, now on all fours and spitting blood, began laughing even as he fell into a coughing fit. "Fuck," he muttered. "You lost, private dick. You lost and you don't even know it. You don't know how much you lost."

He coughed up more blood that turned foamy on his lips, and as he turned his face up to us, a wide grin plastered on his lips, a fountain of scarlet froth bubbled up and poured down his chin. His cheeks then forehead went purple, and his eyes bulged, and soon his whole head was consumed in this blood-tinged frothy mess. This is what had become of everything but the skeleton, for soon only his skull was left, and the same was apparent for his hands and then he collapsed, his bones clattering on the hard concrete floor and shattering into fragments and splinters.

"You pack quite the punch," Beck said, sidling up beside me and handing me the gun.

I took it and returned it to my holster. "Them's the breaks," I answered. "Let's head to the safehouse."

Twenty minutes later, as we rounded the bend and the first rays of morning sun were peaking in the east, I caught the flash of blue patrol lights at our destination, and soon we were in the parking lot. Uniforms stood around the safehouse entrance, and there was tape stretched across the doorway. As we pulled up, I met the glare of the captain and knew I was in for it. Beck hadn't even shut off the engine before I was out of the car and the captain was in my face.

"Where's Jake?" I asked.

"Dead!" he snapped and hitched a thumb over his shoulder. "What in god's name is going on, Phillips?"

"And the girl?" I asked, ignoring him.

He poked a finger into my chest. "You don't get to ask the questions, Straker. I've got a dead detective and a missing girl, and you are at the center of it. Now tell me what the hell is going on!"

I sighed. Beck had exited and the captain gave her a cursory look. "And you brought a fucking reporter?"

"She's with me," I said.

"I don't give a good goddamn if she's with the pope. I asked you a question. You better answer before I slap the bracelets on you and haul your ass downtown."

As if to reinforce this, several of the dozen or so patrolmen surrounded me.

I looked at Beck. "Let her go. I'll answer your questions."

The captain looked from me to her and then back to me. "Haul his ass down to the station." The patrolmen were on me like flies.

☙❧

Now, I've sat through a number of interrogations and led a few more, but I'd never been on this side of the table. Not as a suspect. The captain was in there, but so far, he'd let Stodger take the lead, and I wasn't impressed. You see, an interrogation is meant to do a number of things. Ultimately you want information, but you also want the perp scared. You want them to think you know more than what you really know so they'll give you everything you need to know. If you're working off evidence, then you want the information to corroborate the evidence you've acquired. If you're working off a hunch, then you need the perp to fill in the blanks. You want them to think, no matter their part in this, that their very livelihood depends on giving you what you need. They should be so scared of being sent upriver that they are willing to sing any verse you want to hear.

Maybe it's because I understood all this that I wasn't in the particular desired state of mind. Maybe it's because Stodger was a string-bean of a cop who kissed ass to get his promotion and couldn't scare the pants off a hooker if he'd already paid her. Whatever it was, I wasn't knocking knees, though I was giving them all I knew.

Susan had hired me to find her brother. Her brother and a couple of other cats had been hired to find some merchandise. When they realized the danger involved, Susan, her brother, and the other two had elected to keep the merchandise for themselves. The Sley siblings were hellbent on getting their things back. That was the long and short of it. I didn't go into detail about magic or ghosts or any such things because they'd only reserve me a padded cell at the state hospital with the men in white coats.

"Genevieve Sley is an upstanding member of society," the captain broke in before Stodger could say anything, after I was finished regaling them of my story.

"We didn't find no sign of this man in red down at the storage unit either," Stodger added.

I wanted to say that was because he fucking melted but didn't think that would help my case.

"Meanwhile," the captain went on, "we got you breaking and entering Tritan Pharmaceuticals, discharging your weapon in public, getting into a fight at a local strip club, harassing patrons at a hotel restaurant, and being a general dick."

"To be fair," I said, "I've always been a dick."

"Straker," the captain said, shaking his head. He was smiling, but I knew he wasn't amused. He sat on the edge of the desk and folded his arms across his check, staring at the wall. Without looking over, he said, "Leave us a minute." Stodger slunk out of the room.

"Jake was more than my old partner," I said. "He was my friend."

"Maybe the only friend you had left on the force," the captain said, still not looking at me. "I thought we told you after the strip club to lay low. Let us handle things."

"That big man in red broke into my apartment. Tried to kill me."

"You mean the big man who was shot at that same strip joint? Look, Straker," he said and leveled his gaze at me, "We can confirm he existed, but we don't have an identity and we don't even have a body after it was stolen from the morgue. What we do have is enough circumstantial evidence to charge you with murder as well as a number of other crimes. But I'm not in the business of charging former police, especially when they were good police. But you just about tied my hands, here."

I nodded, understanding. He stood and left the room, and ten minutes later I was out on the street under the golden light of dawn, coat in hand, revolver back in my shoulder holster, waiting for Beck to bring the car. Twenty minutes after that, I was unlocking my apartment. By now, the sun shone through the curtains brightly so that I didn't need any kind of light to see my way around. Trench and fedora hung up along with my suit coat, and my holster with gun back on the scuffed-up dining table. I still felt a little queasy, that had never gone away, but I was tired more than anything. A few hours of shut eye was just what the doctor ordered.

He didn't order a transparent image of Susan, weeping over my shoulder, forcing me to jump when I saw her, or the black-out that quickly followed.

CREO

As the world came into focus again, I recognized that I was no longer in my apartment and that I was laying on a couch. I sat up and blinked, saw the windows, the pocket door, the ornate décor and through the window to my left, the dead grass and dried up elm much as it was the last time I was here, staring out that same window with Genevieve Sley.

I tried to sit up, but my throbbing head felt like it weighed a thousand pounds and I had to wince my eyes shut against the light and pressure in order to upright myself.

"You're fortunate, Mr. Phillips," came the deep voice from behind me. I chanced a glance as I stood and saw an older gentleman with perfectly coiffed white hair combed off his brow, a trimmed mustache, holding a drink in his hand. "Care for a drink?" he asked, a bit of a smile turning the mustache up.

"How am I fortunate? And no, thank you. I'll pass on the drink this time."

"I thought you might. You are fortunate, Mr. Phillips, in that our brother, RG, was eager to meet you, but Genevieve and I thought it best if I were the one to welcome you to Sley House. Allow me to introduce myself. I am Charles Sley."

He took two steps and held out his hand. His fingers were long, and the nails manicured. He smelled of an exotic cologne. "Straker. That's an interesting name."

"Cut the crap, Sley," I said, stepping back, drawing my Magnum from its holster. "Where's the girl?"

His free hand returned to his pants pocket, and he took a casual, unhurried drink. "I'm afraid I have no good news on that front. You're welcome to tour the home yourself if you don't trust my word. I'd love for you to meet my dog." This last he said with a widening grin that revealed teeth impossibly straight and blindingly white, but there was no humor in that smile. His eyes narrowed like a predator as what felt like a great shadow rolled over the room.

"I think she's here. I think you did something to her. It's all ending today."

"Oh, she is, Mr. Phillips. Down in the reliquary filming with Mr. Gladney. I just don't believe that's a location any sane person would want to go. Not now."

I scoffed. "More of this magic stuff, huh."

He took another drink, shrugged noncommittally, and looked around as though our conversation disinterested him. "It was always bound to return, Mr. Phillips. That's what you, what everyone, fails to understand. The spell Gladney's friend performed at the end of the war was merely a salve. Humanity was always in danger."

"So, you thought, why not usher in the apocalypse yourself?"

He frowned, a look of disappointment darkening his brow. "No, my dear boy. We knew we couldn't stop it, but we hoped, for humanity's sake, we could control it. Harness it, much as Solomon did when he constructed the temple. For the sake of humanity."

"Mighty altruistic of you."

He ushered to the door. "Tour Sley House, Mr. Phillips. If you dare. I do hope you encounter neither my dog nor our older brother, as neither will be as hospitable as Genevieve and I have been. But outside this room you'll find a foyer. The stairs that lead up lead to our living quarters, a private library, and other such personal space. The hallway stretching east and west just beyond the stair leads to more accessible rooms, one of which is the kitchen. There you will find three doors. One leads outside, another to the pantry, and the third has stairs that wind down. Take those stairs and you'll find RG's laboratory and our reliquary, and perhaps, Mr. Phillips, you'll find a bit more than that. Again. If you dare."

"I just might, Mr. Sley. Why are you helping me?"

To this he laughed and shook his head. "Oh, my dear boy, I'm not helping you. Believe me, I am not helping you at all. Just engaging in your curiosity and eager to see how it all plays out."

I made for the door, never turning my back on him, keeping the gun drawn, until I stepped out into the hall. Before I could close the door, he called out, "If you get lost, just follow the screams."

But I didn't get lost. I found the kitchen quickly enough, then found the stairs leading down. It was as I was starting down the wide stone steps, the stairwell lit just barely by gargoyle faced torchieres screwed into the wall, winding down, that I heard the first screams. The darkness was thick and tasted like rot, but I couldn't let that stop me. I pressed on until I reached a dirt floor and saw a door to my right and another to my left. I wasn't sure which was the reliquary, but the door to the left contained the screams that had grown louder as I'd descended, so I opted for that one.

☙❧

Several sounds slammed together. The creak of the hinges as the door opened overwhelmed the dying screams that ended as I became aware of a steady and rhythmic clicking noise. I saw upon entering a rectangular room some twenty feet across, whose end was not readily visible to me thanks to the free-standing shelves obstructing my view. Along each wall were more shelves, and stacked on these were a varied assortment of artifacts and books, the likes of which I couldn't begin to describe. Suffice it to say, the books looked old and thick, great leather-bound tomes with Latin names or names in other languages. Not just European languages, either, as I could recognize those titles for their native tongues even if I couldn't translate them. Some were written in characters known to the Middle East while others were even more distant, the detailed and persnickety script of Asian characters. Of the objects lining the various shelves, these were just as strange. Trinkets and medallions, artifacts and statues. All manner of material made up these very unique items, with some adorned by jewelry or laced or made of gold, and others looking just as plain. I received a hint that they were all of different ages as well, and all of the things collected on these shelves were old.

I rounded the free-standing shelf and saw a wide-open space and a sight that left me completely horrified. Gladney stood behind a camera, cranking through the film with the lens pointed at such a subject I cannot, even now, linger on, for fear of going mad. Still, for this story, I will try.

First there was Susan. She was dead. Her eyes were open, and she stared up at the camera, mouth agape, a rivulet of blood trickling down her cheek. She'd been dressed in a white gown now stained with her blood. The gown and her torso were shredded. A bloody pulp mass suggested a cavity there, and if that were all, seeing this dead girl so mutilated, then that would have been enough, but it wasn't.

Gladney, I realized, was laughing. The click I heard was the click of the film rolling through the camera, as he'd captured her murder in the movie he'd undoubtedly hoped to release.

Along the far wall a figure sat balled with head buried, and the figure was weeping. I was not surprised to see the writer when he lifted his eyes. His face was red and streaked with tears.

Next, I noticed Susan's killer. All of this, mind you, took place in the span of seconds. Less even. And maybe not even in this order. This is just the rational way I can recall this memory.

Susan's killer was the very thing I thought I'd hallucinated. The thing the painter had been constructing with his brushes, still legless, though it was working on that. When I fathomed just how it was rectifying its legless situation, I bit into a fist to keep from screaming.

With one claw, it peeled the flesh from her dead body. The other held a paintbrush which it dipped into her cavernous and bloodied torso then stroked through the air below its own waist, where legs were slowly growing. A phonograph spun somewhere, spitting out the staticky chords of a guitar, the soundscape for Gladney's film, and from the mouth of the creature, as it worked, came words that should have been lost in time.

It turned its yellow eyes up to me and it smiled something toothy and horrible.

Gladney, from behind me now, laughed, a sound like the crunch of shattered glass. "Yes! Yes! More! More!"

"What have I done?" the writer asked me. I trained my gun on the creature and crossed to him, kneeling.

"You okay?" I asked.

He looked at me incredulously. "Really?"

"I'll get you out of here."

He shook his head. "It's too late for me. It's too late for all of us."

The music ended and the needle scratched at nothing, projecting only the whir of static. The words echoing from the blackish-gray beast with yellow eyes died down, and even Gladney's ecstatic cries ended. There came the incessant creak of a turning wheel which was, I realized, from a wheelchair. The Sleys rounded the corner of the free-standing shelf: Genevieve and Charles and in the wheelchair, the elder brother RG.

The creature stood and flexed its new legs, then slunk to the corner and dissolved into the shadows. RG offered me a smile that appeared forced. Genevieve stepped forward.

"Satisfied now, Mr. Phillips?"

"What in god's name—"

"God," she said with a bit of a laugh, "has nothing to do with it."

"I told you," Charles said. "We are doing the world a great service, whether it looks like it or not." In one swift move, he stepped up behind Gladney and, producing a dagger, he traced the blade across the director's throat, drawing a line of blood instantly. Gladney collapsed to the ground, clutching at his throat as the blood poured out in sheets between his fingers.

Genevieve stepped closer, and I realized she wore leather gloves. In one she held a powdery substance that she blew in my face. I lost consciousness soon after.

☙❧

I awoke to a rustling sound coming from my living room, wrapped in the linens of my own bed. I awoke wearing only my tee and boxers. Only blackness shone through the windows of my room. There came from behind my bedroom door sounds of movement, of shuffling, and I realized that someone was in my living room. I'd hoped it was Beck.

In the living room, I found the trumpeter instead. His

instrument lay silently beside him as if they'd already said goodbye. He held my gun's barrel just under his chin. I was still getting my bearings when he spoke without looking up at me.

"Cops will be here soon. I'll be arrested for murder. That director, your client lady. Her brother. Others."

"Did you…?" My voice was raspy. Of course, he hadn't.

He shook his head. "No, and it doesn't matter. The evidence the cops have says I did. The evidence the Sleys gave them. That's all that matters, and –"

From afar off, I heard the ding of the elevator.

" – that's also why your shooting is justified. I broke in."

My foggy mind reacted too slowly. The back of his head exploded outward, spraying blood and bone and splinters of skull over my couch back and floor, even as I reached for him to try and stop what was clearly inevitable. I grabbed the gun just as my door was kicked in, and patrol officers filtered inside. They aimed their service revolvers at me, and I set mine down just as easy, then raised my hands.

⌘

A week later, I was having coffee at the diner downstairs. In that time, I'd tried and failed to process all that had happened. My nights were filled with unsettling nightmares that splintered my sleep into bone shard fragments of somnolence, leaving my eyes bleary and red-rimmed and my mind fuzzy, my mouth cottony. Dolores was trying to coax me into eating, but I said I was about to head to dinner at a *fine* establishment. At least, I think the reservation was for today. It had taken all week to clean the blood and bone and brain out of my apartment and even now I sensed the ghost of that smell every time I passed through my own living room.

"You sure, sweetie. You look like a skeleton," she said, thrusting a menu out to me as if I'd ever needed it.

I said nothing, but hunkered over my coffee, I cast a sideways glance and what might be considered a grumble or a grouse.

"Ouch," she said, pretending to be hurt.

"I'm doing good to choke down this swill," I offered as the bell over the door tinkled behind me. Dolores straightened, her eyes wide and staring, the blush on her cheeks losing a bit of the color.

I turned and saw the writer enter. He was wearing a nice suit and drew an envelope from his breast pocket as he crossed the floor then sat across from me. He was well coiffed but his smile was forced. The eyes didn't smile. The lips feigned a smile but couldn't quite grasp the emotion. He had seemed to have lost what pallor colored his cheeks.

"What can I get ya?" Dolores asked.

"I'm not staying long," the writer said.

He slid the envelope across the table. "Services rendered."

It was thin, but I took it anyway. Opened the envelope. A check with a one and more zeros than I'd ever seen was made out to me. I tucked it away in my own pocket and leveled my gaze at him.

"You working for the Sleys then," I said. "Step up from how I found you in that reliquary."

He pursed his lips and shifted his gaze away from me. Perhaps I had cast something accusatory with my eyes. "They claim they're just trying to keep it in check. The magic. Devil you know, I guess."

"You sell your soul?"

He shrugged and squinted at the brightness penetrating the untinted bay windows of the diner, then offered up an angry kind of chuckle. "What the fuck does that even mean?" An idea crossed his mind that allowed another shake of his head.

"I guess I want to keep them in check."

"So, what's next?" I asked.

"What's next? You and I ought to be thankful we didn't go fucking insane."

"After that?"

"Publishing house. Radio work. I have a couple of friends who can help me." He met my gaze and didn't blink. "We'll keep them in line, Mr. Phillips."

I believed he would try. "Well, I hope the pay's good."

"The pay's shit, but I believe in the work I'm doing. I … we have a chance to do *real* good."

"What about the reliquary? What about the record and the book and the paint brushes and all that other stuff they've hoarded?"

"All down in their house still. Safely stored away in their home's basement."

"That doesn't make me feel any better," I said.

"Me either, Mr. Phillips. Me either."

We let a moment of silence pass between us before I downed the last of my coffee and dropped a fiver and a quarter on the table for Dolores' troubles, not that there were many troubles. It's not like people were clamoring to get in and I was taking up valuable real estate. I stood, pulled on the trench coat and adjusted the fedora on my head.

"What's next for you, Mr. Phillips?"

I looked up, but not at anything in particular, snatched up a toothpick and popped it between my teeth. "There'll be other clients, for sure," I said. "But right now, I got a date."

Just then, from outside, a car horn honked. We both turned to see Beck waving at me and blocking traffic. I wouldn't keep her waiting any longer than I had to, and she'd already waited long enough for me. I tipped my hat to the writer, turned, and walked out the diner.